OTHER BOOKS BY LINCOLN JAMES

Coming Spring 2026

All We Wanted

A Supernatural Thriller

They make your dreams come true. Then you disappear.

Spring Formal, 1982—a weekend of open bars, rented tuxedos, and bad decisions at a luxury resort in Las Vegas.

But the casino has unveiled something new.

Buried behind the lobby stands a glass display case housing three mummified figures adorned in gold: a ring, a tooth, an eyepatch.

By day, they're on display. By night, they hunt.

They slip into borrowed skin. They feed on desire, envy, regret.

All they need is one phrase.

I wish.

Because in this hotel, dreams don't come true.

They come for you.

Now Available

The Ninth Layer

A Claustrophobic Survival Thriller

This wasn't a field trip. It was a burial.

It was supposed to be extra credit. A simple research trip into the caves beneath Pendleton University. But the deeper Alex and his classmates descend, the stranger things become.

The air hums. The walls glow. And the silence feels alive.

Then the lights go out.

And something starts screaming in the dark.

By the time they realize there's no way back up, the ground itself seems to shift—breathing—hungering.

In the dark, they know they aren't alone.

And now, they'll have to fight to survive.

Available in print and ebook.

We Are Human

A Gripping Sci-Fi Thriller

They said it was evolution... He knew it was murder.

In 2040, Tyler Alcaster had been living the dream—sun, surf, and no responsibilities. Then he was taken.

He woke strapped to a table, his body screaming in pain, his mind full of static. He was turning into something else—something not quite human. They said it was about immortality. About saving the future. But Tyler knew better.

It was about control.

And he wasn't the only one. There was a silent girl with glassy eyes. A woman covered in scars. They were all being changed.

And they were running out of time.

Available in print and ebook.

All the Time

A Coming-of-Age Sci-Fi Thriller

The past isn't just a memory... It's a trap.

When Carter sets out to reconnect with his dying mother, he never expects to arrive at her house years before he was born. Stuck in the past with nothing but his car, a bag of clothes, and a barely working iPhone, Carter faces an impossible question: how did he get here—and how can he get back?

Time is slipping through his fingers, and every moment spent in the past pulls him further from the future he's desperate to return to.

Caught between what was and what could be, Carter begins to question if time is something you can outrun...

or if it's already run out.

Available in print and ebook.

Devils Like Us

A Tense, Gritty, Chase Thriller

Some devils hide in the shadows. Others look just like us.

Jason Murich thought he was heading home for a quiet weekend—until two desperate runaways hijacked his car. Now he's hurtling through the underbelly of 1990s Los Angeles on a high-stakes chase that spirals into chaos. As secrets surface and loyalties blur, Jason is forced to confront just how far he'll go to survive.

Gripping and raw, *Devils Like Us* is a taut psychological thriller that will keep you holding your breath until the final page.

Available in print and ebook.

The Vanishing Eight

A Pulse-Pounding Survival Thriller

Disappearing was only the beginning.

Eight friends. One missing.

The town of Piedmont had always whispered about them—too close, too wild, too perfect.

Then Roy disappeared.

Now, Jonathan is racing to hold what's left of their group together. But the deeper he digs, the more he realizes: Roy's not the first to disappear. And if Jon's not careful... he won't be the last.

In a town built on secrets, nothing stays hidden forever.

And some friendships don't survive the truth.

Available in print, ebook, and audiobook.

FOREWORD

Content Warning

This story includes themes and depictions that may be distressing to some readers, including emotional abuse, suicidal ideation, confinement, and trauma. There are moments of psychological tension, fear, and emotional vulnerability that may be difficult to read. Please take care of yourself as you go—pause, skip ahead, or step away if you need to.

A Note on Themes

Written Just For You is, at its heart, a story about isolation, memory, and the fight to be seen. Set in a town where silence can feel louder than truth, it follows two young people trying to reach each other through the wreckage of what's been buried.

This book explores themes of control, autonomy, grief, and the resilience of human connection—even in the unlikeliest of places. It's about what it does to a person to be kept small by someone else's fear—and what it means to be truly seen, maybe for the first time.

More than anything, it's a story about love. Quiet, determined, imperfect love. The kind that keeps going, even when it's told not to.

Thank You

To every reader who's picked up this book—thank you. You could've chosen anything else, but you chose to sit with these characters, and I don't take that lightly.

To my friends, family, and trusted early readers: your encouragement and patience helped bring this story to life. Thank you for believing in it.

And to anyone who has ever felt unseen, silenced, or stuck between who they are and who they're allowed to be—this story was written just for you.

Respectfully Yours,

Lincoln James

WRITTEN JUST FOR YOU

LINCOLN JAMES

ISBN-13: 979-8-9904966-9-9 (Hardback edition)

ISBN-13: 979-8-9985731-0-1 (Paperback edition)

ISBN-13: 979-8-9985731-1-8 (Ebook edition)

Library of Congress Control Number: 2025907922

This is a work of fiction. Names, characters, places, and incidents either are the product of the author's imagination or are used fictitiously. Any resemblance to actual persons, living or dead, events, or locales is purely coincidental.

Published by: Lincoln James

P.O. Box 10660 Page Ave # PO 4034

Fairfax, VA 22038-4034

Edited by: E. Lee Caleca

Printed in the United States of America

First Edition: May 2025

CHAPTER ONE

T he Harley growled beneath me, rugged and dependable, like it was chastising me for what was about to be my next move. I rode the last stretch of road between here and nowhere, not even sure if I'd been anywhere. This was supposed to be the end. One more night with the boys before I hit the road for good. Whatever that meant. But something in me wouldn't let it be that easy.

Trees blurred. Power lines hummed. And the ocean—waiting below like it knew I was coming—just breathed, like an enormous tentacled serpent threatening to devour whatever was left of my soul. I coasted to a stop on the bluff, kicked the stand, and killed the engine. Gravel crunched beneath my boots as I pulled off my gloves and unlashed my board. I looked down at the beach. The sky was burning orange, gilding the waves at the edges as they undulated, smooth and secretive. It looked like the world was splitting in two and no one was watching.

Danny spotted me first. "Well look what the cat coughed up."

Charlie raised his beer and shouted, "Holy hell! The legend returns!"

I lit a cigarette, gave them a look. "Didn't realize I was missed."

"Missed?" Danny came up the path to meet me. "Word was you were halfway East by now. Hair slicked back, thumb out, broken-hearted waitresses in your rearview." He gave a mock gesture, like a brooding 1950s James Dean, running a comb through his greased pompadour.

I gave a one-shoulder shrug. "Changed my mind."

Charlie snorted. "You don't change your mind. You disappear. Big difference."

I didn't answer.

That was the thing about this town. You leave too early, they call you reckless. Stay too long, they call you scared. I never figured out which one I was. Though sometimes I wondered if I disappeared, how long it'd take anyone to notice. How long before the town swallowed the space I left. The thought used to scare me. Now it just felt... true. Inevitable.

We stood looking at the water. The tide was low, exposing black rocks like the bones of something long dead. Shiny. Prehistoric. Dragons buried with their gold.

The breeze smelled like rust and salt.

"I can't believe it's really over," Danny muttered. "Twelve years of school, and for what? A lousy paper and a handshake from Hoover."

Principal Hoover, not the federal kind. Though both had a way of making you feel like you'd done something wrong.

"He called me George," I said. "I think he thought I was my old man."

Charlie raised a brow. "How'd that feel?"

I flicked ash off the cliffside. "Like a bad joke."

The silence that followed was a little too honest.

None of us said it, but we all felt it. This was the last time it'd ever be like this. The last night where we were still boys pretending to be men—and not the other way around.

Danny tried to break the tension. "So, what's next, Will? You takin' that garage job or what?"

I shook my head. "Nah. Place smells like rubber and regret."

"You got a real knack for optimism," Charlie said.

I smirked. "Optimism's for suckers."

Charlie rolled his eyes. "You ever think maybe you're runnin' from something?"

"All the time. But I never figured out where I was supposed to run to."

That shut him up.

I didn't hate this town. But I didn't trust it either. Places like this... they keep secrets. And I was starting to think I might turn into one of 'em. If they keep you too long, they turn you into furniture. Make you forget you had legs to begin with, and you best believe I wasn't planning to forget anytime soon.

"So, you coming out with us or what?" Danny asked, clapping Charlie on the shoulder. "You know I'm leaving next week for school. C'mon, let's make a night out of it!"

"Yeah, yeah. I'll be down in a second." I huffed, grinding out the cigarette on a flat rock. I grabbed my board and started down the path toward the beach.

I hit the bottom of the slope and pried my boots off. The sand, still warm from the day, held a memory, like déjà vu; something forgotten that lingered, trying to come to the surface; something rejected long ago.

The tide was pulling out slow and steady—like the ocean was sucking its teeth.

Danny whistled from the shallows. "Hurry up, Romeo! The sun won't last forever!"

I flipped him a look, then peeled off my shirt in one motion—tossed it over the rocks behind me. The air hit my skin like a dare. I unbuckled my jeans and stepped out of them, swim trunks ready underneath, red with a faded white stripe down the side. Lucky pair. Maybe the only thing I still believed in.

I ran a hand through my hair—dirt-brown, slicked back but always falling loose when it counted.

Charlie used to say I looked like trouble.

Danny used to say I looked like someone who'd already caused it.

I waded in slow, letting the cold hit me in stages—ankles, knees, gut. My breath caught, not from the chill, but from the weight of it. Like something out there was watching. I don't believe in myths or fairy tales, but there was something...

The wind shifted. Just a flicker. Like the beach wanted to warn me, but held its breath. I pushed off and paddled. The water was rough, but familiar. I'd grown up in it. Learned to breathe through the salt. A wave rolled in—tall, sharp at the crest. I turned my board, caught it clean. Rose with it easy. Balanced. Cut left. Let the ocean carry me for once.

Charlie whooped farther out. "There he is! Our very own Neptune!"

Beside him, Danny shouted, "Show-off!"

I rode it to shore and stepped off like it was nothing. Shrugged. Rolled my eyes. "Alright," I called. "You want a show?"

I spun and headed back out—deeper this time. The water climbed past my ribs, then chest—colder here, where the sun didn't bother to reach, knowing its authority was not where the deep lives, where things swam and plotted and killed beyond the curious gaze of man.

The next wave was already building. Big. Angry. Like it had been waiting for some arrogant fool to devour... to prove its might. I turned, angled, paddled hard. Felt it lift beneath me. Clean catch. But something in me flinched—like I wasn't supposed to. I popped up too fast. Slipped just a little. Not enough to fall. Yet. I corrected. The board jerked. The wave tilted. My balance broke, and the sky turned to foam.

Instantly, the ocean swallowed me whole.

It was cold. Unfeeling. A hand at my throat, dragging me under like I owed it something I couldn't pay back. Salt burned my lungs.

For a split second, I felt that old panic rise—like I was back there again. The cold. The silence. The way time stopped just before everything cracked. Then my ears filled with that low, endless roar—the kind that reminds you how small you really are. The kind that says, *you were never in charge of any of this.*

I twisted. Fought. Kicked like it mattered.

The ocean didn't care. It never does. That's its whole thing. It takes. Footprints, names, memories, whole lives—gone with the next pull of the tide. You could scream your whole damn soul into it, and it wouldn't even blink.

For a second, I let it have me.

Then—air.

I burst through the surface coughing, eyes stinging, arms swinging like some half-drowned punk too proud to call for help. Which, okay—fair. My lungs clawed for breath. I slicked my hair back, blinking against the water dripping down my face.

The sky overhead was bruised purple and gold, bleeding out at the edges like someone stabbed it, wanting to watch it die.

My board bobbed a few feet off. I should've been swimming toward it. Should've been paddling back out before Danny could start running his mouth.

But I wasn't looking at the board.

I was looking at the cliffs.

At her. Standing on the volcanic edge like a lily in a field where it couldn't possibly be growing. A waif caught in a time warp, looking like she was lost.

But she was not lost. I could see it in her posture, her gaze. She was looking directly at me.

At first, I thought it was the light—the cliffs cutting weird against the sky. My eyes were full of salt, still stinging. But I blinked, wiped my face, looked again.

Still there.

A shape. A shadow. Perched between the rocks like the sea carved her out of stone and left her behind to watch the rest of us drown.

The primordial Ceto telling me I should have known better; should have understood the dangers of the sea.

My chest went tight—not from the wipeout. Not from the cold. From something else.

The cliffs looked different now. Like they knew something I didn't. Like they'd been waiting for someone to notice her. A wisp of light, a scent on the breeze, a stone tumbling down the path like someone had just walked it.

And I did. Notice her, that is.

She didn't move. Didn't flinch. Just watched. Still as the tide. Sharp as a shark's tooth.

Somewhere above, a gull let out a single cry—and then stopped short, mid-call, like it got swallowed by the sky. The wind, which had been steady and restless all evening, dropped away in an instant. Nothing moved. Nothing breathed. Even the waves seemed to hold back, quieting just long enough to notice.

Her hair moved, ever so slightly, slow motion, as if borne on her breath, an enigma, a ghost, a whisper.

I pulled in a breath, forced my brain to work again. Blinked, shook my head, tried to shake off whatever the hell this was. The wind picked up again and tugged at my hair, the tide pulled at my feet, suddenly demanding—but she didn't move. Like the world didn't get to touch her. Aurora, breaking the spell of a past secret; a character out of a novel.

Then—

"WILL!"

The shout cracked the air like a slap.

I blinked, heart thudding in my chest like I'd been sleepwalking with my eyes open.

"Hey! You comin' back out?"

Danny's voice echoed from beyond the break. He and Charlie were bobbing in the surf, grinning, waving, yelling something about me being a coward.

I turned, shook my head like it meant something, grabbed my

board, and started swimming in. The water clung to my skin, colder than it had any right to be. My breath came hard and uneven—but it wasn't from the swim.

It was from her.

Because when I looked back—she was still there.

Watching.

My vision became a telescopic lens, zooming in, everything enlarged and brilliant, like something out of a Hitchcock movie.

I dragged myself onto the shore, water dripping from my shoulders, my board tucked under one arm. Laughter crackled from farther down the beach, the kind that came easy when everything still felt simple. Bonfire smoke tangled with seaweed and salt—sweet and familiar.

But I wasn't in it. Not really. Not tonight.

I was still looking at her.

She sat now with her spine straight, hands resting easy in her lap, like she belonged there. Like she'd always been there. A Buddha of sorts. She didn't look scared. Didn't look delicate. It was like she wasn't waiting for anyone or anything, but someone had been waiting for her. That kind of stillness? You don't fake that. You earn it. And she wore it like a second skin.

The wind lifted her hair, catching the blonde strands and making them float like they weren't even part of her. Like they belonged to the air instead. An eerie Medusa.

But I had not been turned to stone. Not yet anyway.

The last slice of sunlight spilled across the beach, catching her face and painting her in gold and something softer—something the world doesn't hand out often.

And still, she didn't move. Didn't blink. But she was real.

God help me, she was real.

I walked toward the cliff, slow. The sand sucked at my feet, cold and damp, wanting to keep something, some part of me. The wind dropped to a whisper, like even it didn't want to interrupt. Far off, the waves still crashed, but it felt quieter somehow—like the whole damn ocean was holding its breath—keeping its distance against a power it knew.

The bonfire's glow didn't reach this far. It was like this part of the beach didn't belong to the rest of the world.

I pumped my way up the dirt path to the top of the bluff, but before I could say anything, she looked at me. Like she already knew I was coming.

Something shifted. Not big. Just enough. The air around me felt cooler all of a sudden—sharper. Like it had passed through a tunnel no one else could see.

My skin prickled. A wave of goosebumps crawled up the back of my arms before I even knew why.

"You spying on me?" I tugged at the corner of my mouth, like maybe I'd smile. I didn't.

She tilted her head, calm as anything. "You looked like you were drowning."

I huffed and shook out my hair, salt flying. "Yeah? Wiping out's half the fun."

She didn't laugh. Just lifted a shoulder. "Maybe. But for a second, you were gone."

Something in the way she said it made my chest go tight. Like she hadn't just been watching a stranger—like she'd been counting the seconds I was under.

I ran a hand through my hair, trying to shake the feeling. "You could've looked away."

A flicker of a smile. Small. Sharp. "I thought about it." But she didn't.

I dropped into the grassy dirt beside her, arms draped over my knees. Close, but not too close. She looked like something the tide forgot to drag back in. Wind-tangled hair. Pale skin. A dress that didn't belong to 1962—maybe didn't belong anywhere. A dream that forgot to wake up.

"You come here often?" I asked, half teasing.

She looked out at the waves. "I used to. Not anymore."

I frowned. "Why not?"

She didn't answer right away. Just stared past me, out toward the water. Danny and Charlie were still out there, just silhouettes now, riding the last of the light. Laughing like the world hadn't started changing yet.

"Do you think they see me too?" she asked.

I followed her gaze. They didn't. Too far. Too loud. Too in their own world. I didn't need them to notice I was gone. But maybe I wanted someone to. Just once.

I let out a breath. "I dunno. Why? You some kind of ghost?"

Another one of those small smiles. No twitch. No tell. Just... there. "Aren't we all?"

It didn't sound like a joke. And it didn't sound wrong. For a second, I wasn't sure if I was dreaming. Or if I just didn't know how to wake up anymore. Maybe I was still underwater.

I watched her a second too long, trying to figure out if she was pulling my leg—or if I'd already tripped.

"You from around here?"

She nodded. "I've never been anywhere else."

I blinked. "No shot."

Her lips pressed together, almost amused. "That's a strange thing to say to someone you've just met."

I looked out past the cliffs. The lighthouse sat dead and hollow, a skeleton against the sky. No light. No warning. Just a tower full of nothing.

"Depoe Bay's small," I said. "If you've been here this whole time, I would've seen you."

She didn't argue. Just tucked a strand of hair behind her ear, casual. "Maybe you weren't looking."

She said it soft, but something about it felt aimed. Like a dart thrown underhand that still found its mark.

I glanced back toward the tide. "So, what's your excuse?"

She blinked. "Excuse?"

"For hiding out here all by yourself."

There was a pause. Then—"I snuck out."

The way she said it—careful, quiet—landed in my chest like a secret, something I wasn't supposed to know existed. Like she wasn't supposed to tell anyone.

"Snuck out from what?"

Her eyes drifted, her fingers digging gently into the sandy dirt. "My mother doesn't like me going anywhere."

She said it with a laugh in her voice, but her hands told a different story.

That explained a few things. Not everything.

"Does she know you're out here?"

A soft breath. Almost a laugh. "No. That would defeat the purpose of sneaking."

I watched her. Waited. She didn't say more.

So, I pushed it. "Let me guess. If she catches you, you're grounded till you die."

She tilted her head, thinking. "No. I don't think so."

I raised an eyebrow. "No?"

"Not at all," she said. "If she finds out—she won't let me leave again."

A beat passed. A breath.

"And if that happens..." Her voice dropped—not afraid, just honest. "I'd rather not know what life looks like after that."

The waves hissed up the shore, then slipped away like they thought better of it. A gull cried out in the distance—sharp, hollow, lonely.

I dragged a hand down my face. "Jesus. That's dramatic."

She smiled, just a twitch. "Might be."

"So, you ran away for the night. Risked getting locked down for life just to sit out here in the cold?"

She let her fingers trail through the sand beside her, soft and slow. "It's a beautiful beach."

I glanced over. She was watching the ocean like it was the first time—like she didn't trust it to stay the same for long. Like it might vanish if she blinked.

Then— "You gonna be here again tomorrow?" she asked. "Tomorrow morning?"

It caught me off guard. Felt like a trick question.

"I don't know," I said. "Should I be?"

That smile again—quiet, easy, but not empty. "If you want to," she said like it didn't matter, though we both knew it did.

She stood, brushed the sand off her dress. The wind picked up, grabbed at the loose fabric, pulled through her hair like it knew her name. She didn't fight it. She just let it take her.

She turned toward the cliffs and started walking—barefoot, steady, the dusk swallowing her up one step at a time, a spirit returning to an alternate dimension.

I didn't move. Should've. Should've said something. Called after her. Asked her name. But my chest was tight. My breath off rhythm. And by the time I found the words, she was already gone.

Behind me, the ocean stretched out forever.

"Hey—Will?"

I flinched. The world snapped back into place.

Charlie's voice was closer now. He and Danny had come in from the surf—boards slung under their arms, salt still clinging to their skin. Laughing, talking, alive. I climbed down as they approached. He squinted toward the cliffs. "Who you talkin' to?"

I looked back at the spot where she'd been.

Nothing. No sign she was ever there.

The back of my neck prickled—not just from the cold. Like I'd lost something. Or someone. Again.

I swallowed. "I don't know."

Then Danny snorted. "Didn't your ma teach you not to talk to strangers?"

Charlie laughed. Too loud. Too easy. The kind of laugh someone uses when they don't like the way something feels.

They drifted past me, shaking off the moment like water from their hair. They were already talking about the fire. The next set. Whether anyone had beer left.

The night kept moving.

But I didn't.

There were stories—kids that had gone missing, shadows on the cliffs. I never believed them. But something about that interaction seemed off. *Different.*

I stayed there, staring at the cliffs. At the dark stretch of sand where she wasn't anymore. At the ocean, pulling pieces of us away with every breath.

The lighthouse stood quiet in the distance, tall and dead and watching. Only thing besides me that saw her. The wind curled through the rocks like it had a secret it wasn't done telling.

She didn't feel like a stranger. She felt like a secret someone buried—like something half-remembered that still knew your name. Like she'd stepped out of some half-forgotten dream and dared me to remember her.

And somehow, I did. But I couldn't place the details.

There was something about her. She was still as the tide, sharp as a blade, and already too deep in my blood... And I already knew, somewhere deep in my gut—

I'd be here tomorrow.

CHAPTER TWO

I got there early. Not on purpose—at least, that's what I told myself.

The dark fog hung low, thick and heavy, curling over the cliffs like it had done this before. Like the mist that blurs the vision of the dying, it was searching for something it already lost—and would never stop trying to find. The ocean worked in slow pulses—pulling in, reaching out, pulling in, reaching out. The sky was still waking up, all pale blues and gray streaks, with just a hint of warm pink bleeding over the horizon. The kind of morning where everything felt too quiet. Too still.

I parked my bike up the street and walked down the pavement, board tucked under one arm, the salt air thick in my lungs. I wasn't looking for her. Not really. That's what I told myself, anyway. But some part of me was already hoping I'd see her again. Which made it worse. Which made it *real.*

I had on a worn red windbreaker—lightweight, a little too big in the shoulders, the kind you kept even when the zipper stuck. Underneath, a simple white tank—cheap cotton, damp already from the mist. My swim trunks were my same lucky pair from yesterday, red with a single white stripe down the side, cinched at the waist with a drawstring that was unraveling at the ends, the hem brushing just above the knee.

Against my better judgement, I was barefoot, my ankles already crusted with sand from where it had pooled in the parking lot, and I moved quiet over the warming tar like I'd done a thousand times before. My hair was still damp from the morning rinse I gave it in the sink, combed back but already curling a little at the edges from the fog. I looked like someone trying not to look like they cared. Trying real hard.

The wooden stairs under me creaked—old wood settling under the wind, or maybe something else. Maybe the town itself was shifting in its sleep, deciding whether I belonged here.

Mornings like this always felt a little off. Too still. Like the cliffs were holding their breath. Like the fog was watching, trying not to get caught up in the melee only it knew existed behind the veil.

I scanned the beach, but there was nothing but the usual morning crowd—kids darting along the shoreline, shrieking like gulls, laughter breaking against the tide. Two older women strolled near the dunes, arms looped and heads bowed like they were trading secrets, their coats pulled tight against the chill. Just past them, I thought I saw someone—just a flicker, like it was being played on a hand-cranked 35mm movie camera from the 1920s. But when I looked again, it was gone.

Probably a trick of the fog. Or maybe not. Hard to tell, some mornings. And finally, there was some older man leaning on the wooden railing near the cliffs. Probably some tourist. Stiff. Silent. Staring out to sea like it might give something back he'd lost long ago. A memory, a time, a person.

Damn. No sign of her.

I shifted my board higher on my hip and turned toward the kids. "Hey," I called. "Sam!"

The boy with the striped shirt turned. Same dusty-brown hair, same lanky frame I remembered from summer barbecues and pickup games behind the gas station. Danny's little brother.

"You seen a girl out here?"

They slowed, exchanging glances.

"A girl?" Sam squinted at me. "Who?"

"I—uh. I don't exactly know." I gestured toward the spot where I'd seen her last night. "But she's got blonde hair, pale, probably wearing some kinda dress. She was here."

The kids stared at me like I'd spoken a different language. Then—

They laughed.

Not mean. Not mocking. Just the kind of laugh people do when something doesn't make sense.

One of the girls, maybe nine or ten years old, leaned toward Sam and whispered something. I didn't catch it all—just a word.

"Ghost."

Sam paused. Just for a second. Then he laughed. Too quick. Too loud. Like it was funny. Like it *had* to be. A gull screamed overhead—too sharp, too close. I flinched without meaning to, the sound echoing longer than it should've.

"Nope," he said, grinning now. "Haven't seen anyone like that."

I exhaled and turned toward the boardwalk.

The old man by the railing didn't move. Didn't acknowledge me at all. Just kept staring out over the waves, face unreadable.

I looked to the two women near the dunes. One of them—Mrs. Kellerman, the bank teller—gave me a glance over her shoulder. The second she saw I'd caught her, she turned her head and muttered something to the woman beside her.

"Excuse me," I called. "Did either of you see a girl here earlier?"

They stopped walking, but they didn't come closer.

The bank teller looked at the other woman—could've been Mrs. Boyle, the funeral director's widow, hard to tell under the scarf and glasses—and nodded like they'd already decided how this was gonna go.

Mrs. Boyle opened her mouth like she might say something— just a flicker. But Kellerman cut her a glance, sharp and quick.

"No girl," she said.

Boyle closed her mouth. Looked down.

"No one's been here but us," Kellerman repeated, voice flatter this time. More practiced.

And the way she said it—like a prayer. Or a warning. Like she'd said it before. Like I'd asked the wrong question. A deflection given, a secret held.

The wind came in sharper now, biting through my sleeves. I stood there a second longer, just long enough to feel the silence settle back in. The sand beneath my feet felt heavier. Like it had soaked something in and didn't want to give it back. Even the kids had gone quiet. I glanced once more toward the cliffs, where the mist curled, hiding something it didn't want anyone to see.

Whatever. Maybe she hadn't come down yet.

Didn't matter.

I had time to kill.

I tucked my board closer and headed for the water.

AFTER A WHILE, I pulled myself back in.

By the time I landed on dry ground, all the noise had stopped. The kids were gone. The women were gone. The old man at the railing—gone. Like they had never been there in the first place. Even the gulls had stopped. No screech, no wingbeat. Like the beach had swallowed its breath along with everyone else.

No laughter. No footsteps. No hushed voices drifting down from the street. Just me. Just the ocean. And the town, still pretending not to notice me.

The sand still held footprints—but the breeze was already smoothing them out. Like it wanted no one to know who'd been here.

I wasn't sure when they left. Or why it felt like they had to. Like whatever I'd said had changed something. Like I'd knocked on a door and everyone inside went quiet.

I ran my hands through the sand. It was fine and damp beneath my fingers, clinging to my skin, cool where the tide had washed up.

The waves rolled in. Pulled back. Rolled in again. A slow, steady rhythm, like the breathing of an orca hidden beneath the depths was causing it to pulse. The only thing moving now.

I leaned back on my elbows and let my eyes slip half-shut. *Nothing to do but wait.* Didn't know what for. Just knew I had to.

The fog clung to the cliffs, draping itself over the rocks like a bulky shroud, moving strangely—not just rolling through with the wind, but curling, twisting, as if it were fighting something. Grappling, holding onto it. Maybe waiting for something, too.

It curled over the water, surrounding me, listening, like it knew I'd asked a question and was waiting to see if I deserved an answer.

I deserved an answer to the question I asked silently, but maybe I hadn't asked the right one.

The air felt different now. Not colder. Not warmer. Just... different. Like the pressure had shifted. Like the tide had turned, even though the waves still dragged in and out at the same slow pace.

Like the world had tilted, just a little... or slowed down or moved into another dimension, a parallel universe where all things that are broken are made whole again.

I wasn't broken, or so I kept telling myself. But here, I felt whole. Confused but whole.

I sat up, my pulse pressing against the inside of my throat. Scanned the cliffs.

Nothing.

Just rock and fog and the lighthouse standing silent in the distance.

Maybe she wasn't coming. Maybe she was just some tourist playing games with me. Maybe she never even intended to show up. Or worse, maybe she'd never been here at all. Maybe I made her up. Maybe I needed to. God, why'd I even come in the first place?

My breath fogged in the air and vanished. The gulls didn't come back. The waves kept moving, but nothing else did. Not even me.

I was starting to feel like the only thing left alive on the beach. But then—the fog shifted—not caught by wind, but like it had changed its mind. Or like something was compelling it to do so.

It peeled back slow, like it had been guarding her. Like it wasn't sure it wanted me to see.

And there—where nothing had been seconds ago—

She was.

CHAPTER THREE

She was right beside the water's edge. Too still. Too sudden. Like she'd always been there. I hadn't seen her walk up. No sound. No footsteps. No trace. Like the tide gave her back. One second, nothing. The next—there she was, barefoot again, wearing something light that moved with the wind. The color of seafoam, like she belonged there more than I did.

I didn't say anything right away. Just watched her.

She looked the same as yesterday. And yet—not. Something had shifted. Or maybe I had.

I pushed myself to my feet, brushing the sand off my hands.

"You always show up like that?" I asked.

She tilted her head, watching me like she was already in on the joke. Like she knew something I didn't.

"What, would you rather I clomp around and announce myself?"

"Maybe," I shot back. "At least then I'd hear you coming."

That got a smile out of her. Small. Like she was trying to keep it to herself. She wandered closer, letting the tide skim over her toes, the water washing in and then pulling back like it wasn't sure whether it was allowed to touch her.

"You wiped out again," she said, nodding toward my board.

I scoffed. "You weren't even here yet." My heart scudded at the words. *How could she know that?*

"I was," she said softly.

"No, you weren't." I meant it to be a joke, but it came out too sharp.

She just smiled. Like she knew I wouldn't believe her—and didn't care.

A chill worked its way up my spine, slow and careful. I hadn't seen her come down the same way as yesterday. I would've noticed. Would've heard her. But the way she moved, the way she watched— it felt like she was always one step ahead of me.

I didn't like the way that made me feel.

So I changed the subject.

We started walking along the shore, our steps falling into rhythm without even trying. It felt easier this time. More natural. Like shadows who knew each other's algorithm.

She was quick, sharp. Teasing in a way that made my brain scramble to keep up. A rhythm all her own, smooth like the tide rolling in. And I—well. I didn't mind it. Not one bit.

It should've felt normal. A morning like this—crisp air, salt on the wind, the tide rolling in and out like it always had, with all the time in the world. I mean, she was just a girl, right? Different, yes, but still just a girl. And girls—I could handle them.

But then—

Small things. A sharp snap in the woods behind the beach. Nothing weird. Just a branch breaking, maybe a bird darting through the brush. A natural sound. But she *flinched*.

Not a big thing. Not a startled jump. More like muscle memory. Like her body knew something her mind wasn't saying out loud.

A little while later, a car rumbled by on the highway above the beach. Not close. Not even that loud. She tensed.

And every now and then—like clockwork—she'd glance over her shoulder. Not like she was bored. Not like she was zoning out.

Like she was waiting for something to happen. Or waiting for *someone*.

I let it sit for a while. Let the tide keep moving, let the waves do their thing. Then—

"Expecting company?" I asked, keeping my voice easy, like I hadn't already noticed.

She didn't answer right away. Just kept her eyes on the water, her toes skimming the tide like the ocean was the only thing worth listening to. A connection.

Then, finally—

"Not exactly."

I watched her, trying to figure out what that meant. She didn't look scared. Not really. But the way she carried herself—light on her feet, never fully still—like she was waiting to hear a gun go off at the start of a race.

"You got a name?" I asked, tipping my head toward her.

That seemed to amuse her. She turned toward me, lips twitching like she was deciding whether or not to give it up.

"Jean."

I nodded. "Jean." Let it roll off my tongue, testing the weight of it. It fit her. Simple, but not small. A name that could belong to someone in a story—someone who disappears from photographs but still lingers in the air long after they're gone.

"And you?" she asked, tilting her head slightly.

"Will."

"Will," she echoed, like she was measuring it. Then—"You don't seem like a Will."

I huffed, smirking. "Yeah? What do I seem like?"

She tapped a finger to her chin, pretending to think. "Something bigger. A name with more weight. William, maybe."

I groaned. "*Nobody* calls me William."

"Not even your mother?"

"*Especially* not my mother."

Jean smiled, small and knowing. Then let it go.

Some people cast shadows, but Jean cast questions. She didn't take up much space, but somehow the air bent around her anyway. She was stunning, quiet—an enigma wrapped in calm. Like she saw the world for what it was, but was still going to let you figure it out for yourself.

I couldn't put my finger on it, but being near her felt familiar. Like I'd known her my whole life—even though I'd only just met her. And I'd never had to think this hard just to keep up with someone, but I liked it. I liked *her*.

We walked a little farther, our steps sinking into the clean damp sand, keeping time with the lazy rhythm of the tide, leaving tracks that would soon disappear, like we were never there—or here. The waves stretched out, pulled back, stretched out again—never stopping, never still. They caught up to our ankles at the same time. Then pulled away like they were listening, waiting for an answer to the questions they were implying, prodding, insistent.

"You always come out here alone?" I asked, glancing at her.

"Not always," she said. "But a lot."

"Why?"

She hesitated, just for a second. "It's quiet."

"You like quiet?"

She tilted her head slightly, considering. "I like how the ocean never stops moving. Even when it's quiet, it's still alive."

I watched her as she walked, her gaze fixed somewhere out past the waves, somewhere I couldn't follow.

"You used to come here a lot, then?"

She nodded. "A long time ago."

She couldn't have been more than seventeen or eighteen, so 'a long time ago' must have meant when she was a kid. I imagined her then, a slight girl of seven or eight, playing on the beach, collecting shells, mystified by the vastness of the ocean. And in my mind's eye, she wasn't laughing—the way children do. She was an old soul.

"But not anymore?"

Her steps slowed just slightly. "No."

I frowned. "Why not?"

A pause. Then—

"I'm not allowed to."

The way she said it—calm, like it wasn't a big deal—made something in my chest twist.

I studied her, waiting for more. Some kind of explanation. But she just kept walking, arms loose at her sides, the wind catching the hem of her dress.

"You talk like you're writing a book," I muttered, mostly to myself.

She finally glanced at me, a small glint of something in her eyes. "Maybe I am."

"Yeah?" I smirked. "And what, I'm in it?"

"Maybe."

That caught me off guard. I let out a short breath of a laugh, shaking my head. "You always talk like that?"

"Like what?"

"Like you're halfway between a poem and a riddle."

She smiled—small, secretive, unreadable. "Maybe I just like keeping you guessing."

I let that sit between us. Noticed the wind pull at the edges of her dress. Let the sound of the waves drag the moment into something slower, something weightless. She didn't just talk like she was from another world—she made me wish I could live in it. Then—

Another car passed on the highway. Far enough that the sound barely touched us. But I felt it when she tensed.

Not much. Just a flicker. Just a shift.

I stopped walking.

"Jean?"

She looked up at me.

"Who are you waiting for?"

A gust of wind came off the water, kicking up the scent of salt and driftwood.

Jean looked down, her hair falling in front of her face, hiding whatever expression she wasn't ready to show.

Then, just as softly—

"No one."

A lie.

Or maybe not. Maybe she wasn't waiting for anyone. Maybe she was hiding from someone. I didn't ask again.

Instead, I just stopped walking. Planted myself onto the sand and extended my forearms over my knees.

"So, did you go to Taft High?"

Jean shook her head before sitting right beside me. "Home-schooled."

Right. That made sense. I would've run into her before otherwise.

But something about the way she said it—it wasn't shy. Wasn't proud, either. Just a fact. A wall I wasn't supposed to climb over.

Thing was, I wasn't great at leaving things alone. Never have been.

"What about after?" I pressed. "You're my age, right? Eighteen? Good ol' class of '62?"

She nodded. "Yeah. My birthday was back in April."

I laughed. "Well happy belated! You said you've lived here forever —ever think about leaving Depoe Bay?"

She hesitated. Just for a second.

"Sometimes," she said, voice soft. Like the word wasn't even meant for me.

Then, just as quick, she steered the conversation somewhere else. Like she'd already decided I didn't need to know more than that.

I let it go.

For now.

Jean turned the question back on me. "Why do you ask? Do you have plans to leave?"

I leaned back on my hands, staring out at the water.

The tide came in slow, brushing against the sand like it had nowhere better to be. The horizon stretched wide and empty, a thin line between sea and sky, endless to the eye; limitless to the spirit if you knew where to look.

I sighed. "I've been planning my escape since I was a kid," I admitted. "Depoe Bay's small. Too small. It's the kind of place where you grow up with a story already written for you. Old men sit on porches, watching like they already know how your life's gonna end. The roads all lead back to the same places. No one leaves—not really. They either die or disappear. You don't get to decide who you are. The town does. And once it decides— that's it."

Jean hummed, considering. "Like a script?"

I nodded. "Yeah. A script. And no one ever thinks to ask who wrote it."

She tilted her head, watching me now.

I let out a short breath, shaking my head. "I don't know. You ever just feel like you're supposed to be somewhere else?" I glanced at her. "Like you got dealt the wrong cards? Born in the wrong place? The wrong time?"

Jean didn't answer right away. She looked past me, out toward the ocean, like maybe the answer was buried somewhere in the waves.

"Not the wrong time," she murmured. "Just... trapped in the wrong story."

I frowned, shifting toward her. "Yeah? What kinda story you think you're in?"

She smiled faintly, dragging her fingers through the damp sand.

"I don't know yet. But I know how it ends."

"How's that?"

Jean's voice was light. Simple.

"The girl never gets out."

Something about the way she said it sent a strange feeling through me.

"Sure she does," I argued. "Every story's gotta end somewhere. She's got just as good a chance as anyone else. The trick is you gotta rewrite the script. Be your own showrunner. Don't let them get in your head."

Jean let out a quiet laugh, like she wasn't sure if I was serious. Then she turned back to the water.

"Maybe. But for you... why do you want to leave so badly?"

I studied her, but she wouldn't look at me now. Like she already knew how this one was gonna go.

"I guess I never really fit," I said. "People think I'm trouble. Maybe I am. Got into my fair share of fights. Egged my fair share of houses. Stole a couple road signs. Drag raced down the coastal highway at two in the morning."

I smirked a little, tapping my knuckles absently against my knee. "Earned a scar for my efforts."

Jean's eyes flicked to my hand, tracing the faint white line across my knuckles.

"From a fight?" she asked.

I shook my head. "Not exactly, but... it led to one. Few months ago. Some guy ran his mouth about a buddy of mine. I should've walked away, but... that's never been my strong suit."

Jean smiled a little. "No, I don't imagine it is."

I glanced at her. "What gave it away?"

She just shook her head, amused.

Then—before I could say anything else—I noticed something.

Small. Barely there.

Faint white lines on her fingers, just below the knuckles.

I tipped my head, nodding toward them. "What about you, though? Those little marks on your hand. They got a story, don't they?"

Jean blinked, then—so subtly I almost didn't catch it—she covered her hand with her palm. Then she smiled, small and hesitant. "Not as exciting as yours."

I waited.

Jean turned her hand over, stretching out her fingers, her eyes flicking down at the pale, thin indents. They caught the light, delicate and quiet.

"It's stupid, really." Her voice was fragile, but there was something behind it. Something heavier. "And I guess I deserve to be reminded of it." She hesitated. Like saying it out loud might make it real again. Then— "It's from a fork."

That threw me.

"A fork?"

She nodded, still looking at her hand.

"I was young. Maybe six, maybe seven. I don't remember what I said. Just... I wanted to know why."

Something in the way she said it made my stomach turn.

"Why what?" My voice was quieter now.

She exhaled, tilting her palm, watching how the scars caught the light.

"Why I couldn't play outside."

A slow chill pressed against the back of my neck.

I didn't speak. I couldn't. Something about the way she said it— quiet, flat—landed too deep.

Like a story told so many times, it stopped sounding like pain.

Just memory. Another life; another time. Maybe another person altogether.

"And that was the answer?"

Jean didn't say anything. Just stared ahead at the waves, the wind shifting the sand beneath us.

Then, after a long moment, she curled her fingers into her palm again, hiding the scars like they were something she wasn't supposed to let me see—couldn't fully understand or explain even if she tried.

"Guess I should've walked away too," she murmured, hollow, half to herself.

She was good at this.

Good at making things disappear.

I ran a hand through my hair, looking back at the ocean. That was the one thing I'd miss about this place.

"I figure I'll take off soon," I said, voice softer now. "Ride my Harley across the country. Maybe settle somewhere like the Outer Banks. East Coast's still got the ocean, but it's far enough to feel different."

Jean didn't speak for a long time.

The wind pressed against the tide, sending foam skimming across the sand in uneven streaks. The morning fog was beginning to lift, not in any rush—just thinning in slow, hesitant swirls, reluctant to give up its sway. It pulled back in patches, revealing pieces of the beach, but never everything.

Like it knew we couldn't handle knowing everything at once.

Still hiding... something.

Then, almost too soft to catch—

"Do you think you'll ever come back?"

There was something in the way she asked it that made me pause. It didn't sound casual. Didn't sound like small talk.

It felt more like a question she already knew the answer to.

Like she was testing whether I did.

I turned to look at her, but she was already watching the ocean, her face unreadable. Not guarded—just quiet. Still.

Waiting.

I swallowed, my throat tight. "Maybe," I said.

Jean nodded once. Nothing more.

But there was something about the way she did it—slow, knowing, like she was agreeing with something I hadn't even said out loud.

I let out a breath, stretching my legs out in the sand, trying to shake the feeling pressing against my ribs.

"You don't think I will, do you." It was a statement more than a question.

Jean hesitated.

"I think," she said, picking at a loose thread in her dress, "some places don't let you leave so easily."

The way she said it—it wasn't a warning. It wasn't even a challenge. It was a fact.

I wanted to argue. Say I wasn't like the others. That I'd leave and never look back. But the words didn't come. Because maybe... maybe she wasn't wrong.

I scoffed. "Depoe Bay? Don't think it's got much of a grip on me."

Jean turned toward me then, really looking at me.

"Not the town," she murmured.

Something about the way she said it made my smirk falter.

I frowned, shifting toward her. "Then what?"

Jean's eyes flickered down, like she was measuring her words before she gave them to me.

"It's easy to say you'll leave," she said finally. "Harder to actually do it."

I let out a short breath. "I'm not just talking, Jean. I've got plans."

She didn't flinch. "Plans are easy. Life's not."

I stared at her, watching the wind tangle through her hair, the way her fingers dragged idle shapes in the sand without really thinking about it. She wasn't being combative—just honest. Like she'd lived the difference. I opened my mouth to tell her I'd make it out. That I wasn't like the rest. But for some reason, the words felt heavier than usual.

"You sound like you're speaking from experience," I muttered.

Jean gave a small, secretive smile. "Maybe."

I narrowed my eyes. "You ever try to leave?"

She tilted her head toward the sky, letting the question settle. The breath she let out was slow, careful. Like she was going back in her mind, dusting off something she hadn't looked at in a while.

"Didn't get far," she said.

There was something in her voice that made my chest go tight. Not sadness, exactly. Just weight.

"Why not?"

She didn't answer right away. For a second, I thought she wasn't going to. Then, just above the wind: "Some things hold you back."

I frowned. "Like what?"

She looked out toward the ocean again, her expression unreadable.

"Like a fork," she said quietly.

A chill crept down my spine. I glanced at her, trying to read her face, but she wouldn't look at me now. Wouldn't explain.

And somehow—I knew she wasn't going to.

The wind shifted again, colder this time. I swallowed hard and turned back to the water. The tide was rolling in. Slow. Steady. It didn't care what was said up here. It would continue to exist long after we were gone. Words didn't matter to the vastness of the sea, whose mystery never unraveled, never revealed, never intruded without provocation.

The waves crept up the shore, stretched their fingers into the sand, and retreated again. Over and over. Like they couldn't make up their collective mind. Moving as one under some force beyond our understanding. Like they wanted to stay but didn't know how. Automatons under the will of some god.

Or maybe they intended to remind us of their power over us, of their control; that their opportunity lay just beyond the edge of the foam, a place where they made the rules.

Jean sat beside me, her hair tangled from the wind, eyes locked on the horizon. I couldn't tell if she was seeing something specific, or if she just liked the idea of looking that far ahead. I had the sudden urge to ask what she saw—but I didn't.

Instead, I said, "I should probably head back soon."

She didn't turn to me. "Then go."

She said it like she already knew I wouldn't.

I flexed my hands against my knees, swallowed the sentence that didn't matter anyway. The air felt heavier now, like the conversation had tilted into something else. Something we weren't sure how to carry.

"I meant what I said," I murmured. "About leaving."

This time, Jean looked at me. Her face gave nothing away.

"I know."

And that was the problem.

Because suddenly, I wasn't sure if I did mean it. I wanted to mean it. Told myself this is what I'd been planning for, had everything in place. But somehow, it rang hollow to me now.

Some things are easier to say than they are to do. Some roads look open until you try to take them. And some places—some people —don't really let you go.

The wind shifted. Just slightly. Enough to make the hair rise at the back of my neck.

"Same time tomorrow?" she asked, not looking at me. Just watching the horizon.

It was like she already knew the answer. Like she always had. Like maybe she just wanted to hear me say it.

The tide rolled back again, pulling away from the shore. But it never got far. It always came back. Reminding.

I wondered if the tide ever really meant to leave—if it had the power to leave—or if it just learned how to pretend. Maybe I had too.

Sometimes, we live in our heads, where things that are broken can become whole again.

"...Yeah." I said, quieter now. "I'll be here."

CHAPTER FOUR

Jean's words stuck to my brain like gum on pavement—gritty, stubborn, and too old to scrape clean.

"Some places don't let you leave so easily."

Yeah? Well, I'd like to see them try.

The road stretched ahead, winding and cracked, the pavement fighting to hold itself together like the rest of this town. I rode my Harley through it, past the mile markers, past the ghost-town storefronts, past the memories clinging to every damn street corner like cobwebs in a film noir Western.

Mile marker 126 blinked past me. It felt like a checkpoint. Like a test. Like if I hit the gas just a little harder, I could break the spell, the enchantment that threatened to hold me; leave it all behind.

I knew I was supposed to go. Knew there was something waiting for me somewhere else, something real, something better. After all, she was just another girl. But ever since I met Jean, my head had been a tangled mess of questions, like a ball of yarn I couldn't pick apart.

I mean... It's not like I could take her with me.

The roar of the engine should've been enough to drown it all out, but the thoughts just wedged themselves in deeper.

As I rolled into town, I felt the weight of every dead-eyed stare press against my skin. Same old faces. Same sweaty beer cans clutched in the same tired hands. Same voices, worn thin from telling the same stories like they were trying to remember how to forget.

Outside the boat rental shack, Old Man Duffy sat in a metal folding chair with one leg stretched out and a busted radio tucked against his shoulder. He didn't look up, just thumbed the dial like he might tune into something worth caring about. Outside the barbershop, Hazel Cooper perched herself against the dirty tile wall, curlers in her hair and a cigarette trembling between her fingers. Across the street, the Monroe twins—Sadie and Sarah—paused their sweeping of the bait shop steps, brooms angled like weapons.

I could hear them now. The whispers curled around the telephone wires, tucked between the cracks in the pavement, slithering up through the vents of corner-store coolers.

"There he goes. The one who's gonna wreck himself and take the town with him."

"Another one trying to run. He'll be back."

"They always come back."

It wasn't said with hope. It was said like a threat disguised as small talk. It was a prophecy. Like the road just looped back around, no matter how far you thought you got.

Maybe they were right. Maybe no one ever really leaves this place.

But I had to try. A calling more than defiance.

The wind pressed against my back, like it wanted to push me forward, push me out.

Then—home.

The neighborhood perched up on the cliffs, stubborn against the wind, against time, against me. The ocean stretched out behind it, hidden under a low-hanging fog that made the whole world feel like it ended at the tree line.

I pulled into the driveway, my Harley giving one last grumble before falling silent.

And then—

"Whoa, Will!"

Charlie's voice, cutting through the quiet. I turned.

There he was, leaning out the window of his black '57 Chevy, one arm draped over the side, fingers tapping on the chrome trim like a slow heartbeat. His red hair was a mess of soft curls, sun-warmed and wind-tousled, like he'd been driving with the windows down all morning. He wore a faded white tee, sleeves rolled just enough to look like he hadn't meant to roll them at all.

He looked like a summer that hadn't ended yet. Like he'd never known what it meant to worry.

"Glad I caught you 'fore you peeled out," he said. "What time you hittin' the road?"

I shrugged, kicking down the stand. "Not sure yet. Might push things back to tomorrow."

Charlie's grin slipped—just a flicker, like a hairline crack in a windshield. Gone before you could be sure you saw it.

"Tomorrow, huh?" He drummed his fingers against the wheel. Slow. Thoughtful. Like a clock ticking down. "Didn't peg you for the waiting kind. Not after—"

He cut himself off. Cleared his throat. Rolled his shoulders like he could shake something off.

"Well." He forced a grin. "One more night never hurt nobody."

We both knew that wasn't true.

I hesitated, shifting my weight. Then, like it wasn't a big deal, like I wasn't really asking—I said, "You ever hear of a girl named Jean?"

Charlie blinked.

"Jean?" He paused—barely—but it was there. A flicker. Then gone. "Can't say I know one."

That was it. No follow-up. No questions. Just a flat, easy dismissal, like the name meant nothing. Like he'd never even heard it in passing.

And then, before I could press it—

Charlie let out a low whistle. "Hey, you around later? I got a date with Polly tonight—figured I'd see if she's got a friend hangin' around. Bridget's single again. Thought you might wanna tag along."

Polly.

Used to be louder with me. Now she talks like we're neighbors who wave instead of friends who remembered things we're not supposed to. And when she did, it was always the same—neutral, distant. Never mean, just careful. Like she was holding me at arm's length without making a show of it. Like she didn't want to act different, but she didn't want to act the same, either. I used to think it was because of that night. It probably still was.

I cleared my throat. "Last night was supposed to be our last night. Wouldn't wanna ruin the memory."

Charlie smirked. "You sure? Word is Bridget's finally lit up a smoke. Guess she's really leanin' into the whole bad decision lifestyle."

I laughed, shaking my head. "Nah. Last thing I need is a reason to stay."

Charlie nodded, his smirk softening. "Yeah. Yeah, I get that." He exhaled, rolling his shoulders back again, like the air felt heavier all of a sudden. "Bay's gonna feel kinda empty without you."

I swallowed, glancing past him. Past the road, past the rooftops, past the cliffs. The ocean was out there somewhere, buried under the fog. The waves reminding.

"Take care, Charlie," I said, quieter now. Then, after a beat— "And, uh... thanks for being a friend."

Charlie's grin faltered—just for a second, just enough for me to see something behind it.

Then he threw the Chevy into drive. "Anytime, man. You know where to find me."

The car rumbled off, gravel kicking up in its wake.

I stood there a moment longer, listening. The wind curled through the cliffs, brushed past the trees, tangled in the power lines, whispered across the roof of my house.

This place had always felt too small. Too predictable.

I had spent years waiting for the moment I could leave.

And yet—there it was. That old, ugly feeling. Like something had its hooks in my ribs, keeping me tethered. Like the town itself was waiting, patient, almost mocking, knowing I'd never make it past the county line. Not this time. Not the last time.

I used to think leaving was easy. Then I learned some roads don't end where you expect them to.

Some places don't let you leave so easily.

Maybe. But I knew I still had to try.

INSIDE, the house was warm—but not the kind of warm that made you want to stay. It was tight, heavy, like the walls had been holding their breath for too long. Like they didn't know how to let it out. The kind of heat that lingers after a fight or a funeral. The kind that feels more like memory than comfort.

It smelled like dinner—something hearty, heavy. The kind of meal you made when you didn't know how to say goodbye. But beneath it, always, that stale cigarette smoke soaked into the walls, woven into the couch cushions, clinging to the floorboards like a shadow that could never leave. You could scrub all you wanted, throw open every window, light every candle in town. But some things don't fade. They burrow deeper. They wait. The smoke, the grief, the memories—they cling to this place, the only home they've ever had, part of a town that kept its grip on every mind, body, and soul, real or imagined. Any attempt to leave would... well, I wouldn't know that yet but I was willing to find out. To see what I was made of. To take my chances against a half-imagined force that made this place a town whose reality was a constant grimace of... of what? Fear? Suspicion? Threat?

The radio was on in the kitchen, the dial set to Mom's usual station. A voice hummed through the air, old and smooth, carrying something slow from another lifetime.

Eddie's voice rang out from the hallway, bright and upbeat, like he had been waiting for me to walk through the door.

"Hey! Look who finally made it home!"

I heard him before I saw him—moving around Mom like they were running some old routine, the kind that never needed talking through. A well-oiled machine.

"Mom made meatloaf," he called. "Set the table and everything. Figured you might want a bite before you, y'know... took off on your grand adventure."

He said it with a smile in his voice, but the words hit harder than he meant.

Because I hadn't told them.

Hadn't said out loud that this wasn't a trip. Not really. Not the kind you came back from.

Dad used to say goodbyes don't mean anything if you don't stick to them. I guess I didn't see the point yet. Mom, though—she knew. Or at least she had an idea. You could see it in the way she moved, careful and quiet, like naming it would make it real. It was in the meatloaf and the way the table was set. A grand gesture to be remembered one day. Some day.

Eddie? Eddie was different. He'd be sixteen next month, but he still looked at me like I hung the stars. Like I had some kind of secret map for how to get through the world. For being cool. Like I wasn't just some burnout with a motorcycle and no plan.

I couldn't do that to him.

"Yeah," I called back, forcing my voice lighter, brighter.

"Figured I'd stick around one more night. Outer Banks'll still be there tomorrow."

Eddie leaned into the doorway a second later, a dish towel slung over one shoulder, freckles faint under the kitchen light. His brown hair was tousled from running his hands through it too much—he did that when he was thinking, or nervous, or just bored. He wasn't tall yet, not quite, but you could tell he was growing into himself. A little lanky, a little awkward in that in-between way, all limbs and good intentions.

He wore his jeans cuffed at the ankle like he'd seen in a magazine once, paired with a tucked-in Henley that had a faint grease stain near the hem—probably from helping Mom fix the toaster again. One sock was bunched at the heel. He didn't notice.

There was something unshakably clean about Eddie, like no matter how tired the world got, he'd still be standing there holding out a glass of water and asking if you were okay.

I passed through the living room, through the quiet hum of the old television set, through the echoes of voices that weren't here anymore.

The kitchen window was open, the cool salt air drifting in. Sam Cooke played low on the radio, crooning about bringing it all back home. A voice full of ache. Like he'd already lost something, and knew it wasn't coming back.

Mom was at the stove, pulling the meatloaf from the oven. The orange glow hit her in the face, and for a second, she looked younger. Or maybe I was just remembering her wrong.

Her cigarette burned out in the ashtray on the counter, but the smoke still curled like the fog on the cliffs—thin, quiet, and impossible to shake. Secrets and memories. Reminding.

"The man of the hour," she said, lifting the pan onto the stovetop. "Didn't think we'd see you tonight."

But I knew she'd hoped. Her 'perfect dinner' proved that.

I leaned against the counter, hands shoved in my jacket pockets. "You know me. Gotta keep the people wanting more."

Mom smirked, tossing a dish towel over her shoulder. Her smile didn't quite reach her eyes. Not all the way. Like she was still trying to forget the sound of sirens. Still trying not to imagine me bleeding out somewhere in a ditch. "So, what? Had a change of heart while you were out?"

I shrugged, aiming for casual. "Did some thinking, sure. Do that a lot, really."

Mom scoffed. "Twelve years of report cards say otherwise."

I huffed a laugh as she nudged the oven door closed with her hip.

"Take a seat," she said, waving a hand at the table. "We've got everything handled here. Dinner's ready in five."

I took my usual seat. The one that used to be Dad's, before it became mine. Funny how that happens. You keep sitting in a chair long enough and suddenly, it remembers you instead of the ghosts of those who came before.

Eddie plopped down next to me, all grins, all energy.

"So, what's the first stop gonna be? The beach? I hear the Outer Banks are full of pirate stuff. Blackbeard and all that."

I smirked. "Sounds fitting for a guy like me." I leaned back in my chair, stretching my arms behind my head. "If I find his treasure, I'll send you a piece."

"Nah, bring it back yourself," Eddie shot back. "Save it for my birthday. Definitely save it for my birthday. I'll trade it in for a hot rod."

Mom placed the meatloaf onto the table, shaking her head. "Don't go getting any ideas."

Eddie just grinned, unbothered. "What? I mean—unless you've already got something lined up for me."

Mom smoothed a napkin over her lap. "You can save up like everyone else," she said, giving him that knowing look. "Get one when you're nice and ready."

Eddie sighed dramatically, slumping back in his chair. "Guess that's a no, then."

"Sorry, kid," I said, offering a lopsided grin. "Think I crushed that dream for you."

Eddie shrugged, still smiling. "Eh. We all know I'm the responsible one, anyway."

I chuckled, but Mom's voice cut through the moment, softer now.

"Don't dwell on the past, Will."

I blinked. Looked up.

She was looking right at me. Not scolding. Not teasing. Just—looking. She reached out, placed a hand over mine. A small touch, but enough to send a crack through something in my chest. "What's done is done," she said.

I nodded, but my throat felt tight. Mom was never the type to lock us in the house. But she didn't chase us when we left, either. She just stayed behind, setting the table. The conversation shifted after that. Forks scraped against plates, Eddie filled the silence with stories, and I let the noise of it all wrap around me, warm and familiar. But my mind stayed somewhere else.

How much longer would it be like this? The three of us, sitting at this table. Same meal, same voices, same sounds. Just like it was before Dad left. Just like it'd be after I left. Except—quieter.

Would Mom still set three plates by accident? Would she pause, mid-motion, realizing too late? She never talked about when he left. But sometimes her silence was loud enough. She'd still set one for him, the first few weeks. I caught her once, frozen with a fourth fork in her hand. She tossed it in the drawer like it bit her. And what about Eddie? Would he still crack jokes, or would that weight settle into his shoulders before he even hit seventeen?

I didn't know if I'd be missed. Or just remembered. There's a difference. One leaves the porch light on. The other lets it burn out.

Ghosts weren't real. I knew that. But I wondered if I'd become one anyway. Lingering in the spaces I used to fill. In the laughter I used to share. Just a glimmer, an impression, a suggestion that I had once been there. Or would I disappear altogether from this house the way Dad did?

I swallowed, pushing the thought away. For now, I let their laughter fill the air. For now, I let myself pretend I'd come back.

Then, somewhere between bites of dinner, Eddie said,

"Hey, you remember that old ghost story? The one about the girl on the beach?"

I glanced up, startled and hiding it. "Which one?"

He waved his fork. "Ghost Girl of Depoe Bay. Supposedly she shows up just before people go missing."

I paused, staring down at my plate.

"Yeah. I've heard it," I said. "Little girl, right? Runs up to strangers in the fog, asking for help. But when they turn around, she's gone. Drowned out there years ago." I cleared my throat. "One of my... buddies used to love that one. Swore he knew her, back when they were kids. Called her Jenny."

Eddie blinked. "That's not the version I heard."

I looked up. "No?"

He leaned in like he was telling me a secret.

"This one's about a woman. Blonde. Pretty, I guess. Shows up to guys in the early morning—always on the beach. Sometimes in the fog, or when it's raining. Calls to them. Then walks straight into the ocean." He stabbed a green bean, casual. "They follow her in. And no one ever finds the bodies."

I gave a quiet laugh. Mom laughed too. But she didn't look at me when she did. Like if she met my eyes, she'd have to admit I was already gone.

"Yeah, well, I don't believe in ghosts. But if it *were* the same one, I'm pretty sure it wouldn't *age*." I pushed a piece of potato around my plate. "Either Depoe's got a few too many legends... or maybe we've got a new serial killer on our hands."

It was a joke. But then I saw her again—Jean, barefoot in the fog, eyes full of something that didn't belong to this place. And just for a second, I wasn't sure I was kidding.

Mom, who had been quiet until now, spoke up. "This town's always had legends."

I looked at her. She stared past the table, past the room, into something else.

Eddie snorted. "Yeah, but not real ones."

Mom set down her fork. Didn't look at me. Didn't look at Eddie either. Just stared out the window like she was looking for something, waiting for something.

"Believe me. They all start somewhere," she said.

The room felt smaller. Eddie didn't notice, he just kept talking, moving on like it was just another dumb story. Forks scraped against plates. The house hummed with warmth, conversation, and the rhythm of something normal. But underneath it, the crack had already formed. And I couldn't stop staring at it.

AFTER DINNER, the house settled into that kind of quiet that only happens when everyone else has gone to bed.

Eddie knocked out first, barely making it past nine. Mom followed not long after, slipping onto the porch for one last cigarette before calling it a night.

Now, all that was left was the imprint of her habit—the smell of smoke hanging in the air, curling down the hallway, sinking into the floorboards, mixing with the scent of old pine and saltwater pushing in through my open window.

I sat on the edge of my bed, elbows on my knees, staring at the wall like it might suddenly say something worth hearing. But the only thing in my head was her.

Jean.

The way she moved—like she wasn't entirely tethered to the ground. Like she belonged to someplace else, someplace just outside the reach of this town. She spoke in sharp edges and quiet hesitations, like every word was part of some bigger riddle. Like she knew more than she was letting on and figured I wouldn't understand it even if she told me.

She didn't make sense.

And she didn't leave footprints. Or was I imagining that? Of course she did. We all do.

She was a mystery without a key. A story someone started but never finished. A puzzle missing half the pieces and all of the corners.

And maybe that was the point.

Maybe she wasn't supposed to make sense.

Still, I couldn't stop trying.

I leaned back, ran a hand through my hair, and let out a long breath.

"Getting attached isn't an option," I said out loud, like that might make it true. Like if I said it with enough conviction, it would start to sound like something I actually believed.

Because I was leaving.

That had always been the plan—long before I met her, long before I even had a good reason. I'd been telling myself for years that places like this don't let you grow, don't let you change. They just hold you in place, like amber. Preserve you in silence until the memory of you becomes more valuable than you ever were. Unless you lay lost, buried in the ground forever.

But the more I tried to keep Jean out of my thoughts, the more she pressed in. Like static I couldn't tune out. An old ham radio sending messages from another time. A melody I couldn't name, but couldn't stop humming. Like it had been written for me and I just didn't know the words yet. A flicker of something in the corner of my eye that vanished every time I turned my head.

She lingered.

She wasn't going anywhere, not in my head. Not anytime soon.

And the worst part was—I didn't want her to.

I smirked, shaking my head at myself, at the whole stupid mess of it. I was starting to look forward to tomorrow.

And that—more than any ghost story—terrified me.

CHAPTER FIVE

Somehow, it seemed like Jean slipped through my fingers like fog through floorboards—there, then gone, leaving the space colder than before. A tease, a smile, a subject change so smooth I'd almost forget I'd asked anything at all. *Almost.* But I wasn't stupid. I knew when someone was hiding something. And Jean? She was hiding a lot. And the next time I saw her, I wasn't about to let her slip away so easy. I wanted answers, though I wasn't sure I had a right to any of them.

The sky sagged, gray and heavy, like an old canvas stretched too thin. A storm was out there somewhere, coiling up over the horizon, waiting for the right moment to make itself known. The wind had that sharp, electric bite to it, the kind that made the hair on the back of your neck stand up. The ocean below moved slow, steady, like it was thinking something over. It rolled up against the cliffs, then pulled back, like it had a secret it wasn't ready to spill.

There was that smell, thick with salt and pine—like the ocean had been chewing on the trees and spitting them back out. The air was damp enough that it stuck to your skin, the mist curling through the rocks like restless hands reaching for something just out of grasp.

There was a weight to the silence, too—like the whole town was holding its breath, waiting for my next move.

Jean stood at the shoreline, her toes sinking into the wet sand, arms crossed against the wind that tangled her hair into something wilder than she probably liked. Her dress—pale blue, the kind you'd find folded in a hope chest—fluttered like it wanted to leave without her, insistent in its tug and flap.

She looked like she belonged here. Not just part of the landscape, but something embedded in it, like a watermark on a photograph, colorized, faded over the years. Something that had always been here and always would be.

I walked up beside her, the surf licking at my ankles—cold enough to shock, to remind me I was standing here, real and breathing.

I'd left my motorcycle at the landing and kicked off my boots at the edge of the rocks, set them down where the tide wouldn't reach. My jeans were cuffed and damp, clinging to my legs, and the wind tugged at the hem of my white tee beneath the weight of my leather jacket. The jacket creaked slightly when I moved, stiff from sea air and too many years of wear, but it still felt like mine. Like the one thing that fit when everything else was shifting.

The sand sucked at my heels as I stepped closer, slow, barefoot, each step pulling something down out of me.

"You always this much of a mystery?" I asked, tilting my head, watching her from the corner of my eye.

Jean didn't look at me right away. Her gaze stayed on the horizon, her expression thoughtful, distant. Like maybe she hadn't heard me. Or maybe she was deciding whether or not I deserved an answer.

When she finally spoke, her lips curled—barely. Not a smile, exactly. More like she was amused by some joke I wasn't in on. "And you? Always this determined to solve things?"

"That depends." I dug my hands into my jacket pockets, rocking back on my heels. "You got something to hide?"

Jean hummed, soft and almost melodic, tipping her face toward the sky. "Don't we all?"

She said it lightly, but it hit wrong—like she wasn't asking me to agree. She was warning me not to ask again. The mist curled in tighter, swallowing the space between us like it wanted to keep her hidden, keep us separated. Even the wind quieted, like it didn't want to interrupt her lie. But I wasn't one to back down.

"Nah." I scoffed, kicking at the sand. "I don't buy that."

She finally turned her gaze on me, studying. There was something in her eyes, something flickering and unreadable, like she was flipping through options in her head, deciding which version of herself she wanted to give me. Then, with a slow breath, she looked back at the ocean.

"You ever think that maybe knowing everything takes the beauty out of things?" she asked. "That maybe a little mystery's good for the soul?"

"Sounds like something someone with a secret would say."

Jean exhaled a quiet laugh, shaking her head. "Maybe. Or maybe I just like the idea of something being left untouched."

I narrowed my eyes, trying to read between the lines. But Jean had this way of talking that felt like poetry—like she could make you believe anything was profound if she said it softly enough.

"Sometimes hiding's the only way to survive being seen," she continued, voice low, like it was a line from a book she wasn't supposed to be reading. The kind of book that got banned from libraries because it was too deep, too controversial and profound, and told of things that children should not know.

"Yeah, well. Can't say I've ever been the type to leave things untouched." My voice was lighter now, but I was watching her closer than before. "But I'm just trying to get to know you, Jean. That's all."

Jean didn't flinch. Didn't even blink.

For a long second, she just watched me, like she was measuring something, like she was trying to decide if I was worth the weight of an answer.

Then—so casual it almost felt careless—she shrugged. "Maybe some people just get tired of being the wrong version of themselves in everyone else's story."

"Yeah?" I smirked, tilting my head. "Well, I'm not asking for a version. All I want to know is..." I paused, taking her in. "Who's the real Jean?"

Jean's lips twitched, but she didn't smile. "Wouldn't you like to know." It wasn't quite sarcastic. Just a hint of rebellion and contempt.

I let out a short laugh, shaking my head. "Alright, fine. Keep your little secrets."

Jean lifted a brow. "Oh? Giving up already?"

I grinned. "Not a chance."

The waves kept rolling in, steady, patient. The mist curled low over the sand, winding itself through the rocks, around our ankles. Jean kept her hands tucked into the pockets of her dress, but her shoulders had relaxed, just a little. Like maybe she was starting to believe I wasn't a threat. The wind dipped, just for a second. Enough to let a lock of her hair settle against her cheek instead of clawing at it. Like the world had paused to watch her breathe.

"C'mon," I said, nodding toward the cliffs. "I wanna take you somewhere."

She hesitated, just for a second. "Where?"

"You'll see."

Jean studied me for a moment, quiet, thoughtful. The wind tugged at her hair, whipping loose strands around her face, and she made no move to tuck them back.

Then, finally—

"Alright," she said, slipping her hands from her pockets. "Lead the way, detective."

And just like that—

She was coming with me. The hard cliffs loomed behind us, glaring, demanding us to stay. I held my breath for a second, feeling like something was telling me it didn't want us to go. Like if I took her off this beach, something terrible would happen. Removing the Golden Idol that held the place together.

But I didn't care.

In the distance, the lighthouse stood like an old sentry, waiting for something that had already passed—and wouldn't return. Like it was stuck in a moment it couldn't get out of. I knew that feeling.

THE SCENT HIT ME FIRST—SALT and rust, like the air inside an old work garage, where parts no longer fit cars and tools gave up their tasks long ago. Made me think of things I hadn't thought about in a long time. Things I didn't like dragging into the light.

The lamp here didn't work anymore. Hasn't for years. But people still check, still hope maybe this time it'll flicker back on. Like they need it to. Like something is coming home and they don't want to miss it. It used to guide people. Now it just watches the sea and remembers what is lost.

The wind sliced through the cracks in its walls, whispering old secrets that had long since washed away with the tide. But the waves remember and bring them home, over and over, wanting someone to notice, to remember. The ocean stretched out before it, vast and hungry, the kind of hungry that didn't rush—just waited. It had been trying to swallow this place for years, but even the sea got tired eventually.

Rust climbed its ribs like ivy, flaking white paint peeling in sheets off railings and stairs that wound their way up the tower. This place had once mattered; it had once stood tall and proud, and maybe it still wanted to, but time had stripped it down to its bones. Useless in the modern world.

The Pacific crashed against the cliffs below, sending up mist that clung to my skin like a film.

Jean stood a step behind me, arms crossed against the wind. She looked up at the lighthouse the way people look at old photos, like she was trying to see something that wasn't there anymore. *Had she been here before?*

I ran my fingers over the old metal handle. The corrosion bit back, rough and uneven. It had seen too many storms, too many years.

"Ready?" I asked.

Jean's brow furrowed. "Are we supposed to be here?"

I smirked, glancing over my shoulder. "You trust me?"

She let out a soft breath, half a laugh, but there was something careful in her eyes—something like hesitation, like a maybe disguised as a yes. The wind caught a strand of her hair, twisting it across her cheek. She tucked it away, thoughtful.

"That's the sort of question you ask before taking someone to an abandoned place," she said. "Not after."

The wind howled through the cracks in the cliffs. I almost told her it was safe. But that would've been a lie—and she'd know it.

I shrugged. "What, you scared?"

Jean gave me a look. "You really want the answer to that?"

I grinned, rocking back on my heels. "Nope. What's the verdict, then?"

She hesitated just long enough for me to notice. Then she exhaled, like she was tossing the question into the wind.

"I guess I'll have to find out," she said.

And when I held out my hand—

She still took it.

Her fingers found mine like they remembered how. They were small and cold from the wind, but they curled into me like maybe she didn't mind. The wind softened then. I held my breath. The world noticed.

I shoved the door—pushed a bit with my shoulder before it gave in. It groaned open, the hinges screaming in protest.

Inside, the air was thick, dense, stale with dragon's breath—a beast who'd been asleep too long. The walls didn't echo. They swallowed sound. Just another fixture that held its breath, like the rest of this town. A blip on the radar of time.

The scent of seawater clung to the walls, soaked deep into the bones of the place. The metal staircase twisted upward into the dark, the steps groaning under the weight of years. Rust veined the stairs like brittle bloodlines—like the lighthouse had once been alive, pumping something vital through its bones. Now it was just iron and memory. Dust and salt had settled into every crevice, abandoned, but not forgotten.

I glanced at her. "You afraid of heights?"

Jean tilted her head, considering. "Never really thought about it," she said, her voice light but distant. Then she looked at me, eyes sharp with something like a challenge. "But I guess now's not the best time to start."

I huffed a laugh. "That's the spirit."

Jean rolled her eyes, but I caught the whiff of a smile as she stepped past me into the dark.

CHAPTER SIX

We climbed. Our footsteps echoed up the winding metal stairs. The higher we went, the colder the air became, until I could see my breath in the dim light filtering through the cracks in the walls. The fog stung my eyes, sharp and sudden—weak tears began to slip out before I could stop them. I blinked hard. Pretended it was just the wind.

The place had been empty for years. But standing there, it didn't feel empty. It felt paused. Like someone had left something behind, and time had stopped moving, waiting for them to come back. Something was alive in this place; untouchable and unknowable. The spirit of the wind and sea, the waves always reminding of the potential for destruction. Of fragility. Of the moments we spend that seem like eternities but end before we can blink our eyes.

At the top, another rusted-out door led to the gallery outside the watch room, the wind rattling against it like it was impatient.

I pushed it open. The air hit me first—sharp, biting, tasting like salt and something older. It wrapped around the tower, the metal railing warped from years of sea air and neglect. Rust clung to it like a second skin, flaking off where my hand pressed against it.

Jean stepped up beside me, fingers grazing the rail before she pulled away.

The ocean stretched out forever, dark and endless beneath us. She looked like she could call out to the sea—and it would answer. Like it knew her name already. It had the kind of vastness that makes you feel small. The kind that makes you wonder if it's looking back at you.

How many men had walked this catwalk, bundled in their Cossack hats and alpaca wool seaman's coats, defying the frigid Northwest cold, battling the wind as they looked to sight the last ship that should have been coming in, dutiful to the last? How many nights did they spend away from loved ones for the love of the sea? How many perished in storms that rode up to heights and washed them away. Into the waves that always remind us.

I shook the thought and let out a slow breath, leaning against the railing. "Hell of a view, huh?"

It was strange. The way the ocean stretched out like it had no end. The way it could swallow up anything, anyone, and never even blink. I looked into the horizon, saw the shelf at the end of the sea, like if I were standing on the edge, I would see another world of cities and clouds and pastures and gods.

Jean stared at it like she was trying to solve something.

"It's funny. You grow up looking at something every day, thinking you know it," she murmured. "Then you step inside, and suddenly it's like seeing it for the first time."

I smirked, leaning against the railing. "Don't get used to it."

She turned to me, frowning. "Why not?"

I shrugged. "Some guy bought the place. Says he's fixing it up. Wants it back in factory setting. Work starts in a few days."

Jean scoffed, shaking her head. "That's ridiculous."

I watched her for a moment. The way the wind caught the edges of her dress. The last bit of light turning her hair to copper. Some people just looked like they belonged in stories.

"You been here before?" she asked.

"Yeah. Once."

"With your friends from the other night?"

"Nah." I glanced back at the sea. "Someone else."

Jean didn't push it. Just let the silence settle between us. The waves crashed below, a relentless barrage that didn't try, it just was. The distant moan of a foghorn rolled through the air. Then again, long and low—a sound that didn't feel like warning anymore. More like grief. Like a cry that had never been answered.

Finally, I exhaled.

"My buddy, the one who took me here, said places like this made you feel free." I ran my fingers over the rusted railing, tapping against the metal, waiting for it to answer back. "I think he meant it, too. Back then." I paused. "Thing about freedom is, you don't really notice when you have it. Just when it's gone."

Jean tilted her head, watching me carefully. I felt it. The weight of her looking. But I shook it off, forcing a smirk.

"Also told me this place was haunted."

Jean raised an eyebrow. "Oh?" Her voice was lilting, skeptical. Then, after a pause, she grinned. "Well. That's a little predictable, don't you think?"

I huffed a laugh, looking up at the burnt-out lightbulb hanging above us. "Yeah, well. The classics are classics for a reason."

She crossed her arms. "Alright. Let's hear it, then."

I leaned against the railing, voice dipping low, just enough to make the wind carry it.

"Story goes, back in the 1920s, some guy was stationed here. Kept watch over the water. He was waiting for his wife to come back from sea—except she never did. Whale watching boat wrecked in a storm. One of those sudden ones, the kind that doesn't give you time to say goodbye."

Jean was staring at me now, lips pressed together, but I kept going.

"They say he stayed up here, night after night, watching the horizon, waiting for a boat that never came." I tapped the railing again, letting the metal ring out. "One night, they found his boots right here, where I'm standing. Just his boots. He was gone."

Jean shivered. "I don't care for ghost stories." Her voice was quieter than before, like maybe she'd just realized it. Like she hadn't thought about it until now.

I chuckled, trying to lighten the mood. "Hope I didn't spook you. If it helps, I don't believe in any of it."

She didn't answer right away. Just glanced toward the ageless cliffs, where the fog curled over the rocks, shifting with the wind. The primeval siblings that marked time for us, yet remained after all else was gone.

"Definitely been hearing a lot of them lately, though." I added, adjusting my grip on the railing. "My little brother was just telling me about one. Some lady—this ghost—who haunts the beach. Shows up in the fog. Calls out to guys. And if you go to her, you never come back."

Jean's gaze flicked back to me.

"Had me wondering," I half-joked. "Seems like the town's looking for a girl who matches your description."

Jean didn't smile. She didn't even look surprised. Then, quietly, almost like it wasn't meant for me:

"Not all ghosts want to haunt. Some just don't have anywhere else to go." She exhaled, barely a breath. "I promise you, Will. No one's looking for me. No one ever has."

The clouds thickened above us. A low rumble cracked across the horizon—not thunder, but close. Like the sky had a bone to pick and didn't know who to blame. I wanted to argue. Tell her it wasn't true. But something in the way she responded stopped me. What did I really know of her anyway? She didn't sound angry. Just... sad. Like it was something she'd known forever. Something she had long since accepted.

The wind pulled at her hair, and for a second, I wasn't sure if I was looking at a real person or something the town had already forgotten. Like if she jumped, I didn't even think the ocean would drown her. It would just keep her. Hold her. Like she had already been part of it. One of its own.

I hesitated. Then, quieter—

"Hey."

She turned toward me again, eyes searching mine.

"What's your life like?" I asked.

Jean blinked.

For a moment, she looked caught off guard, like it wasn't the kind of question people asked her. Or maybe the kind she never let herself answer.

She glanced toward the ocean, and I let the silence stretch. The waves crashed below, rolling in and pulling away, over and over, like they were waiting for something.

Jean turned back to me then, her gaze sharper now—like she was measuring something. Not me, exactly. Maybe the space between us. The things we weren't saying.

Then, just as quickly, she looked past me, stepping away from the railing. Without a word, she started walking, her footsteps light against the metal platform.

"Meet me here tomorrow," she said over her shoulder. "Same time. I—I have something to give you."

It sounded rehearsed. Like she'd said it before. Maybe to someone else. Maybe in a story that didn't end right. But it also sounded like a dare. Like a promise. Like a future I wasn't sure I deserved—but wanted anyway.

I blinked.

"Wait, Jean!" I called after her, but my voice was lost in the wind.

She didn't look back. Didn't hesitate. Just kept walking.

The hollow clang of her footsteps on the stairs was the only answer I got before she disappeared into the darkness.

Just like a ghost.

The next day, I showed up at the lighthouse.

The front door was bolted shut. A NO TRESPASSING sign nailed right into the wood, the edges curling from wind and salt.

Damn.

I let out a slow breath, rolling my shoulders against the cold. I'd thrown on the same leather jacket from yesterday, the sleeves still stiff with sea air. My jeans were the same pair too—dirt at the cuffs, a small tear at the knee that hadn't been there before. I hadn't shaved. Didn't see the point. My white tee clung to me beneath the jacket, and the wind cut through it like it had something to prove.

The whole place already felt different—emptier somehow. Like I was standing outside a memory, not a building. Like last night had been some kind of fluke. Some half-remembered dream that slipped away the moment I woke up.

The air was thick with the scent of rain, that sharp, electric smell before another storm. The sky hung low and heavy, a patchwork of charcoal clouds with slivers of gold where the sun still fought to break through.

I barely had time to turn when I saw her.

Jean.

Standing exactly where she had yesterday.

Something clutched in her hands.

Not just something.

A book.

She didn't speak right away. Her hair was damp with sea mist. The same kind of damp that clung to you after a funeral on the beach. Where ashes were thrown to the four corners, to the spirits of the wind, rain, sun, and earth. For protection, a sacrifice, a tribute to the waves. It was the kind of smell that stayed in your clothes long after the service was over. Maybe that's the way it was supposed to be. Maybe we aren't meant to forget so quickly, so easily, so cavalierly.

She stepped forward and pressed the book against my chest, fingers lingering for a fraction of a second too long before pulling away.

"Here."

I blinked, looking down.

The cover was worn, the edges frayed like it had been held a hundred times before. The seams along the spine were hand-stitched —loose in places, tight in others, like someone had pulled the thread too hard and kept going anyway. It looked like she'd patched it together from scraps of other lives—pages torn from fairytales, margins filled with things she wasn't allowed to say out loud. This wasn't just a book. It was a reconstruction. A confession in stitches.

The words

Written Just For You

were scrawled across the front in careful, deliberate handwriting.

Jean swallowed, tucking a strand of hair behind her ear. Her fingers hovered there, lingering at her temple like she was trying to steady herself.

"It's me," she whispered. "Everything I can't say out loud. Everything no one wanted to hear."

I ran my thumb along the stitches again. The thread tugged beneath my skin, rough and real. She'd built this thing out of pieces of herself. Not polished. Not pretty. But true. Some of the corners were curled from water damage, edges browned and soft like decay. Like this book had been buried somewhere before it made its way to me. But I held it like it was her heart, ripped out and stitched back together.

"Jean—" I started, but she shook her head.

"I can't stay long."

A pause. Just a fraction of a second. Barely anything at all.

"Just... read it, okay?"

She said it quick, like if she didn't get it out now, she never would. But then—for just a second—her eyes flickered up to mine, like she wanted to say something more.

Like she wanted me to understand.

I almost asked. Almost caught the words before they slipped away.

But then she turned, her dress kicking up in the wind as she disappeared down the path, each step echoing in the silence she left behind.

Like she hadn't just dropped something heavy between us.

Like it hadn't meant anything at all.

I almost called after her, but something about the way she left—quick, decisive, almost shy—made me stay quiet.

This felt real. But so do dreams just before you wake up.

Slowly, I sank down onto the steps of the lighthouse. The icy cold of the rusty metal seeped through my jeans, an appropriate response to the way I was feeling. Confused by a turn of events I could not justify. Could not understand.

I flipped open the first page.

It wasn't a diary. Not exactly.

Inside were stories—pages upon pages, some copied by hand, others just pictures or torn fragments from books. Some I recognized. Some I didn't. Whole passages were underlined. Notes filled the margins, some in careful script, others in rushed, slanted lettering, like she'd written them in the dark.

Passages. Poems. Lyrics from songs I'd never heard.

Sketches of things half-remembered—waves crashing against rocks, the silhouette of a lighthouse, a girl standing at the edge of the world. Even the mist, shades of grey blotched onto the page with a watercolor sponge. An intentional obscuration? A Freudian message?

I flipped through slowly. Some pages were written in neat cursive, others in frantic, tilted script. Some were ripped down the middle. Some had whole paragraphs crossed out so violently I could still see the pressure of the pen marks beneath them. Others were untouched, frozen in time, like she'd been afraid to finish the thought.

I tried to make sense of it, but it was like reading someone's mind mid-dream—scattered, half-formed, slipping through my fingers just as I got close.

This was her world. The things she couldn't say, the things she tried to bury—they were here, scattered in ink, torn edges, crossed-out thoughts. I ran my fingers over the words, over the places where she had pressed the pen too hard, like she was trying to make something permanent.

Like if even one person saw her, maybe she wasn't invisible. Maybe she was real.

And she had given it to me. Her thoughts, images of her reality or some alternate mind; a Nostradamus of sorts, intentionally masked in bits and pieces, waiting for me to figure her out.

CHAPTER SEVEN

That night, the book sat heavy in my hands. Not just in the weight of its pages, but the kind of weight you carry in your chest—like a name you whisper for the first time in years, or a memory that shows up without being asked. It was the weight of something unfinished. Something waiting. Like I was holding pieces of her. Fragments of a story she had never told out loud.

I flipped the cover open, careful. The spine cracked, like it had been waiting too long to be touched. But how? Surely this was something she had recently put together. Yet, it physically seemed to be some ancient artifact, mired in history, heavy with sentiment and grief, like the last stages of life before we move on.

My fingers lingered at the edge, slow, deliberate—like hers must've, once. Same motion. Same pressure.

Written Just For You

The words looked handwritten, but not delicate or neat. No,

Jean's title was a little slanted, a little rushed. Like she was in a hurry to put it down before she could change her mind.

I swallowed, ran my thumb over the letters. The ink had smudged a little. Or maybe that was just the way she wrote.

Outside, rain slicked the windows of Gracie's Diner, running in long, winding streaks, carving paths that never ended. The neon "OPEN" sign buzzed against the fogged-up glass, flickering like it wasn't sure it wanted to be here either. Like it belonged to another time. Another place. Living a parallel life for the sake of appearances. Longing. Like her. For a second, the sign stuttered—blinked out entirely—before it flared back to life. A weak, pulsating heartbeat in the dark.

I glanced outside. The streetlights burned dim through the mist, their reflections stretching long across the pavement—distorted, warped by the rain, casting weak shadows where there should have been none. For a second, they looked like figures. Reaching, shifting, disappearing before they could fully form.

If I didn't know better, I'd think this place existed outside of time, floating somewhere between yesterday and never. The kind of place spirits would stop for coffee. The kind of place that remembered who you were, even if no one else did. And maybe I didn't know better.

As I lifted the page, it felt like opening a door in a house that didn't want to be entered. Haunted. Secretive. Guarded.

Slowly, I turned it.

There was a time when I wasn't afraid. Or maybe I was, but I didn't have the right words for it yet. Back then, fear felt like something else—like running too fast down a hill and laughing because you can't stop, or standing on the edge of the dock just to see how close you can get before the water swallows your toes. It was a thrill, not a warning.

I stared at that last line for a second, thumb tracing the crease in the page. The paper was old but sturdy. A little rough. Like something that had been handled a lot but never quite fell apart.

On the side, there was a drawing. Two stick figures, legs blurred like they were mid-run, arms stretched out like they could catch the wind. The name *Sandra* was written above one. It felt like something out of a dream. Or a memory I almost had, but not quite.

Somewhere behind me, a voice pulled me back.

"You gonna order, Will, or you just here to make my tables look pretty?"

I looked up.

Norma stood beside my booth, notepad in one hand, the other braced against her hip, pen shoved over her ear. Her hair was done up in that eternal diner-waitress style, curled and pinned like time had left her untouched since at least 1935. A cigarette sat unlit between her fingers. Her eyes—sharp, but not unkind—narrowed at me like she'd already seen a thousand boys like me in a thousand rainy nights just like this one.

I cleared my throat. Scratched at the back of my neck.

"Coffee," I said. "Black."

Norma clicked her pen against the paper. The scratch of it matched the rain against the window, steady and unhurried.

"You look like you've seen a ghost," she muttered, tearing the receipt from the pad. The paper crinkled between her fingers like a whisper. "Or maybe you're waiting for one."

She winked like she knew something and left before I could answer. The smell of cheap floral perfume and distant cigarette smoke lingered in the air.

I exhaled, rubbing a hand over my jaw before turning back to the book.

The world felt enormous then, and I was just this

small piece of it, eager to know everything, to touch everything.

There was a drawing on the page—a rough, uneven sketch of a coastline done in dark, inky lines. The sea stretched wide, shaded in with the side of a pencil, smudged where the waves should be. On the land, tiny dots marked trees, little rectangles for houses. But only one had a name written beside it, scrawled in looping cursive.

Home.

It sat on the edge of the cliffs, right where the land started to break apart, like the earth was trying to decide whether to stay or go.

A little further down the page, she had added another note. Smaller handwriting. Like an afterthought. Or a secret.

"I used to think the world went on forever. That if I just walked far enough, I'd find the edge of the map. And past that, something else. Something new."

There was a small, circular burn mark near the bottom corner, like a cigarette once rested there too long. A pressed wildflower was taped at the edge—a sprig of Queen Anne's lace, brittle now, its petals the color of old paper.

Next to it, Jean had written:

I read somewhere that these are called 'the devil's breath.' Funny, isn't it?

The jukebox hummed in the background, spitting out some Roy Orbison song that barely reached past the rain hammering against the roof. The sound was warped, stretched thin under the weight of the storm.

A few booths down, Earl Danning—a long-haul trucker who

only stopped through when the roads flooded—stared into his coffee like it was supposed to say something back. I wasn't sure if he'd moved since I walked in. Maybe not even before.

Near the counter, an older couple sat, Marge and Gil Benner, their hands folded between their plates. They weren't eating. Just watching the rain. Just waiting. They'd run the hardware store for most of their lives, before their son took it over and gutted the place with new shelving and fluorescent lights. They hadn't stepped foot in it since.

I paused. Part of me braced for what was next, like the story might change depending on how I touched it. I flipped the page. It felt different—lighter, almost. Like something fragile. The paper stuck to my fingers, like it didn't want to be let go. The edges curled, worn by hands that had turned these same pages again and again, like a prayerbook.

The ink bled in places. Smudged. Like it had been caught in the blur of movement, of hesitation. Like she had pressed too hard.

Like she needed these words to last. Like she needed them to mean something.

Like she had been afraid they might disappear.

> *I used to chase the wind through the trees behind the house, and my sister—God, she was always right behind me.*

The sentence cut off at the edge, unfinished. Like she had started to write more and stopped herself.

The page wasn't hers originally—a scrap from another book, torn and taped into place. The words beneath, faded and typewritten, described golden afternoons, forests stretching on forever.

She had underlined two lines, carving them deep enough to leave an impression on the next page:

"There is a kind of magic in the way light filters through the trees. A world that belongs only to those who are young enough to believe in it."

There was a faded photo tucked into the corner, not quite stuck down, just slipped between the pages. An afterthought? Another secret to be decoded. Two girls in a clearing, all sunlight and movement. The older one turning back, laughing, a shell necklace around her neck. The younger one staring at her, slightly out of focus.

I swallowed. Tucked the photo back where I found it. Then, below it, her handwriting again—jagged, uneven, like she was in a hurry.

We were anything we wanted to be. Pirates, explorers, queens of a kingdom no one else could see. We built thrones out of broken branches and gave names to the rain, pretending it was music only we could hear.

I could see it. Jean as a kid. Carefree. Back when life seemed easy. Wild-haired, barefoot, laughing. The way she smiled now—small, careful, like she was holding something back—I doubted it had always been that way.

There was a smudge at the bottom, like she had pressed her thumb into the ink before it dried. Like she had hesitated before turning the page herself.

In the margin, smaller, fainter:

And somehow, she always let me win.

Something about that stuck. The idea of her, all sharp words and steady hands, letting someone else win. Letting her win. Not just once, but every time.

A ceramic clink pulled me from the words.

Norma slid a steaming cup of coffee onto the table without breaking her stride.

"On the house," she said, voice softer this time. "You look like you need it."

I wrapped my hands around the cup, the heat bleeding into my fingers, grounding me.

Norma lingered.

She glanced at the book, eyes flicking across the tattered pages, the messy handwriting. Then she looked back at me.

"Someone else's story?" she asked.

I hesitated. Then nodded.

Norma hummed, pulling the cigarette from behind her ear and tucking it between her lips. She didn't light it—just let it sit there, like an afterthought.

"Well," she said, tilting her head toward the book. "Don't stop reading now. Ain't nothing lonelier than words left unread."

She walked away, apron swaying, heels clicking soft against the tile.

Jean's words. She needed me to read them.

The kitchen hissed behind the pass-through window as I turned the page. The booth creaked under me, the vinyl growing warmer the longer I sat. The smell of bacon clung to the air, sharp against the ink.

On the next page, Jean's writing curved tight across the margin, like she'd run out of space or patience or time.

My mother says the world is dangerous.

I remembered hearing that too. Not the same words, maybe. But the same tone. The kind that walls you in while pretending it's love.

I think she believes that if she just says it enough, it'll be true. Like a spell. Like she can keep me here just by telling me there's nowhere else to go.

There was a news clipping below it, unevenly glued, the ink bled from time and rain.

I skimmed the article.

There was a photo of a woman. Betty Weinhart, according to the article, standing stiff on a porch. Arms crossed. Face like someone had told her to smile, and she tried, but it just didn't take.

Jean's handwriting, curling at the bottom like an afterthought:

You should hear her talk about ghosts.

I exhaled, slow. *Alright.* And flipped the page.

Another passage, underlined three times:

"The ocean is beautiful, but it can pull you under in an instant. It will never love you back."

Beneath it, in Jean's small, slanted script:

She never forgave the water. Not for what it is, not for what it did, not for the way it takes and never gives back. Not for taking my sister.

I stopped breathing. I could almost feel the ocean pressing against the glass. Like it had heard Jean's words. My fingers curled against the edge of the page. *Jean never talked about her sister. Not once.* I felt the words settle heavy in my ribs.

But in truth, nobody here forgave the water. Drownings happened all the time. Town just goes quiet about 'em. Stops talking. And hopes the tide will forget what it took.

But the waves never forget. They're always reminding.

There was another piece of paper tucked behind the entry, barely held in place. A newspaper scrap, brittle with age.

"Depoe Bay Drownings on the Rise."

Exactly my point. I sighed. There were no names. No photo. No byline. Just a handful of words. The article wasn't long. Just facts boiled down to fog. Half the words were gone, like they'd been eaten by time. Or maybe torn out on purpose. The only names left were the ones meant to survive the story.

Jean had written something at the bottom, the ink smudged like maybe her hand had shaken:

It stole her away.

I closed my eyes for a second. Just a second. Each page felt like a piece of her she didn't want to keep but couldn't throw away. I wanted to hold them all for her. *I'm sorry, Jean.*

Outside, the rain had gotten worse. Fat droplets pounded the pavement, the sound blending with the low hum of the jukebox. Water streamed down the diner window in shimmering streaks, rivulets turning the neon lights outside into a blur of color—red from the "OPEN" sign, yellow from the streetlamp, green from a flickering motel vacancy light down the road. Glacial art informing the school of drip painting.

I stared down at the book, more pages curling slightly at the edges from wear, from use. From years of someone else's hands lingering on them, someone else's breath whispering over the ink.

I turned the next page.

After she was gone, everything changed.

The handwriting here was different—sharper, pressed so hard into the paper that the indentations caught the light when I tilted the page. The ink had bled slightly, feathering out like a bruise. Below it, faint scratch marks ran across the margin—like she had started to write something else and scraped it away with the side of her nail.

I ran my thumb over the words, feeling the pressure behind them, the weight of the pen bearing down. The ink had depth. Like it had been pushed in—not written, but carved. Like she needed them to stay. Like she was afraid they might disappear.

Before, I was allowed to talk to people—the grocer, the pharmacist, the doctor's children.

Grocer? That was probably Greaves. Or his old man. The market's been there forever—peeling green sign, crooked floorboards, bell over the door that always rang half a second too late. I used to buy licorice ropes there as a kid. Still does that thing where he bags your change like he's doing you a favor.

The pharmacist... maybe Mrs. Larrin. Or her sister. I remember someone in a stiff white coat who always smelled like lavender and rubbing alcohol. Never smiled much. Still doesn't.

The doctor's children, though—that one gave me pause. *Which doctor?* There'd been a few over the years. Some stuck around. Some didn't. The clinic sat off Cedar, always waiting for the next tragedy. I remembered getting stitched up there after—everything.

I closed my eyes, refusing to fall back into it.

The past is in the past, Will. You're stronger than it.

I ran my thumb over the words again, like maybe she could feel it, wherever she was. The way she wrote it—like it was normal. Like she used to walk past those storefronts, wave to those people, laugh at something someone said in passing. Like she was part of this town. *But now?* Now nobody seemed to know her at all.

The page was slightly uneven, a faint outline pressed into the paper—a square, just empty space now, like something had been there once. A photograph. *Had it fallen out? Or had someone taken it?*

It didn't feel like an accident. Not the way the edges were clean. Not the way the page bent around it, like it was still holding on. *Someone removed it. Maybe her. Maybe not.* But whoever did—it wasn't because they forgot. It was because they remembered too well.

I traced the edges where it should've been, my pulse picking up. The scrapbook had been handled so carefully—every picture, every note placed with intent. But here, there was a gap. A piece missing. A hollow where something had been. Like a tooth pulled from a smile.

I turned the page, scanning the others, but the absence sat heavy in my mind.

What had been here? And why was it gone?

After, my mother told me it wasn't safe. That bad things happen to girls who wander too far. That if I just stayed inside, I'd be okay.

I swallowed. Something about the way she wrote it—how the words seemed caged between the lines, trapped in the margins— made my chest tighten. *God, she'd been through hell. Still going through it, really.* But I still couldn't believe someone like her looked at someone like me like I was something good.

A gust of wind slammed against the diner window, rattling it in its frame. Marge and Gil looked up from their coffee, barely fazed. Then they went back to their conversation, like nothing outside could touch them.

I flipped the page.

This one was warped from water damage, as though someone cried over it and never dried the tears. A ripped passage was glued in place, slightly crooked. The glue had bled through the paper, warping the edges, making it look old before its time. Something about small hands pressed to glass, watching the world move without them.

Jean's handwriting curled around the printed text, slipping into the empty spaces like it had always belonged there.

I remember what warmth feels like.

A picture—taped just below the words. Betty, younger, standing on the porch. Hair pulled back in a perfect knot. Staring at the camera like she knew something you didn't, but she wasn't going to tell you. Below it, crossed out so violently the paper nearly tore:

But not from her.

She'd tried to erase it. But it was still there. A phantom of itself under the ink. Like a secret that refused to stay buried.

A burned matchstick was taped in the corner. The charred tip flaked when I ran a finger over it. Beneath it, Jean's writing, smaller than the rest. Like she wrote it late at night, when the house was too quiet.

Sometimes, I wonder what she was like before the world got to her. Before she stopped believing in warmth too.

Turned another page.

Still, I know it exists.

I exhaled through my nose, tilting my head back against the booth. I could see her in my mind. Younger. Smaller. Standing by a window, tracing the rain with her fingertip. Watching a world she was no longer allowed to touch.

Just then, another shadow passed over my table.

And I glanced up.

CHAPTER EIGHT

Norma stood there again, one hand on her hip, watching me like I was a puzzle she wasn't sure she wanted to solve. Something about her presence had shifted, but I couldn't tell if it was caution or just plain boredom.

"Still reading?" she asked, eyebrow arched.

Christ Almighty. I nodded. "I am."

Norma didn't move. Her gaze flicked to the book, the way I had it spread open like evidence, like something that needed solving. Then, instead of walking away, she did something else. She slid into the booth across from me.

"You mind?" she asked, tapping out another cigarette from the carton tucked in her apron. "You're the liveliest thing in here tonight."

I smirked a little, leaning back. "That bad?"

Norma jerked her chin toward the rest of the diner. "See for yourself. Like the walking undead."

Earl was still staring into his coffee; still waiting for it to tell him something he hadn't asked about—a message in a bottle that might drag him into a better life. Marge and Gil had gone quiet again, watching the rain without speaking. They knew what the rain meant; the memories it held for them. The jukebox droned out something slow and crackling, a phantom dispatch from a bygone era, barely keeping up with the rhythm of the storm outside.

Yeah. It was that bad.

Norma lit up. The cigarette flared between her fingers, smoke curling toward the ceiling, soft and slow, the orange glow of the lit end brightening as she dragged on the stick. She turned back to me. "So, who's it belong to?" she asked, nodding toward the book.

I hesitated. Then, careful, I said, "A girl I met. Name's Jean."

Norma hummed, exhaling smoke out the side of her mouth. She tapped her fingers against the tabletop, her rings catching the neon light.

"Jean," she echoed, almost to herself. There was a pause, a flicker of something behind her eyes. Recognition. She took another drag, then let the smoke slip past her lips, slow, measured. "Used to know a Jean. Sweet girl. It's a shame what happened."

The words sat wrong in my chest. I sat up a little straighter. "You know her? What happened? Betty's girl, right?"

Norma's gaze flicked to me, then—just for a second—she glanced toward the cutout window between the kitchen and the dining room.

Through the opening, the cook stood motionless, one hand resting near the ticket rail. He was wiry and weathered, with sleeves rolled up to his elbows and a faded anchor tattoo winding around one wrist. His name was Red. Just Red. The kind of guy who never left town, never left the grill. Been flipping burgers and frying eggs since my dad was a teenager. He didn't speak much. Didn't need to. You always knew where you stood with him. When Red looked at you, you felt it.

His eyes flicked toward Norma, then toward me. Not long. Just enough.

Then the air in the diner shifted.

Earl finally looked up. Not quick. Not startled. Just slow, steady

—like he'd been waiting for this. Marge and Gil stopped pretending to watch the rain. Gil turned his head slightly, just enough to see me from the corner of his eye. Marge didn't turn at all, but her fingers curled tighter around her coffee cup, like she was bracing for something.

Norma looked back at me and exhaled slow. "You oughta be careful reading things like that."

It wasn't a threat. Not exactly. But it felt like a warning wrapped in a lullaby. I frowned. "What do you mean? Like what?"

She tapped her ash into the tray beside her, the cigarette resting easy between her fingers. She didn't move away, didn't fidget. Just sat there. Watching. Thinking.

"Like things that ain't yours to know."

The silence in the diner felt different now. Like it was stretching, pulling around me. I heard Red shift behind the counter. Earl leaned back slightly in his chair, his gaze still set on me in the reflection of the window.

At the sound of Norma's voice dipping lower, Marge and Gil finally turned. Just slightly, just enough. Their eyes didn't just watch —they remembered. The kind of silence that builds when you're trying not to let something surface. Like my voice had knocked loose a memory they'd boarded up years ago.

I glanced at the scrapbook, my fingers resting against the worn edge. "It's just a scrapbook."

Norma exhaled through her nose. "Yeah?" She met my eyes. "Then why's my gut telling me to tell you to walk away? When I said you look like you've seen a ghost... well."

Something about the way she said it made my skin prickle. I shifted in my seat, trying to shake the feeling.

Earl adjusted his spoon against his saucer, the quiet clink somehow louder than it should've been. He wasn't drinking his coffee. Just watching, waiting.

I swallowed, adjusting my grip on the book. I wasn't cold, but a chill threaded through my spine. Not from the weather. From the way everyone had gone still. Like the air had rules now and I'd just broken one.

Norma sighed, tapping ash into the tray again.

"You ain't the first, you know." Her voice softened, like she was afraid saying it too loud would bring the others back.

I looked at her. "First what?"

She hesitated. Then—another glance toward the kitchen. Red didn't move. Didn't speak. But I saw the way his mouth pressed into a thin line. Like he already knew what she was about to say.

Norma shook her head once, like she was deciding against something. Then, leaning in just slightly, she said, "First fool boy to follow a ghost."

My grip on the scrapbook tightened.

Norma's voice dipped lower. "Couple months back. Military guy. Came through town, real quiet-like. Said he saw somethin' down by the cliffs. Next day? Gone. Never made it to his next post. Never heard from again."

She flicked her cigarette, watching the embers flare and fall. Then, softer—like she was pulling something up from a place she didn't want to go, "He ain't the only one."

I swallowed, my pulse slowing into something heavy.

Norma let the smoke curl from her lips before speaking again.

"Before him, there was some kid. Summer worker at the docks, just passing through. Swore he saw a girl standing in the surf one night. Said she was callin' to him. Next morning, his bunk was empty. Bags still there, no note. Just gone."

She tapped her ash, eyes on the storm outside. "And before him? Tourist. Maybe sixteen. Sandy blonde hair. Full of life and enthusiasm. Had a boat he liked to take out late. One night, he went out and never came back. Coast Guard searched for days, never found a thing. Just his boat, washed up near the cliffs, empty. Said they found a scrap of material clung to the floorboards, like it was tore off a little girl's dress or something."

Earl exhaled through his nose, like he'd heard this before. He shifted his gaze. He didn't look at Norma. He didn't look at me. Just stared down at his coffee, squeezing the mug tighter.

My grip on the scrapbook turned to stone. "I don't believe in ghost stories. She's real—"

Norma sat back, shaking her head. "It doesn't matter what you believe. All I'm saying is, you start askin' the wrong questions, people notice. And if they notice?" She shook her head. "Well. You best be sure you wanna be noticed."

I hesitated. "Why?"

For the first time, Norma didn't just look at me—she studied me. Her fingers tightened around her cigarette. "We all know what happened that day," she murmured. "And it's best to let the dead rest."

The air changed. It thickened. Like even the walls had ears—and they didn't like what I was hearing. The rain picked up harder outside, hammering against the diner windows, like it protested the conversation inside. A forewarning. I opened my mouth, but something in Norma's face stopped me. It was final. Like she wasn't just cautioning me—she was telling me to drop it.

Earl finally pushed his mug away, half-full, like he'd lost his taste for it. Marge and Gil turned back toward the window, conversation forgotten.

Norma exhaled, slow and steady. Then, like she was telling me a secret I wasn't supposed to hear, she said, "This town ain't seen much in you, Will. But I do." She stubbed out her cigarette, crushing it flat. "My advice? Get outta here. Forget whatever you think you saw."

The lights in the diner seemed dimmer now. Like something had leaned in close to listen; last scene before the play ended. Something about the way she said it—low, like she already knew I wouldn't listen—made my stomach twist. Then—

The diner door slammed open. Wind and rain blasted through the entrance, dragging in the sharp scent of wet sand and grime on pavement, musty and metallic. A guy stumbled inside. Soaked head to toe. He looked about my age, but I'd never seen him before. His clothes—dark slacks, a jacket too modern to fit—clung to him like he had walked straight out of the ocean. He looked around, blinking hard, like he didn't know where the hell he was.

Something in my gut went tight.

Norma stubbed out her cigarette, already pushing up from the booth.

"That's my cue," she said, smoothing her apron.

She turned, voice shifting back to its usual no-nonsense hum as she called over, "Alright, sweetheart—how can I help you?"

But I barely heard her. My mind was whirling miles away. *Jean... what are you caught up in?*

I hesitated before looking back down at the book. My fingers twitched as I turned the next page.

A torn-out map was taped across the next two pages—the coast of Oregon. The whole damn thing. Depoe Bay was circled in thick, dark pen strokes. But there were other places, too. Newport. Lincoln City. Portland. A bus ticket was taped next to it. The ink was faded. The date was smudged. But the destination was still clear.

Seattle. Unused.

Jean's handwriting at the bottom:

Sometimes, I trace the roads with my fingers and pretend I'm already gone. I think I was always meant to leave.

I let my hand hover over the words. Like I could feel them. Like I could touch the longing in them.

I knew that feeling. I'd done the same thing once. Tracing the roads on a crumpled map the night before we left. Back when I thought running meant freedom. Before I learned what it cost to vanish.

I wondered how many nights she'd stood with that ticket in her hand. Wondered if she folded it like a prayer. Wondered what stopped her from getting on that bus—and what would stop me, if it came to that.

Outside, the rain picked up even harder, like it was trying to get my attention; trying to get me to listen, hammering against the pavement in a fury. The neon glow of the "OPEN" sign flickered against the window again, bleeding red into the storm.

I turned another page. Kept reading. But something started to bother me. It wasn't just what was here. It was what *wasn't*. The gaps. The way some stories started and never ended. The way her handwriting shifted when it got close to something she didn't want to say. Like she was giving me a version of her truth—but not the whole thing. Like she was protecting me. Or protecting herself. I wasn't sure which one scared me more.

I flipped through more sections. Then another. More passages. More images. More pieces of her, stitched together in someone else's words. Stories about girls who ran away and never looked back. A torn section of a novel, the edges burned, like maybe she tried to get rid of it once but couldn't go through with it. Perhaps an indication of how she felt about what was written there. A single sentence underlined in deep, slashing ink:

Some people are born with their feet already on the road.

A line from a song I didn't know, circled in red:
"There's a world out there waiting."

My throat tightened. Beneath it, her handwriting again. Smaller. Like a thought spoken under her breath.

Maybe you knew that already. Maybe that's why you're here.

I swallowed, my chest feeling too small, too tight.

She had been waiting for this. For something. For someone. Not just for love. For proof. Proof that the world was still out there. Proof that she wasn't wrong to want it.

I stared at the words, my fingers twitching against the worn pages, smudged where too many hands had pressed too hard. *But whose hands were they? Had I mistakenly assumed no one else had ever read this...*

The storm raged outside. The diner lights buzzed against the dimness, flickering slightly as the wind howled, as if the whole place was held together by static and stubbornness.

And for the first time, I felt it—the full weight of what I had walked into. A weight that settled deep, curling in my gut, heavy and unmovable.

Jean wasn't just trapped. Not for days. Not for months. No, this kind of waiting stretches farther than that. It felt like something out of time. Like the longer I sat here, the more I could feel her waiting bleed into the walls. This wasn't just waiting. It was *becoming* the wait. Letting it hollow you out until you forget what it was like to move freely. The kind that changes you. The kind that makes you wonder if you'll still be yourself when someone finally arrives.

My fingers stilled over that last page. The edges curled like petals. She had been patient. And she had been writing. Not just hoping for someone to find her, but for someone to hear her. For someone to see her— She wanted to be known. But only in pieces.

And maybe that's what surviving looks like. Not telling the whole truth—just the part that lets you keep breathing. She wasn't a ghost, or a siren, or some curse. She's a girl. Still alive inside the story someone tried to bury her in.

CHAPTER NINE

Jean's book didn't just tell a story—it unraveled. Piece by piece, word by word. Like something meant to be whispered instead of read.

She was careful with it. Like every sentence had weight, and she wasn't about to drop something too heavy in my hands. Not when she knew I was already carrying enough on my own.

The next night, I returned to the beach.

Same jacket. Different perspective.

The leather creaked as I moved, shoulders stiff against the wind. I'd thrown it over a button-down this time—pale blue, sleeves rolled just enough to show I didn't care if it got wrinkled. My slacks were clean, pressed yesterday, scuffed at the knee from kneeling beside my duffel earlier. Boots on again—shined up just enough to fool somebody who wasn't looking too close.

I'd even combed my hair back, though it didn't hold. The wind kept catching it, tugging it loose, strand by strand. I hoped it would make me more believable. But it didn't matter. I wasn't here to impress everyone. Only her.

It was later than usual. The sun had already started folding into the ocean, bleeding the sky red and orange, spilling light over the waves like a Monet before the dark swallowed it whole.

The water moved, alive and restless. Like it wanted to pull the whole damn world under with it.

I kicked at a rock, hands shoved in my jacket pockets, waiting. And then—just as the last light sank beneath the horizon—she appeared.

Jean stepped onto the sand, her hair catching in the wind, her dress twisting around her legs. She was fidgeting with the hem, winding a loose thread between her fingers like it was all that tethered her to here. The mist curled tighter around her as she stepped into view, like it hadn't decided whether to keep her or give her up.

"Took you a while tonight," I said, watching her approach. "Was it hard to slip out?"

She let out a breath—half a laugh, half something else.

"Hard enough," she murmured, her voice carrying just enough defiance to make it sound like a challenge. She stopped a few steps short of me, arms wrapped around herself. The ocean wind was colder now, curling between us, tugging at the space we hadn't quite closed.

"You're freezing," I said, suddenly aware of how cold her arms looked beneath that soaked-through dress. "Here, take my coat." I was already shrugging it off, halfway through the motion before she had a chance to stop me.

And of course—she did.

"Don't," she said, quick, brushing it off like it didn't matter. It wasn't about the cold. It was about control. About not needing someone else's warmth to survive.

"I'm fine." Her voice softened after a second, her gaze still fixed on the horizon. "Did you read my book?"

I paused. "Got through several pages," I said, raking a hand through my hair. My eyes followed the shoreline, anywhere but her. "Had a couple distractions."

Jean's lips twitched like she might smile, but didn't let it land.

I hesitated, then asked more quietly, "How long's it been like this? With your mom?"

She glanced up at me for the briefest second before turning away again, her expression unreadable.

"Fourteen years, give or take."

The number sank like a stone in my chest. *Fourteen years. Nearly our whole damn lives. Locked in a house while the world moved on without her.*

"Since you were a kid?" I asked.

She nodded once. "As long as I can remember."

That was it. No tears, no story, no explanation. Just that. She wasn't just beautiful. She was brave. Even when she didn't want to be. Especially then. Especially *now*. But suddenly, the silence between us felt heavier than before—like it had been waiting to show up all along. The fog thickened around us, curling low to the sand. Like it didn't want her words going too far. Like it was trying to keep the secret too.

Fourteen years in the same house. The same air. The same walls pressing in like a set of hands, shaping her world into something so small it could fit inside a locked room.

A seagull shrieked overhead, cutting through the silence.

Out past the tide, the cliffs loomed, half-swallowed by mist— hiding the secrets it couldn't share. How many people had walked those cliffs, looking out at the waves, remembering, wanting, waiting, hoping.

We walked along the shoreline, the waves pulling back, whispering things we were meant to hear but couldn't decipher.

"What about the rest of your folks?" I asked. "They gotta think this is a bit much, right?"

Jean hesitated.

"It's just me and my mom. Betty."

"That's it?"

She nodded, slow. "I used to have an aunt once. She moved to Washington years ago. Piedmont, I think. I've never been."

I watched her out of the corner of my eye, but she didn't look at me—just kept her gaze ahead, like the ocean might have something better to offer.

"They didn't really get along," she said. "My mom and her. Not ever, really. But things got worse after my dad proposed. He gave her this ring—orange stone, looked like amber. Used to belong to her mother. My aunt always thought it should've been hers."

She paused. Her voice had gone softer. Not sad. Just... distant.

"After that, she just up and left. Never came back. My dad even bought a cabin out there, on some nearby mountain, hoping my mom would visit. But she never did."

A beat passed. Jean's steps slowed.

"I think about it sometimes. Going there. Finding that cabin. Seeing if she's still around. But... I don't know. I don't think she'd want to see me."

"You don't know that," I said.

Jean shrugged. "She probably doesn't even care I exist."

Silence stretched between us, thin and delicate as the fog curling over the water.

"Where's your dad now?" I asked.

Jean didn't answer at first.

"Not around." she finally replied.

I nodded, dragging a hand through my hair.

"Yeah. I get that."

Jean's eyes flicked toward me, searching my face like she was looking for something between the words. "Yeah?"

I let out a short, humorless laugh.

"Used to think my dad was some kind of war hero. Big-shot adventurer. Real man of the world." I shook my head. "Then I got older and realized he was just some coward who ran from responsibility. Funny thing is, I used to think running meant freedom."

I hesitated. Just for a second. Then—

"Now I'm not so sure. Maybe freedom's just another word for nothing left to lose." I smirked. "I mean, being alone, not having anyone tell you what you can or cannot do, no clock to follow, no judgements... that's freedom, right?"

Jean caught it—my tone, the weight behind the joke that wasn't one. And maybe she saw something I wasn't ready to admit yet.

"Do you really think so?" she asked, her voice softer now.

I glanced out at the horizon. Half-smirked. "Maybe not always, but I guess someone's always left behind in the end." My voice didn't land quite the way I wanted it to. "Most we ever hear from my dad now is a monthly check for the bills. We're lucky if we even get a Christmas card."

Jean was quiet for a moment. The ocean filled the space between us. Then, finally, she shook her head. "It's not like that for me."

I wanted to ask what that meant. But something told me I already knew. She wasn't abandoned. She was caged. The wind wove through the cliffs, pulling at the mist, making it shift like something was breathing into it.

Jean's voice cut through it, soft but steady.

"So, it's just you and your mom then?"

"Me, my mom, and my little brother," I said. "But I raised myself in a lot of ways. Got into trouble young, and school wasn't exactly my thing."

Jean gave me a look. One of those sharp, knowing ones. The kind that made my stomach twist in a way I wasn't used to.

"That, I could've guessed."

I smirked, kicking up sand as we walked. "Yeah? What gave it away?"

She laughed under her breath, shaking her head. "The fact that you ride a motorcycle and smirk like that, for starters."

I grinned, the wind tugging at the collar of my jacket. "Guilty. Cars and I don't really get along." I sighed. "But yeah—got into trouble early. Never had much of a leash. No one ever really stopped me."

Jean tilted her head, like she was weighing something. "That sounds like freedom," she said, but not like she believed it.

I shrugged. "Sometimes. Other times it just felt like floating. No one holding on. No one noticing if you drift too far."

Jean was quiet for a moment, then said, almost to herself, "I wouldn't know. I was always locked in place. Held too tight to drift anywhere."

I looked at her, but she didn't meet my eyes. Something in me tightened. I wanted to be the first person who didn't try to hold her back. The first who just... stayed. But I didn't know what to say.

"Guess we got the opposite problem," I said.

Her lips twitched. "Funny how they both end the same way, huh?"

"Hey, at least we survived high school. Not everyone can say they graduated—I mean, I barely did."

Jean tilted her head slightly. "Ah, yes. And let me guess—you had a teacher that believed in you? Thought you were something special?"

I scoffed. "Maybe some of 'em." I shrugged. "Could've saw potential or whatever. Let me scrape by out of hope—or maybe just exhaustion."

Jean laughed and, for a second, it was easy. Light. Like we weren't two kids carrying more than we should.

"Well," she said, "I never had teachers to disappoint or impress. Just my mother. And she was never really the encouraging type." A small, sharp smile. "Still, I graduated top of my class."

I huffed a laugh. "Impressive. I made it out by the skin of my teeth."

Jean tipped her head at me, her eyes glinting with something unreadable. I studied her—the way the dimming light softened her face, the way her fingers curled into the pockets of her dress.

"So, you got any friends?" I asked.

She didn't answer right away. Then, without looking at me—

"Do you?"

She shot the question back like it was a game, but her voice caught on the edge of it. Like she didn't expect it to land so hard. I took a moment, staring up at the sky as it deepened into richer shades of blue.

"Yeah. Something like that. Those guys you saw me with at the beach, the night we first met. We're kinda close. Grew up together, caused trouble together. Like our own little misfit crew."

Jean's smile was small, but something about it felt distant. Like a wisp of smoke before the wind could take it.

I squinted at her.

"C'mon, you're telling me I'm the first guy you've ever talked to? No boyfriends or nothin'?"

Jean let out a soft laugh, looking down at her hands.

"No," she said, a hint of amusement threading through her voice. "I suppose you have that honor. Though I'm not sure if that speaks well of you or poorly of me."

Something about the way she said it made my chest tighten.

I hesitated. Then— "What about the doctor's kids? What happened to them?"

Jean's laughter faded. For a moment, I thought she wasn't going to answer. Her hand drifted to the hem of her dress again. That same loose thread. She tugged at it once—twice—until it snapped. Just a small sound. But somehow, it echoed louder than it should've. She smoothed her hands over the fabric of her dress, gaze drifting toward the water.

"Well... After Sandra..." She took a slow breath. "My mother wouldn't let me leave the house anymore. Wouldn't even let the doctor see me. Not really. She said she'd take care of me herself."

She didn't say it with anger. Just fact. Like someone describing a window being boarded shut. But there was something else she wasn't saying. Maybe something I wasn't ready to hear yet.

The mist stopped moving, just for a second. A catch in its breath, listening. A strange, heavy quiet settled between us. Jean still wasn't looking at me. Just watching the tide, like she could disappear into it if she tried hard enough. Maybe she already had.

I swallowed. "So that was it?"

She nodded. "That was it."

The wind stirred between us, lifting strands of her hair, sending them drifting like silk against her cheek.

I rubbed at my jaw, shifting my weight. "So, I really am the first."

Jean's lips parted slightly, like maybe she wanted to say something. Maybe she wanted to argue.

But in the end, she just smiled—small, fleeting, barely there.

Then, glancing at me through her lashes, she said, "What about you?" Her voice softened, teasing. "On your third marriage yet?"

I snorted. "Not quite."

She tilted her head, lips curving just a little. "So?"

I thought about it for a second, then shrugged.

"Had a few things here and there. But they were short-lived. Unremarkable."

Jean raised an eyebrow. "That bad, huh?"

"Nothing compared to you."

I didn't mean to say it like that. Or maybe I did. Maybe I wanted to see if she'd run. But she didn't.

Jean stilled, just for a moment. She looked at me—really looked —like she was trying to memorize the shape of my face, the way my voice sounded in the wind. And then, slowly—she smiled.

It wasn't fair, the way she did that. Like she had no idea she was capable of knocking the air clean out of my lungs.

CHAPTER TEN

The sky had softened into indigo, and the dark didn't just fall—it grew. Crawled in through your sleeves, settled behind your ribs, whispered to you if you were quiet long enough.

The tide rolled in steady, waves folding over themselves in a slow, hypnotic rhythm. Like breathing. Like something asleep but still listening.The air smelled thick with salt and wet driftwood, something faintly metallic lingering underneath, like the remnants of an old storm still clinging to the coastline. Like blood on a coin. Like something left behind that shouldn't have been.

I liked that smell. It was the kind that made you feel like you were standing in the middle of something ancient, something bigger than you—something that had been here long before you took your first breath and wouldn't even notice when you took your last. Nothing has changed here since civilization took over the West. Hundreds of years. Centuries. Still the same cliffs, the same ocean. The same waves. Jean sat cross-legged beside me, fingers digging absently into the sand, leaving behind little trails like she was writing something only the ocean could read. Like she was trying to remember something the rest of her had already forgotten. She wasn't really looking at anything, but her eyes were fixed on the water, watching the waves drag themselves forward, then retreat. Always leaving. Always coming back. Always reminding.

The wind caught the loose strands of her hair, twisting them around her face in wild, sun-bleached tangles. She didn't seem to notice. Or maybe she didn't care.

I watched her for a moment, the quiet stretching out between us like an open road, then cleared my throat.

"Want me to walk you home?"

Jean's hand stilled. It was small—just a fraction of a second—but she hesitated.

The wind, which had been tugging at the edges of her dress, stopped. Just for a breath. Like it didn't want to carry her answer any farther than it had to. And in that moment, I knew the answer before she even said it.

She shook her head. "That's okay."

I smirked. "What, does it bite?"

That got a small laugh out of her, short and quiet. She tucked a strand of hair behind her ear, looking at the ground like the words weren't quite ready to meet my eyes.

"Not exactly. It's just..." She trailed off, her fingers curling into the fabric of her dress. Then, after a breath, she let it go. Let it all go. "It's nothing special."

I raised an eyebrow. "You're saying your castle on the hill isn't all it's cracked up to be?"

Jean gave me a dry look, but her mouth twitched like she was fighting a smirk. "More like a shack on a cliff," she said, her voice light, but her eyes weren't. "With a cellar that floods every time it rains."

Cellar. The word slipped from her lips like something she didn't mean to say. Something too heavy to leave behind but too dangerous to hold onto. Something about it made my skin prickle. Not in a *ghost stories and things that go bump in the night* kind of way. More like... a red flag. Something quiet. Something ignored. Like she was hoping I wouldn't notice.

"Creepy," I muttered, only half-joking.

"It's nothing," she murmured. "We just don't use it."

Not *we don't need it*. Not *it's useless*. Just: *We don't use it*.

That sat between us, an open door neither of us wanted to step through. I let the thought hang in the air, then pushed myself to my feet, brushing the sand from my jeans.

"Alright, then. How about your phone number? I'll call you sometime. As much as I enjoy our spontaneous meetings, it would be nice to plan something. Just you and me."

Jean let out a laugh—a real one. Quick and sharp, like I'd just told her the most ridiculous thing she'd ever heard.

"We don't have a phone."

I blinked. That didn't sound like a choice. It sounded like isolation disguised as simplicity. Like someone had gone out of their way to keep the world from reaching in.

"You don't—what do you mean, you don't have a phone?"

She shrugged, like it was nothing. Like it wasn't a big deal. Like it wasn't *insane*. My stomach twisted.

A house with no phone. A girl with no friends. A mother who never lets her leave. No one to call. No one to check. No one to notice. She could disappear, and the world wouldn't even blink.

I exhaled sharply, rubbing the back of my neck.

"You know, I worry about you, Jean."

She looked at me, brow slightly furrowed.

I swallowed. "If something were to happen... nobody would even ask. They wouldn't look for you." My voice came quieter now. "Because they already think you're gone."

Jean's smile faltered. "What?"

I hesitated, watching her carefully. Then, softer— "You've become a bit of a local legend, you know?"

She blinked. "What do you mean?"

She had no idea.

I shifted my weight, forcing my hands deeper into my pockets. "The ghost story. The one I told you at the lighthouse? People are really starting to believe it's you." I let out a slow breath, shaking my head. "Every version I've heard is worse than the last. They say there was some massive tragedy. What it was? I don't know. But some people swear they've seen you—standing by the cliffs, walking in the fog."

Jean stared at me, lips slightly parted.

I swallowed. "They talk about you like a shadow. Like you're some figure out there haunting the place, waiting for the tide to take someone else."

Her gaze flickered, her expression shifting—something unsettled. Something uncertain.

"But—" Her voice was softer now, almost distant. "Of course, people see me. I'm here. I've been locked away, sure, but... I'm still here..." She trailed off.

I watched as she tried to piece it together—the quiet flicker of doubt in her expression, the way her brows pulled together just slightly, as if something wasn't fitting the way she thought it should. Like a puzzle with a missing piece. Like a memory with a gap. The wind pulled at her hair, twisting it into thin ribbons of gold against the dying light.

I shifted my weight, swallowing hard. "I know you're here," I murmured. "But the rest of the town?" I exhaled. "They think you're gone, Jean."

Jean's hands curled slightly at her sides. She didn't answer. Didn't argue. Just stood there, listening. Like maybe she was hearing it for the first time. Then, finally—

"I wish I was."

My heart plummeted. "Me too," I broke a sorry smile. "But you said it yourself. Some places don't let you leave so easily."

The wind howled through the cliffs, shaking the bones of the coastline. It crawled through my jacket, pressed cold fingers against my ribs. I forced my hands deeper into my pockets.

"Tell me, do you at least have a radio? Something to keep you sane?"

"Just KXV8," she murmured. "Only station we get. The voices don't come in clear," she added after a second. "Sometimes I think they're saying things I'm not supposed to understand."

I frowned. "Damn, we don't even get that one!" I smirked, trying to lighten the mood. "How do you?"

Jean's mouth twitched—something small, almost sad. "Just special, I guess," she said, but the words sat hollow in her throat, like she didn't quite believe them.

I tilted my head, watching her. "So, you don't even have a record player?"

Jean shook her head. "Nope."

I let out a low whistle. "That's tragic. You'd like music. The good stuff, I mean. I'd make you a whole collection if I could."

Jean turned her head toward me, smiling a little.

"What about books? You seem to love 'em—" I laughed. "Or hate 'em, considerin' your diary looks like a crime scene."

Jean's smile stretched, just a little. "It's not a diary, it's a scrapbook."

"Scrapbook, diary—same thing."

"Not even close."

I grinned. "So, you got a whole library, or what?"

Jean shook her head again, and I extended my hand. She grabbed it, her small fingers coiling in mine. Cold. I pulled her to her feet, and she brushed the sand from her dress. The moonlight caught in her eyes, turning them glassy, almost silver.

"Only the books I get for my birthday."

I frowned. "That's it?"

She nodded, her fingers absently tracing patterns in the sand. "It's funny," she murmured. "I've been everywhere. Paris, Cairo, the stars. But only on the page." Her voice dipped. "The real thing... that's still locked away."

Her voice was light, almost teasing, but underneath it—something else. Something heavy. Something aching. It settled between us like a weight neither of us could name. I swallowed, forcing my voice to stay even.

"Maybe we can unlock it one day... if you want to."

Jean was quiet for a long time. The wind rolled through the cliffs, pulling at the tide, carrying the scent of salt and storm and things left unsaid. Then, finally—

"I do." Her voice was soft. "More than anything."

I exhaled, watching the tide roll in, stretch itself thin, then pull away again. Always moving, always shifting, always trying to get somewhere it was never gonna reach. Kind of a sad thing, when you thought about it. Didn't stop it from trying, though. The wind caught between us, tangling in Jean's hair, catching on the edges of her dress. She stood there, arms loose at her sides, fingers twitching like she wasn't quite sure what to do with them.

"797 Point Drive," I said, letting the wind take my voice, tossing it out to sea like a cigarette butt.

Jean glanced at me, one eyebrow raised.

I smirked. "That's me. My address. In case of emergencies."

That got a laugh out of her—small, breathy, like she wasn't sure if she was actually amused or just humoring me. "Oh really?"

"Yeah, really." I shoved my hands into my jacket pockets, leaning into the breeze. "C'mon. What's yours?"

She hesitated. Not long. Just long enough to be noticeable. Then, she looked toward the cliffs, like she was waiting for them to answer for her. When they didn't, she sighed.

"19 Crescent Avenue."

The wind stopped. Just for a moment. Like it didn't want to carry that name. A pause. Then, quieter—

"Really, it's nothing special."

I blinked. Then straightened.

"You're kidding."

Jean gave me a look—half-curious, half-wary. "What?"

I let out a short laugh, shaking my head. "No way; we used to have legends about your place! Used to say an old witch lived there—"

And that's when she looked at me. Not amused. Not surprised. Just... still. Like something ancient had stirred in her chest and didn't want to be touched. Like something about what I said had hit a pressure point, like I'd knocked on a door neither of us had realized was there. And now we were both waiting to see if something knocked back.

I cleared my throat, rocking back on my heels. "Alright, well, Miss Crescent Avenue," I said, forcing my smirk back into place. "Same time tomorrow?"

Jean let the silence stretch for a second longer, then smiled. But it was the kind of smile that made my stomach feel weird.

She dusted off her dress again, shaking off the sand that had settled there, then turned toward the path winding up the cliffs. The wind pulled at her hair, twisting strands into the air, curling around her in the way that made it seem like maybe it knew her personally.

"Maybe." The wind caught her voice, soft but certain.

She started walking, slow, steady, like she wasn't in any kind of hurry. But then, just before she reached the foot of the path, she looked back at me. And there was something in her eyes—something sharp, something distant, something knowing. The kind of look that made your skin prickle before your brain could figure out why.

"We'll see if you're lucky."

My smirk faltered, just slightly. Her words landed like a dare, and the air twisted in the space between us.

The wind didn't just howl—it clawed. It whipped through the cliffs, rattling against the rocks, wrapping cold fingers around my ribs. Something about the way she said it made my skin crawl. Like she already knew something I didn't. Like she'd read the ending to our story, and she wasn't going to tell me if either one of us made it out alive.

"Let's hope I am."

CHAPTER ELEVEN

The scrapbook was my way of keeping her close. Figuring her out when she wasn't around. Like trying to solve a mystery when half the clues are written in a language you've only ever heard in dreams.

It was right where I left it—beside my bed, waiting. Like a dog by the door. Like something that knew I'd come back eventually.

The leather cover caught the weak glow of my bedside lamp. Worn down in spots, edges all scraped, corners curling in that way leather does when it's starting to give up. Years of turning pages, of thumbs pressing against the spine like they could squeeze the truth out of it.

I was still half-dressed—slacks creased and dusted with sand from earlier, the pale blue button-down now untucked and hanging loose around my waist. I'd unbuttoned the collar but hadn't bothered with the rest. The leather jacket was slung over the chair across the room, forgotten the second I walked in. My sleeves were wrinkled and still rolled halfway up my forearms. I looked like someone mid-sentence—with nothing left to say.

The room was quiet. Dim. Lived-in. The kind of quiet that feels borrowed. Like the silence belonged to someone else and I was just holding onto it. The type of place that held onto things—scents, memories, shadows that never quite left. It smelled like engine grease, salt air, and the burnt-out wick of a candle I'd forgotten to snuff out. Or maybe just hadn't bothered to.

The walls used to be pale. Maybe white, once. Now they wore the muted yellow of time, streaked with fingerprints and smudges of oil from afternoons spent fixing up my bike in the driveway. A history of touch, pressed right into the paint.

The floor was a battlefield of dog-eared paperbacks, some stacked, some flopped open, mid-thought, like they'd been dropped in a hurry. Like I'd planned on picking them up and never did. A half-drunk bottle of Coke sat on my nightstand, next to an ashtray full of cigarette butts—some mine, some from people just passing through. People who never stayed long enough to explain why they left.

The window was cracked just enough to let the ocean in. The slow, rhythmic crash of waves folding into the cliffs, the kind of sound that makes you feel like the world is breathing around you. The wind pushed against the curtains, making them billow—slow, steady, like a hibernating beast exhaling in its sleep. The house felt like it was listening. Like it was waiting. Like it had been holding its breath for this moment.

Against the far wall, my desk sat in its usual state—an organized mess of thoughts I never finished. Records stacked against rusted pocket knives, scraps of paper covered in half-done sketches, words scrawled in the margins of things I never planned to share. A radio hummed in the corner, its antenna bent at a weird, desperate angle, whispering static into the silence. Searching for something, trying to reach someone with a message no one was left to hear.

And the bed? Just a tangle of blankets, flannel shirts and my lucky pair of shorts kicked to the foot of the mattress. The only thing in the room that time hadn't gotten its hands on.

I picked up the book, its pages thick. Distorted. Heavy. Weighted down with newspaper clippings yellowed at the edges, ripped-out book passages, and ink-scrawled confessions meant for no one's ears. Least of all mine.

I let my fingers drift over the rough edges, over words that had faded like an old song you can almost remember but not quite.

The last time I opened it, I learned how long Jean had been waiting. And I knew she wasn't just telling a story—she was clawing her way back into the world. Word by word. But this time, I didn't know if I was prepared for what else awaited me. Regardless, slowly, I flipped it open, and I turned the page.

The ink felt heavier now, like the words had been waiting. Waiting for someone to see them. To read them. To understand.

It all started when my father never came home.

That was it. Just those words, sitting alone at the top of the page. No build-up. No explanation. No soft landing. Just a hit straight to the ribs. The kind of sentence that doesn't let you look away.

The paper had yellowed around the ink, the edges curling slightly, like it had been handled too many times. Or maybe just once —really, really hard.

Beneath it, a photo. Taped down unevenly, the corners barely hanging on. Like someone put it there in a hurry and never came back to fix it. The picture was old, the colors faded into that dull, washed-out look that time gives things. A young man in uniform stood by the docks, hands shoved into his pockets, staring off past the camera. The ocean stretched behind him, flat and endless. Like it had swallowed something and was too tired to give it back.

The edges of the photo curled inward, trying to hold onto something that wasn't there anymore.

His name was Patrick Weston. And he saved her.

I ran my thumb over the ink, like I could feel the weight of it. The way she wrote it. No hesitation. No doubt. Just fact.

A new photo, pressed into place below. Different man, different time. A butcher now. An apron instead of a uniform, standing in front of a small, narrow shop. Weston's Meats was painted across the window, the kind of thick, blocky lettering that insisted it had been there forever. That it would never fade. The kind of sign people walked by without thinking, because it was always there; always going to be there.

His arms were crossed, his face soft—like someone who never knew how to pose. Like someone who was only standing still because they were told to.

Jean's handwriting wrapped around the edges of the photo, pushing into every blank space. Like she couldn't leave anything empty.

He was kind. He was gentle. He took her away.
She loved him.

Then, in smaller letters, tucked into the crease where the page bent:

But she never stopped being afraid.

I exhaled slowly, running my fingers over the edge of the page. On the next one, a torn-out passage, pasted down unevenly, like the paper itself had been rescued from something.

"The sea carried him away, and I waited for the day it would bring him back."

The ink was darker here. Pressed deep into the page, like she had traced over it again and again, making sure the words wouldn't disappear. Beneath it, Jean's handwriting, looping careful and deliberate.

But it never did.

And below that, a newspaper clipping, pasted into place. The ink had faded, the edges fragile, but the headline was still there, sharp and unflinching. The tape holding it in place had browned and cracked, curling at the corners. Like even memory was coming undone.

Local Man Lost at Sea.

Jean had left the margins empty. No scribbled notes, no explanations. Like she didn't need to add anything. Like the words had already taken up all the space they could.

Even now, when I ask about my father, I'm told not to speak of ghosts.

The wind rattled the windowpane—sudden, sharp. Like it didn't like what it had heard. That one landed differently. Settled in my chest like a weight, like something I should have seen coming but still didn't know what to do with. I turned the page, and there was a new sentence.

Then a year later, Sandra drowned.

The handwriting changed here. Different from before. Shaky. Pressed too hard into the page, like the pen had nearly torn through. Like the words had been carved instead of written. Beneath it, a list. Books, mostly. Titles about the ocean, about storms, about drowning. Some crossed out so aggressively the ink bled clean through—

like the words didn't just want to disappear. They wanted to ruin everything they touched.

And near the bottom, two lines.

I dream about the water sometimes.

It has already taken so much from me.

The way she underlined it sent something cold up my spine. Stayed there. *Jean still hadn't told me what happened to her sister.* I didn't even know how I'd ask. But there it was. The thing she never said out loud.

I flipped to the next page, but the paper beneath it felt warped, like it had been caught in the rain once. Or in someone's hands, shaking too hard to care.

My mother loved her.

Next to it, another passage, pasted down, slightly crooked.

"She was golden, untouchable, the kind of girl who made the world feel brighter just by being in it."

A tiny, near-invisible X below it. Like Jean was marking something only she understood. Then, her own words, curling in the margins.

I barely remember her.

Another note at the bottom of the page. A single sentence, but it hit like a gut punch.

But I know she is the reason I never got to live.

I let out a slow breath, steadying myself. It felt like trying to exhale after being underwater too long. Like I'd surfaced into someone else's grief. I could feel it now—the weight of this. It wasn't just grief. It was something else. Something heavier than one person could carry alone. I flipped to the next page, letting Jean tell me what came next.

My mother thinks she's protecting me, but I think it's the reverse. I think she's protecting herself.

I blinked. The words sat there, neat, deliberate. A small, fragile paragraph sat beneath it.

Before, she belonged to my father. Then, she belonged to my sister. When she lost them both, she belonged to no one. So, I made myself belong to her.

I turned another page. The words looked different again. Smaller. More rushed. Like she had written them in the dark.

She taught me all she could. But books taught me the world.

The sentence curled around another ripped-out passage, pasted into the paper.

"I have never seen the ocean, but I dream of it. I have never stood in the city, but I know what it looks like. I have never walked down a crowded street, but I can already hear the sound of it in my mind."

Jean's handwriting curved into the margins, quieter now. Almost like she didn't want to say it out loud.

Is that enough?

The ink was lighter here. Like she tried to erase it. Still, Jean's words wound between the lines, curling into the empty spaces like they belonged there.

I have never lived freely. But I have read about it.

The words sat on the page, but they didn't feel motionless. They felt restless. Like something trying to breathe beneath glass. I exhaled, slow. Flipped the next page carefully, as if that would make a difference. As if the words weren't already waiting for me. There, there were more notes. More thoughts. More pieces of her, pressed into paper, refusing to disappear. *This was how she survived.*

I learned young—fighting back only makes things worse.

A memory folded itself into the words, pressing through in the way the ink deepened, the way the pen had dragged just a little slower in some places.

I used to think I could outrun her. That if I could just make it past the dunes, past the jagged cliffs, I'd find something waiting on the other side. I was wrong.

I could almost hear it—the sharp edge of that thought. The way it must have sounded in her head before she wrote it down. A little girl running for her life, the sand slowing her small legs down, her mother easily catching up to her.

The words felt old. They had weight, the kind that settled into your bones, the kind that made you tired even if you weren't the one carrying them.

I didn't make it past the kitchen before the belt found me first.

I didn't flinch reading it. I froze. Because flinching meant you saw it coming. She hadn't. She hadn't even made it to the sand, to the dunes she fought to reach. But beaten? The next line came slower. Stiffer. Like it had been forced onto the page.

The second time, she made sure I wouldn't try again. My scars don't feel like memories. They feel like warnings.

My breath hitched. *The fork.* I could hear her words in my mind, *"some things hold you back."*

A scrap of fabric was taped to the page. Frayed at the edges. Torn from something. Maybe a dress, maybe something else. There was no explanation. Just a note, written in the corner, the ink fainter than the rest.

She told me it was for my own good.

The house shifted around me. A creak. A breath of movement on the roof above. The kind of sound that made the walls feel closer, made the air feel thicker. I knew it was just wood and nails and empty air. But it didn't feel like that.

It felt like something else. Like the house had been listening. Like it had been waiting for me to get to this part. The radio crackled in front of me—static flaring for half a second, then dying again. Trying to speak, then changing its mind. I turned the page—and there it was.

I never fought back after that. But I never stopped dreaming of leaving.

I swallowed, the words settling in, pressing their weight down, heavy and quiet.

I expected the next page to be another passage. A quote. Something borrowed, something stolen from someone else's story. Instead, it was her. Raw. Honest. Undiluted. The words were scrawled fast, slanted, like she had been thinking too quickly to write neatly.

I never wanted to just run.

I could almost hear her saying it. Like a confession. Like an ache.

I wanted to live.

A short list followed.

Read a book outside.
See a movie on the big screen.
Listen to music beyond what the radio plays.
Ride in a car with the windows down.
Feel the world rush past me.

I stared at it. Ran my fingers over the ink. The handwriting near the bottom was smaller, fading, as if she'd pressed lighter on the pen. They weren't goals. They were proof. Proof she hadn't given up on the world, even if it had given up on her. Then, in a different pen, she wrote:

I used to think I would.

I froze. The space between them said more than the ink did. I hesitated before turning the page.

The ink felt heavier here. Pressed harder, like she had known these words were final. Like she had wanted them to last. My chest tightened. Maybe I already knew what I was about to read. Maybe I just didn't want to see it. But I read it anyway.

I started this scrapbook because I wanted proof that I was here. That I existed. That I wasn't just some ghost wandering through her house, waiting for my turn to disappear.

The handwriting was steady. Too steady.

I thought that maybe, if I collected enough—words, images, paper-thin pieces of the world—I could build a life out of them.

A pause. A breath between sentences.

But all I've done is build a history of everything I can't have.

And then—

If you're reading this, maybe you're the one who's supposed to save me. The one who sees past the walls and locked doors and finds the girl still hiding inside. Or maybe... you're reading this because I'm already gone. Maybe the house finally swallowed me whole. Maybe she did. Some nights, I wonder what it would feel like to let the ocean take me. Fast. Cold. Quiet. I think about it more than I should. Not because I want to die—But because sometimes, I don't know how to keep living like this. If that's the case—if I'm gone—then I hope this is enough. Enough to make someone remember me right. The right version of me. The one I've always wanted people to see. Because I tried. God, I tried. But you can only scream in a locked room for so long before the silence starts to feel like your fault. So, if I'm gone, I hope someone reads this and understands. Not forgives—just understands.

I never wanted to disappear. I just didn't know how to stay.

My chest tightened. The words blurred for a second, and I wasn't sure if it was my eyes or the way they had been written. They didn't read like doubt. They read like a goodbye. They felt old, even though they weren't. Like they had been sitting in the dark, whispering to themselves, waiting for someone to find them.

That was it. The final entry.

I shut the scrapbook like it had burned me. Somewhere in the house, a floorboard creaked. A shift. A breath of movement. Like something settling back into place.

The pages held their shape. But just barely. Like even they

weren't sure how much more they could take. The weight of the book didn't feel like paper. It felt like bones. Old. Brittle. Unmovable. Like something that had been buried, only to be dug up again. And now that I'd seen it, I couldn't put it back. They were still breathing. Just waiting for someone to read them again. They sat there, carved into the page, ink pressed deep, like Jean had wanted them to last forever. And maybe they would.

But why won't anyone do something? Or believe she's real—or alive? Why has no one helped her?! What do they know, this town—it has to be hiding something!

My hands shook. I rubbed my thumb over the leather cover, as if that would change what I had just read. As if I could rewrite it. Make it softer. But Jean had written her history in ink—not meant to fade. The words Jean left behind were quiet but crushing, like the weight of the tide pulling back before a storm.

What...what was all this? Why did she choose me? And how can I save her?

CHAPTER TWELVE

Somewhere in the house, a plate clattered against the counter, followed by the muffled hum of the radio in the kitchen. The same station my mom always kept on, playing something soft—Patsy Cline, maybe. 'Crazy,' drifting through the walls like it belonged there. The kind of voice that tricked the house into remembering it used to feel safe. The kind of song that sounds like it already knows how your story ends. It made the air feel thin.

A voice broke through the quiet.

"Mom says dinner's ready."

I exhaled, dragging a hand through my hair, my fingers getting caught in the mess of it. A second passed before I glanced toward the door.

Eddie stood in the doorway, hair still damp and curling at the ends from his shower. He wore a soft flannel pajama top—blue plaid, slightly too big in the sleeves—and a pair of well-worn lounge pants cinched at the waist like he'd outgrown them but hadn't bothered to mention it. His socked feet shifted against the hallway tile, one toe nudging the baseboard like he wasn't sure if he was welcome or not.

He still had that open look about him. Like part of him was still a kid —safe, soft, untouched. He had the kind of trust in people you usually grow out of by the time you stop scraping your knees. Not that he was naïve—just that he hadn't learned yet to expect the worst. Not like I had.

He was everything I wasn't.

Eddie had always been the type to offer a smile before suspicion, to fix things instead of break them. The kind of kid who still said "please" on instinct and meant it.

He helped me with my bike sometimes—mostly just held the tools and talked while I pretended to need the extra hands. He'd do anything to be useful. To stay close.

Tonight, it seemed like what he really wanted was to know what I was doing.

He squinted at the book in my hands. "Whatcha readin'?"

I huffed a laugh, shaking my head. "Would you believe me if I told you?"

Eddie smirked. "Try me, wise guy."

I glanced at him, then down at the book, running my thumb over the edge of its worn pages. "It's a book. From the supposed *Ghost Girl.*"

Eddie's face lit up, eyes wide. "No way! You're pullin' my leg. You've seen her? Like, really seen her? What was she like?"

I hesitated, rubbing the back of my neck. "Very much alive. We've been, uh... seeing each other."

Eddie stared at me like I had just told him I was dating Bigfoot.

"You're serious? You're actually going steady with the Ghost Girl? Man, that's bonkers! I knew that story was a bunch of baloney. Tell me about her!"

I swallowed, glancing back down at the book. "She's... different. Witty. Poetic, in this quiet kind of way. And sad." I exhaled, rubbing at my jaw. "She gave me this. It's basically her entire life."

Eddie's grin faltered slightly, curiosity flickering into something more thoughtful. "Like a diary?"

"More like a scrapbook," I muttered. "Pieces of things she's held onto. Notes, old stories, torn-out pages from books."

I hesitated.

Then, flipping back to the last two pages, I let my voice fill the space between us.

"I never wanted to just run."

I didn't mean to say it out loud. The words just came. Like they wanted someone else to hear them for once. They landed heavy in the room, and I could feel Eddie watching me, but I kept reading.

"I wanted to live."

I swallowed.

"Read a book outside. See a movie on the big screen. Listen to music beyond what the radio plays. Ride in a car with the windows down. Feel the world rush past me."

I let the last words settle. They were small things. Simple things. But they sat between us like something bigger.

Eddie was quiet for a moment, shifting his weight from one foot to the other, like he wasn't sure if he should say what was on his mind. Then, soft but certain—

"That's not a long list."

I glanced up at him.

He didn't say it like a joke. He said it like someone realizing just how little it takes to feel human—and how cruel it is to keep that from someone. He frowned slightly, like he was doing the math in his head and coming up short.

"She doesn't want much," he added. "Not really."

I sighed, shaking my head. "No, she really doesn't." My voice dropped lower, like saying it out loud made it sit heavier in my chest. "But she's never had any of it."

Eddie frowned. "How come?"

I sighed again, rubbing a hand over my face. "I don't know. Not completely. Her mom—she lost it after Jean's dad was declared MIA in the war. 'Lost at sea.' And then her sister, Sandra, drowned." I hesitated, watching Eddie's expression shift as he put the pieces together. "And oh yeah—the Ghost Girl? She has a name." I swallowed. "It's Jean."

Eddie let out a low whistle. "Holy smokes." He furrowed his brow. "So... there's no Jenny, then?"

I glanced at him.

He let out a short laugh. "Guess your buddy got the name wrong, huh? Probably made the whole thing up. Which friend was this anyway?"

I didn't answer. Didn't move. Just gave him that knowing stare.

Eddie sat up straighter. His voice softened. "Oh." He rubbed the back of his neck. "Sorry, Will. I didn't realize—"

I shook my head once. "It's fine."

But it wasn't, and we both knew it. The room went quiet again.

Jean's name still hung between us. But so did the other one—the one I couldn't bring myself to say.

He rocked back on his heels, processing, then grinned. "So, what're you going to do? I can tag along, you know." he nudged my arm. "Be your trusty sidekick. Robin to your Batman. Watson to your Sherlock. I'm flexible."

I huffed a laugh, shaking my head. "What do you think?"

Eddie smirked. "I think if anyone can pull it off, it's you."

I wanted to tell him the truth—that I wasn't some hero. That saving someone wasn't as easy as wanting to. That Jean had already spent so long collecting scraps of the world instead of living in it, and I wasn't sure I had anything real to give her.

Hell, Jean would've probably given anything for a night just like this one. A radio playing. A roast in the oven. Someone to call her in for dinner. But here I was, trying to leave it all behind like it wasn't enough.

Still, Eddie had the kind of faith in people that felt unbreakable. So, I let him have it. Even if I didn't believe it myself—he was kinda right. She'd written her story like no one was ever going to read it. Like whoever did would be too late. But I did—and she's still here, dammit. And I was going to do something about it.

Eddie tilted his head toward the hallway. "C'mon, Sherlock. Before Mom storms in here and whacks you with a dish towel."

I sighed, shoving the book onto my nightstand and pushing myself to my feet. "Yeah, yeah. I'm coming."

Eddie turned, already disappearing down the hall, his footsteps light, easy.

THE SMELL of roasted meat filled the kitchen, thick and warm, curling around the room in slow, lazy waves. Mom pulled the oven door open, heat billowing out as she slid a roast onto the counter. The hum of the radio carried on in the background—something slow, something old.

She turned, wiping her hands on her apron, her gaze landing on us. "There you two are. What kept you so long?"

Eddie didn't miss a beat. "Will's seein' the Ghost Girl. Her name's Jean."

The air changed. Like someone had pulled a curtain tight over the windows.

Her fingers paused mid-wipe. She didn't blink. Didn't breathe. Then, slowly— "Jean?"

Eddie, completely oblivious, grinned. "Yeah! Turns out she ain't actually dead—just been locked up all this time by her mom. Wild, huh?" He leaned against the counter, launching right into it. "Her dad went MIA in the war, then her sister drowned, and then—"

"That's enough," Mom snapped.

Eddie shut his mouth. The warmth of the kitchen felt different now. Like something had shifted.

Mom smoothed a hand over her apron, the movement stiff, like she needed to do something with her hands. She let out a sharp exhale, shaking her head. "That's enough ghost stories before dinner."

The room didn't break. It just held its breath with us.

Eddie blinked. "But it's not a ghost story, it's—"

"I said that's enough." Her voice wasn't angry. But it wasn't light, either.

Eddie turned toward me, eyes wide, looking for backup.

I sighed, rubbing the back of my neck. "It's true."

Mom finally looked at me. Really looked at me. Her lips parted slightly, like she was going to say something—like she wanted to argue, to tell me I was wrong, that I was joking. But she didn't. She just stared, searching my face for something I wasn't sure she'd find. Then, slowly, she turned back toward the roast, grabbing a knife to start carving. The scrape of metal against the cutting board sounded too loud in the quiet.

The silence that followed felt different. Not empty—just full of things no one wanted to say.

Eddie rocked back on his heels, crossing his arms. "So what? You don't believe us?"

Mom didn't answer. She placed a few slices onto a plate and set it down on the table, her movements careful. Then she turned toward the stove, busying herself with the rest of the meal.

Eddie frowned but slid into his seat, glancing at me. I followed, pulling out a chair.

The silverware clinked lightly as Mom set a serving spoon beside the mashed potatoes.

I cleared my throat. "Did you ever know Betty Weinhart?"

The knife hesitated mid-slice. The room felt smaller.

Mom straightened. She turned toward me slowly, like she was

already preparing herself for something she didn't want to hear. "What's this about, Will?"

The warmth of the kitchen had drained away. The glow of the overhead light felt harsher now, casting longer shadows. The mashed potatoes steamed on the table. The roast cooled. But no one moved.

Mom didn't say anything at first, just standing there with her hands braced against the table, her back straight as if that alone could push away everything Eddie had just dumped into the room.

I swallowed hard. "Mom... everything Eddie said is true."

She didn't look at me.

I leaned forward, voice steady, urgent. "I need to know the truth."

Still, she didn't move.

"Mom, please."

Even the radio seemed to hush—its soft hum barely touching the edges of the room.

I thought about showing her the book. About setting it on the table between us, right there next to the roast and potatoes and whatever normal was supposed to taste like. But I didn't.

Finally, she exhaled, long and slow. Then, she pulled out a chair and sat down. She was quiet for a moment, her fingers smoothing over the tablecloth. Then—

"Betty and I went to school together," she said. Her voice was softer now, but still edged with something unreadable. "She was always quiet. Kept to herself. Had a tough life."

She let out a breath, shaking her head. "Then she met Patrick—the town butcher. Weston Meats, it was called. Your father and I used to go there all the time." She gave a small, absent smile. "Best meat in town. Best everything, really. That place was his pride and joy."

Her fingers traced the edge of the plate absently, as if she were remembering something far away.

"Her life was good for a while. They were happy. At least, as happy as folks could be." Then the lightness in her expression faded. "And then the war started."

She went quiet for a moment. I watched as her throat worked through a swallow, her hands folding together on the table. "Patrick was shipped off. Never came back."

The words sat in the air, heavy and unmoving. Mom let out a slow breath, shaking her head again, but this time, there was something bitter about it.

"The war took a lot from this town." She glanced at Eddie, then back at me, her eyes sharper now. "It didn't take your father's life, but it took him all the same. He came back different. A stranger in his own skin. And I watched him walk out again, this time with both feet planted on American soil. Sometimes I wonder if I'd rather he'd died. At least then there'd be a reason."

Eddie stiffened beside me.

Mom pressed her lips together, rubbing her temples before continuing. "I don't expect you boys to understand. You don't remember what it was like back then. You don't remember the notices. The families torn apart overnight." Her voice dipped lower. "Betty wasn't the only one who lost her husband. And she wasn't the only one who never got to bury him."

She let out a shaky breath, her fingers curling against the tablecloth.

"People tried to move on. Some of us did." A pause. "Some of us couldn't."

I swallowed, placing a hand over hers.

She stiffened. The kitchen still smelled like dinner. But it tasted like silence.

"Mom. Jean's not dead." I met her eyes, steady, certain. "She's still out there. Please, you have to believe me."

Mom's jaw tightened. Then, slowly, she shook her head. "No, Will. That's not true."

I had her whole story in my hands. Page by page. A life she wasn't supposed to tell. And still, even that wasn't enough to make someone listen.

I opened my mouth, but she cut me off, her voice firmer now. "I was at the funeral. We all were. You were there, too."

The words knocked something loose in my chest. "What?"

"It was a closed casket," she said. "For both of them."

The room tilted slightly. *Closed casket.* Meaning no one *knew.* They just... *believed.* Like the town needed a funeral more than a body.

"What happened to them?" I asked, my own voice sounding distant.

Mom looked up at me, eyes dark with something I couldn't place.

"They both died in the surf." Her voice was quieter now, as if the words themselves carried weight. "One trying to save the other."

She let the words settle before adding, softer—

"The day those girls died, we were all in mourning. Maybe not for them. Maybe foolishly for ourselves. But we all know what happened that day."

The weight in her voice made my stomach tighten.

"The whole town was there." She swallowed, shaking her head slightly. "I remember seeing Betty at the service. She didn't cry. Not once. She looked like someone who had already buried more than her fair share of family. Like grief wasn't new—just louder that day. And she just... stood there. Staring." She let out a breath, then slowly pushed her chair back. "I've lost my appetite."

Eddie and I both shifted.

"Mom, we're sorry," Eddie said quickly, guilt creeping into his voice.

Mom shook her head, waving a hand. "No, no, it's alright." She turned toward us, something unreadable in her expression. "I couldn't imagine what would happen to me if I lost you both." The air felt thick, too heavy. "When the phone rang that night, I had a glimpse. When I stood in the hospital hallway and couldn't breathe. Not because of your injuries. But because I didn't know if I was about to be the one left behind—again." She inhaled slowly, then exhaled, letting her shoulders relax slightly. "I just... I love you. I love you both so much." She gave a weak smile, her eyes softer now. "Just...please. Let her stay gone. The dead don't like to be dragged back up. And neither do the people who buried them."

The way she said it—it didn't feel like a warning. It felt like a plea.

I swallowed, nodding, but I didn't mean it.

She turned, gathering the plate she'd barely touched. "Betty has grieved enough. We all have." She set them in the sink and disappeared into the living room.

The radio kept playing. Skeeter Davis this time—something about the end of the world and how no one even notices. The volume hadn't changed, but somehow the lyrics felt louder now. Like the house was still listening. Like it always had been. Nothing moved. Not the air. Not us. Like the world was waiting to see if I'd say her name again.

Eddie and I sat in silence. I glanced down at my plate, and suddenly, I wasn't hungry either.

CHAPTER THIRTEEN

Jean was already waiting for me when I got to the beach.

I'd dressed like it mattered. Because it did. I had thrown on my leather jacket—creased and heavy with salt air, the sleeves stiff at the elbows—but underneath, my white dress shirt was still tucked in, though the top button had given up somewhere along the way. Khaki slacks, clean for once, creased from the ride, and boots I'd bothered to polish even if the tide would scuff them all over again. My hair was combed back when I left the house, but the wind had its own ideas.

I looked like someone trying not to fall apart. Like if I pressed the right creases and polished the right boots, maybe the night wouldn't see through me. At least I tried.

The sky was bruised, the last light of day dissolving into something darker, like ink spilled into water, spreading slow and inevitable. The ocean swallowed the sun whole, pulling the color down beneath its waves like it was never meant to be there in the first place. Mist curled around the jagged rocks, thick and heavy, the kind that seeps into your bones if you stand in it too long. It clung like a memory, the kind that keeps its grip long after you try to shake it.

Jean sat in the thick of it, knees pulled to her chest, small against the vastness of the sea. The wind toyed with her, threading itself through her light hair, tugging at the hem of her blush pink dress like it was trying to pull her away. She didn't stop it. She just sat there, watching the tide inhale and exhale, deep and steady, like something ancient, something that had always been here. The mist clung to her like she belonged to it. Like it had shaped itself around her absence and didn't want to let her go.

She didn't look up at first—not until I said her name.

She turned then, slow, like surfacing from something deep, her eyes catching the last scraps of daylight. Blue-gray, the color of a storm that's already passed but left the sky uneasy about it.

"You're late," she said. Not accusing. Just a fact. Like she'd already done the math, already made peace with it before I even showed up.

I smirked, shoved my hands into my pockets like I wasn't cold. "Hopin' you'd still be here."

Jean studied me. The way she looked at things—at people—like she was searching for something just beneath the surface, something she wasn't sure she'd ever find but kept looking for anyway.

"Why?" she asked, careful. Like the answer mattered.

I took a step closer, the damp sand shifting under my boots. The mist curled at my ankles, slow and creeping, like something alive. "Because," I said, "I'm taking you somewhere."

That got her attention. A flicker of something crossed her face—curiosity, wariness. Some blend of both.

"Somewhere," she repeated, rolling the word over like she was testing its weight. "You make it sound like another planet."

I let the smirk stick. "Maybe it is."

A small smile whispered across her lips, brief but real. "Sounds romantic," she murmured, but there was something else in her voice. A kind of wistfulness. A kind of disbelief.

I let the moment stretch, let her wonder.

"It's a surprise," I said finally.

Jean's fingers curled into the fabric of her dress, gripping, just for a second. She was always caught in this in-between place— half-ready to run, half-ready to see what was waiting past the edge.

"Do you always do that?" she asked, after a pause.

It wasn't the question that caught me. It was the way she said it —like she was asking if this was the kind of story she'd survive.

"Do what?"

"Talk like you're leading a girl straight into a story she was never meant to be a part of."

I let out a quiet laugh, but something about the way she said it made my chest feel tight.

"That a bad thing?"

Jean let out a slow breath, the kind that wasn't really an answer but wasn't not an answer either.

Then, just as quickly, something shifted in her expression. That restless spark—always there, even when she didn't want it to be. The kind of curiosity that could get a person into trouble. The kind that made her wonder, just for a second, what was out there.

I held out my hand, palm up. Waiting. "Come on, Jean," I said, softer this time. "Trust me."

She hesitated, just for a breath. The space between us felt thin, charged, like the pull of the tide before it crashes back down.

And then, slowly, her fingers brushed against mine. And for the briefest second—

I wasn't here.

I was back in the dark. The cold. Holding on too tight to hands that weren't there anymore.

I felt it again—the rush of breathless running, gravel scraping skin, headlights carving through the night. The crack of tires skidding, too late. The scream that wasn't mine.

His voice, calling my name— And then nothing. Just nothing.

I blinked hard, forced myself back into the present. Jean's fingers curled around mine, warm, solid. Here.

Not a ghost. Not yet.

And as I pulled her to her feet, I felt it—that shift in the air, quiet but certain. The kind of moment that sticks, like sand in your shoes, like the taste of salt on your skin long after you've left the shore.

The waves crashed against the rocks, the mist hung thick in the air, and somewhere out there, the world kept spinning.

But right now, it was just us.

SHE HELD onto me tight as we rode the twelve miles to Lincoln City, her arms locked around my waist, her cheek pressed against my back like she was afraid to let go. Maybe she was. Maybe I was too.

The road stretched ahead of us, dark and endless, the roar of the wind swallowing up anything that might've been said. It pulled at us, lifted strands of Jean's hair, like ribbons in the breeze, sent them streaming behind her, caught in the headlights of passing cars like something alive. The fog wrapped around the road like a secret too old to speak. But the farther we got from Depoe, the less it chased us. Instead, it waited. And for a little while, it felt like nothing else existed. The wind drowned out everything but her heartbeat against my back. Like we were outrunning time. Or at least pretending we could.

By the time I pulled up in front of the Lakeside Theatre, Jean was staring—eyes wide, lips parted just slightly like she was scared saying something might break the moment.

The marquee buzzed against the night, neon flickering like it was shorting out a heartbeat. Pink and gold light rippled across the pavement, jittery and soft. The kind of light that made people look better than they were. It had stood here forever, part of the town's backbone—cracked tile, soda stains, and all. A place thick with old stories. First kisses. Almosts. Messy breakups. Fights in the parking lot. Nights that should've been forgettable but weren't.

The letters above us—carefully slotted in, some slightly crooked —spelled out the night's feature:

THE MUSIC MAN – 7 PM

A loose crowd drifted beneath the awning. Small-town evening usuals. Groups of teenagers in varsity jackets that hadn't been earned this season, if ever. Girls with ponytails and cherry lip gloss pretending not to look at the boys pretending not to look at them. A few kids from my old math class leaned against the wall, spinning nickels and talking too loud. One of them—maybe Chris Denning or someone who looked like him—flicked a glance my way and elbowed the guy next to him.

They knew me. Or used to. Crowds used to feel different. Now sometimes they press in too close. Like being seen is the same as being cornered.

A couple leaned against a beat-up red Plymouth, sharing a milkshake with two straws like they hadn't moved since '59. Someone had propped open the lobby doors, and the scent of popcorn drifted out—heavy, salty, warm—cutting through the brine of the sea air.

The Beach Boys hummed low from a car parked across the street, windows rolled down halfway. It almost felt like time had paused just for us.

Like somehow, in the hum of the marquee and the rhythm of the waves just down the block, this was a world where Jean belonged. Where she always had. A version of this town without the rot.

Jean's hand tightened on the sleeve of my jacket. Her voice came soft, careful. "The Music Man," she read. And for a second, it sounded like she was reading her own name. She turned to me, something wide and weightless in her gaze. "We're going to see a movie?"

I nodded.

She exhaled, slow, like she was afraid she'd wake up from a dream. "I've never been inside one before."

I knew that. I knew that, and yet somehow, hearing her say it still hit me in the gut, sharp and unexpected, like missing a step on the stairs.

"Well," I said, offering my arm, "guess today's a good day to change that."

Her smile was small at first, careful. Then—real. And for a second, it felt like maybe she wasn't so far away. Like maybe she wasn't a phantom flickering between past and present.

Then, just as quick, something in her shifted. The lights caught the shimmer in her eyes. And from behind us—

"Holy hell, Will. You're still around? Figured you'd be in North Carolina by now. Who's the doll?"

I turned, already knowing who I'd see.

Charlie and Polly loitered by the curb, half-draped in the lazy confidence of people who had never needed to be anywhere else. Like gravity worked differently for them. Like nothing in this town had ever told them no.

Charlie stood a little apart from the crowd, hands shoved deep into the pockets of his worn leather jacket. His red hair caught the glow of the marquee, messy in that boy-who-forgot-to-comb-it kind of way. He wasn't flashy—not like Polly—but there was something steady about him. Like a campfire that didn't ask for attention, just gave you warmth if you stood close enough.

He had one of those soft, crooked smiles—the kind that made you feel like he already knew who you were, but didn't hold it against you. Maybe he did have me figured out. But unlike Polly, there wasn't anything sharp in it. Just something familiar.

That was the thing about Charlie. He never pushed, never tried too hard to be clever. He just had this easy way of talking, like life was something to be endured and laughed at all at once. The kind of guy who'd be the last one left standing at the end of the world— quiet, calm, whistling a song no one remembered the words to.

Charlie looked like someone who'd never left because he didn't need to. I, on the other hand, looked like someone who'd left already and just hadn't realized it yet.

But Polly—Polly was something else.

She leaned against Charlie's black Chevy, one foot crossed over the other, the kind of casual that took work. A cigarette dangled between two fingers, the tip burning a slow, smoldering orange. She exhaled like she was bored, the smoke curling around her like a movie star's entrance.

Her blonde hair was pulled into that sharp, sleek ponytail like she had just stepped out of a doll box labeled—Now with Attitude. Cat-eye sunglasses sat perched on her head, even though the sun had long since vanished. Her lipstick was red—real red—the kind of red that made a statement. And then there were the leather slacks. Black, sharp, shining under the neon glow of the theatre marquee. The kind of pants you saw once in a magazine ad and never again. Like they were made for someone cooler, meaner, and impossible to ignore.

It was the first time I'd seen her since... everything. And she didn't look surprised to see me. Just... unreadable. Like she'd practiced being that way.

Jean stiffened beside me, and Polly just smiled.

She always knew how to make a room look at her, but tonight, it felt like she was looking through me instead.

"Well, well. Look who didn't burn rubber after all." Polly drawled. Her voice sounded the same, but it settled in my chest like a bruise. "Who's this little thing?" she asked, tilting her head, her eyes sharp and glittering. The way she said *little* wasn't about height. It was about power. About putting Jean in a box and sealing it shut.

"You pick yourself up a girl already, Will? That was fast—even for you." Polly continued.

Jean's fingers twitched in mine. I felt it—her whole body shrinking in on itself, pressing inward like she could make herself disappear if she tried hard enough.

Charlie's gaze flicked over her, slow and thoughtful. He wasn't looking at her like Polly was, not trying to pick her apart. More like he was just trying to place her, like some distant memory he wasn't sure was real.

"Don't think I've seen you around before," he said, not unkind, but not exactly friendly either.

"Maybe she don't get out much." Polly murmured like she was saying something casual, something harmless.

Except it wasn't.

Jean's grip on my arm turned rigid. My jaw clenched without thinking—an old habit that kept the noise down. I didn't like the way they were looking at her. Like they were trying to place her. Like if they stared long enough, they'd remember.

"Look, she's just visiting," I said, too fast. The kind of fast that made it obvious I was lying.

Charlie's smirk twitched at the corner, just slightly, like he caught it but wasn't going to say anything. Not yet, anyway.

Polly took a long drag from her cigarette, lips curling just slightly as she exhaled. "Hmm. Cute."

Jean didn't move.

Polly flicked her gaze back to me—sharp, amused. "Didn't think the quiet type was your flavor, Will."

I didn't know what she thought of me anymore. Maybe I never really did. But the way she looked at Jean—it wasn't curiosity. It was a warning.

Jean's fingers found my sleeve, small and tense, curling into the fabric like she didn't mean to. She kept her eyes on the sidewalk. "Are you sure these people are your friends?"

I swallowed. "The guy is. The other... it's complicated."

Polly exhaled another lazy plume of smoke, still watching Jean like she was trying to place her from a half-forgotten story.

Then: "Oh, I get it now." She turned to Charlie, lips curling. "You ever see those dumb little birds that slam into windows? Think the sky's open—then *bam*. Glass."

Jean blinked.

Charlie ran a hand through his hair and sighed. The kind of sigh he gave when he was tired of Polly—but not enough to stop her.

Polly turned back to Jean, eyes glittering. "You've got that look. Like you know how it feels to crash. So does Will. Maybe that's why he's into you."

Jean didn't flinch. Didn't speak. But her grip on my sleeve tightened.

Something hot coiled in my chest.

"Lay off, Pol," I said, voice flat.

She held up her hands, all mock innocence. "What? Can't a girl make conversation anymore? Or you always get this touchy these days?"

Charlie chuckled, shaking his head, but he wasn't all the way amused.

Polly flicked the ashes of her cigarette onto the pavement, then tilted her head toward Jean, like she was examining something fragile. "Tell me. You ever been someplace like this before, sweetheart?"

Jean didn't answer right away.

Polly's smirk widened. "Didn't think so."

Charlie shot her a look, like she was pushing just a little too hard, but Polly just grinned, like she had already decided she was the most interesting person in the conversation.

Charlie, turned back to me. "So, you sticking around, Will?"

His voice was easy, but there was something under it. Not quite disappointment. Not quite relief.

I hesitated. "Not sure."

Charlie nodded like that was the answer he expected. "Yeah. Didn't think you'd be the type to run forever."

"Didn't think you'd be the type to wait forever," I shot back.

He grinned, but it wasn't unkind. "I wasn't—'til recently."

"Yeah, well, as fun as this reunion's been, we should probably get inside. Wouldn't want to miss the previews and all that." I said, tugging Jean gently toward the line at the entrance, like if I just kept us moving, none of this would stick.

Polly smirked, the kind of smile that didn't quite reach her eyes. "Sure. You kids have a blast." She stretched the words out, sweet as syrup, slow as molasses, just enough that they didn't feel as nice as they should.

Then she turned to Charlie, murmuring low, but still loud enough for us to hear. "See? Told ya he'd never really leave."

"Why don't you cut him a break, Pol." Charlie responded lower. "You know he's still having a tough time with—"

"And I'm not?!" Polly scoffed. I turned and met her eyes, but all I could see was the old windowsill at her house. The one we used to sneak out of. She hadn't looked at me like someone who remembered that. Maybe that's what stung the most.

I was just about to push through the theatre doors when Polly's voice called after me.

"Listen, I guess I'll see you around, Will, alright?"

She stopped. Paused, like she was just now realizing something. Her gaze flicked to Jean, a little more focused, a little sharper than before. Her lips parted slightly, but she hesitated.

"Wait— what's your name, sweetheart?"

Jean tensed. Just barely. But I felt it. She didn't answer right away.

Polly waited, tilting her head, eyebrows raised expectantly.

Jean swallowed, then spoke. Quiet. Careful. "It's Jean."

It landed like a dropped pin in a silent room. Polly blinked. For the first time all night, something in her expression shifted—like the air had changed, like the ground wasn't quite as solid beneath her feet as she thought. She opened her mouth, then shut it. Her lips pressed together, a flicker of something unreadable in her eyes before she muttered, almost to herself—"Jean?"

Barely a whisper. Barely there at all. The name hung in the air like smoke. And Polly—she didn't just hear it. She *recognized* it. The cigarette in her hand went still. Her smile flickered, just once.

Jean's fingers clenched around mine.

Charlie shot Polly a sideways glance. "What is it?"

Polly blinked hard, like shaking herself out of something. She forced a small laugh, shaking her head as she flicked the cigarette to the pavement, crushing it under the toe of her pointed black heels.

"Nothing." But the smirk she pulled on didn't quite fit right anymore. "I—uh. She just reminded me of someone I used to know."

I didn't wait for whatever else she might've had to say. I just tightened my grip on Jean's hand and pulled her inside before she had the chance to look back.

CHAPTER FOURTEEN

Inside the lobby, the muffled buzz of the crowd gave way to the low hum of a film projector spinning in the background, the scent of hot, buttered popcorn clinging to the red velvet ropes and the gold-trimmed carpets. The kind of smell that wrapped around you, thick and warm, like something out of a memory you weren't sure was yours. A soft crackle of static played from the lobby speaker, the voice on the other end grainy and distant, announcing the next showing like it was calling people home.

Jean hesitated at the entrance. Just a fraction of a second. Just long enough that I noticed. She let out a breath that could've been a laugh, except it wasn't.

"Your friends think I'm strange."

She didn't say it like it hurt anymore. More like it had become part of the script. Something she could recite without flinching.

I shook my head. "No, they don't." Said it fast, like I wanted to cut the thought off before it could settle.

Jean glanced up at me then, lips pressed together like she didn't quite believe me. Like she was already rewriting the moment in her head, turning it into another story where she was the odd one out, the thing people whispered about when they thought she couldn't hear.

I sighed through my nose, stuffing my hands into my jacket pockets. "Okay, fine. Maybe they do. But they don't matter. And you know why?" I tilted my head, waiting for her to look at me again. "Because screw them. That's why. They're the ones who're strange. I mean, Polly's a high-heeled freak in a Barbie ponytail. Trust me, she doesn't think poorly of you, she just *hates* me. We have history—but not like that. And Charlie—he's okay, I guess, but anyone who hangs with her has got to have something wrong with him."

Jean blinked, then huffed something that could've been a laugh if she'd let it. "Real poetic."

I smirked. "Yeah, well, sometimes the truth don't need fancy words."

I wasn't in love. Not yet. But if this kept up, I was going to fall fast and hard, and no one was going to stop me, including me.

Jean gave me a nod, small but steady, before her eyes broke from mine. And then, something changed. She turned slowly, taking it all in—the grand, glowing marquee outside, the movie posters lining the walls, the ornate ticket booth with its brass accents, polished and glinting under the lights. The way the whole theater seemed to hum with a kind of magic that had never belonged to her before.

For a moment, she wasn't the girl trapped behind a locked door. She wasn't the shadow her mother tried to erase. She wasn't a secret.

She was just a girl stepping into the world for the first time.

And *God*, it hit me then—how wrong it was that something this simple could feel so monumental. That a girl walking into a movie theater could feel like breaking the laws of the universe.

But that's what it was. A fracture in time. A night that shouldn't exist.

And for a little while, I let her have it.

. . .

INSIDE THE THEATER, the air was thick with the heat of too many bodies packed into velvet-upholstered seats. That kind of warmth that stuck to your skin, made your clothes feel heavier. The hum of the projector droned above, steady and constant, like a heartbeat that kept the place alive. The scent of buttered popcorn and caramel candies mixed with the faintest trace of cigarette smoke clinging to jackets and hair—a reminder that people had been loitering outside, sharing quick drags before ducking in, exhaling ghosts into the cold night.

Jean followed me down the aisle, her footsteps softened by the plush red carpeting, her movements slow, deliberate. She moved like someone stepping onto sacred ground. I could hear the soft swish of her dress brushing against the backs of the seats as she trailed her fingers along them, her touch barely there, like she was afraid to disturb something sacred.

We found a pair of seats near the middle, where the screen stretched wide, glowing like stained glass, washing over the crowd in flickering light. As we settled in, Jean let out a slow breath, her fingers pressing into the armrests like she was holding herself in place. Like the moment might disappear if she didn't anchor herself to it.

Then, in that soft, thoughtful way of hers, she murmured, "It's strange, isn't it? How something can feel so real and unreal all at once?"

I glanced at her, the way her brow creased just slightly, like she was trying to put her thoughts in order before they got away from her.

"Yeah," I said after a beat. "But maybe that's the whole point."

Jean turned her head slightly, not quite looking at me, but close. "The point?"

I shrugged, eyes on the screen even though nothing had started yet. "Life's weird. It throws you around, spins you out, makes you feel like you're floating half the time. But then—" I gestured toward the screen, toward the rows of people settling in, the murmurs dying down. "Then you find places like this. Where you can sit still for a while. Where you don't have to be anything except... here."

The silence that fell over the theater felt reverent, like something holy was about to begin. Jean didn't say anything right away. Just held onto the thought like she wasn't sure whether to set it down or tuck it away for later.

Then, the film began.

A burst of Technicolor flooded the screen—vibrant blues, reds, golds—too rich, too full, too much like a world that didn't belong to us. I watched as it washed over Jean, her face bathed in flickering light, her eyes wide and unguarded.

She leaned in ever so slightly, barely moving, but I could feel it. "It's like stepping into another life," she whispered, and I don't think she even realized she said it out loud.

Her gaze never wavered—not once. Not when the music swelled, not when the characters spoke like they carried the weight of the world in their voices. It was all right there, written across her face.

The wonder. The longing. The hunger for something just beyond reach.

At some point, I felt her fingers brush against mine on the armrest. A light touch, the kind you could ignore if you wanted to, if you pretended hard enough.

Neither of us looked away from the screen. Neither of us spoke.

She just curled her hand into mine, small but certain, as if, for just a little while, she could hold onto something steady.

And in that moment, we weren't Jean and Will. We weren't two kids sneaking around, stealing whatever pieces of freedom we could. We were just anyone. Two people in a darkened theater, watching a movie. Just like everybody else.

It was a night that shouldn't have happened. A bubble in the timeline of history. A pause in the story. And we both knew, sooner or later, it would burst.

. . .

By the time we stepped outside, the night had fully settled over the town. The neon marquee still hummed overhead, its glow spilling onto the pavement in streaks of red, yellow, and electric blue. The letters, once so sharp and bright, now felt softer—like the last few words of a story trailing off into the dark. The kind of ending that didn't announce itself. Just faded.

A few last stragglers loitered near the entrance, their voices hushed, smoke curling from the ends of their cigarettes as they laughed in that quiet, tired way people do when the night has stretched long. Not loud. Not hurried. Just lingering. Like they weren't quite ready for the world outside the theater to be real again.

Beyond them, the streetlights flickered, their glow uneven, casting weak halos over the cracked asphalt. The air smelled like salt and exhaust, like warm pavement and cold ocean mist. A little bit of everything. A little bit of nothing.

Just off to the side, near the curb, two girls stood together—one maybe twelve, the other seven, their shoulders pressed close like the night might swallow them if they let go.

"I told you it's too late," the older one said, her voice edged with worry, hands fidgeting at the hem of her sweater. "Dad's going to kill us."

The younger girl looked up at her, wide-eyed, shifting on her feet. "We need to find a payphone."

The older girl exhaled sharply, scanning the street like she was hoping one would magically appear. "Yeah. Yeah, I know." She hesitated, then chewed on her lip. "I don't remember the number."

The younger one blinked. "What do you mean? You call it all the time."

"I know, but—it's different when you have to say it out loud." She shook her head, frustration creeping into her voice. "Just—just give me a second, alright?"

The little one nodded, hands clasped together, shifting from foot to foot as if standing still might be the thing that got them in trouble.

Jean watched them for a moment, her expression unreadable.

Then, so quietly I almost missed it, she murmured, "I remember that feeling."

I glanced at her, but she didn't say anything else. Just stood there, watching as the older girl took the younger one's hand, leading her down the sidewalk, both of them searching for something that might get them home.

Jean hugged her arms around herself, her fingers gripping her elbows like she was holding herself together. Then she tilted her head back, her gaze flicking toward the sky.

The stars were faint. Swallowed up by the glow of the theater lights, by the fog rolling in thick from the coast.

"It's funny," she murmured, almost to herself. "I was just thinking —how something can feel so much like an ending, but not be one at all."

I reached for my keys, the cool metal jangling in my palm. The sound was sharp in the quiet, too solid, too final.

"I'll take you home."

Her whole body stiffened. It was small. Almost nothing. But I felt it.

No.

It wasn't loud. Wasn't angry. But it stopped me cold.

I let the keys settle in my palm. Swallowed. "Jean—"

"I need to go back to the beach." Her voice was thin, unraveling, stretched tight like an over-wound thread.

Not *home*. That word was a lie. A wound pretending to be shelter. The word itself sat heavy between us, weighted down by things she wasn't ready to say out loud. Things I already knew.

She rubbed her hands together, slow, restless. Like she was trying to shake off something she couldn't quite touch. Like something had reached out and left a mark.

Her eyes flicked toward the road. Toward the dark. Toward something I couldn't see.

Something that was already waiting for her.

"I have to," she whispered, but it wasn't meant for me.

I shifted, rolling my shoulders, trying to keep my voice even. "I don't mind driving you, you know. It'd be faster—"

"No, Will."

The words came quick, clipped at the edges, and I caught the way her breath hitched right after she said them.

I frowned. "Your mom's gonna notice either way."

She swallowed hard, her gaze dipping, just for a second. "I know." And then, softer— "But if I don't walk back on my own, it'll be like I really left."

The words landed somewhere deep, somewhere I couldn't quite reach. That wasn't fear talking. It was survival. As if letting someone carry her now meant losing the right to ever stand on her own again. I didn't argue.

"Alright, the beach it is," I said, shrugging off my jacket and handing it to her. "But put this on. It's cold out, and it'll be worse on the bike."

She hesitated for only a second before slipping her arms through the sleeves. The jacket was too big on her, swallowing her frame, the worn leather creasing at her elbows. She tugged it tighter around herself, her fingers gripping the edges.

And just like that, we were off.

THE NIGHT DIDN'T WELCOME us. It swallowed us. The road stretched ahead, long and empty, its faded lines swallowed by the creeping fog. It circled around us—tightening, pressing. Like it had questions we hadn't answered.

Somewhere behind us, the lights of Lincoln City blinked out, one by one. Not fading—vanishing. Like the fog had decided we were done being seen. The mist clung to the asphalt in thick waves, swirling in the wake of our tires, curling in slow, deliberate tendrils, like something breathing. The wind cut sharp against my ears, and for a second it sounded like something else. Like tires. Like metal. I shook it off. The darkness pressed close, heavy and unmoving, like it had been waiting for us to come back.

Storefronts shuttered. Mile marker 126 swallowed by mist. A motel sign blinking like a dying star.

Depoe Bay was pulling us back. It always had been.

Jean held onto me a little tighter as we rode, her fingers gripping the edge of my jacket, her breath warm against my shoulder. I could feel the weight of it—the silence, the thoughts pressing down on her, the things she wasn't saying.

The fog curled around the road ahead, thick and unmoving. Not like it was keeping something out. Like it was keeping something in.

The night watched us go, silent. Anticipating.

Jean didn't look back. Maybe because she already knew what was coming.

Maybe she always had.

CHAPTER FIFTEEN

The ocean never sleeps. It paces. Back and forth, back and forth, like a restless thought trying to untangle itself, repeating itself over and over again, trying to find its way out of your head but never quite making it. The waves don't crash so much as they press—heavy, steady, like the weight of something unsaid.

I cut the engine, and for a moment, the only sound was the low, throaty murmur of it dying out. Then came the tide. I really listened —listened to the way the water pulled itself apart and stitched itself back together again, over and over, like it was working something out. It sounded like a question no one had the guts to answer.

The wind curled through the spokes of my bike, whistling soft and low. The night stretched out around me, deep and starless, swallowed up by a creeping marine layer that blurred the line between sky and sea. The horizon didn't feel like a horizon anymore. It felt like a suggestion. Like if I stepped forward, I wouldn't know if I was falling into water or sky.

The waves kept rolling in, slow and deliberate, their white crests catching the sweep of the new lighthouse search lamp before breaking against the shore. The scent of salt thickened in my lungs—sharp and clean, but underneath it was something older, something earthbound. The faint, oily trace of gasoline from the harbor. The echoes of fried fish from some long-shuttered café up the road.

I let the silence rush in. The ocean had always been loud here—crashing, howling, whispering things I didn't always want to hear. But tonight, it was louder. Or maybe I was just quieter.

Jean slid off the bike without a word.

She landed light, pulling my jacket tighter around herself. It was too big, hanging loose off her frame, but she wore it like armor. Her face was turned away, wind cutting through the strands of her hair, lifting them, twisting them. She looked small like this. Not weak. Just... small.

Neither of us moved. The silence between us stretched wide, stretching as far as the black horizon, as far as the water that went on forever, over the edge and into another world. Even the town behind us—Depoe Bay, with its single strip of neon-lit diners and flickering motel signs—felt distant, like something belonging to another life. Here, there was only the tide, the wind, and everything we weren't saying.

I exhaled, raking a hand through my hair, still wind-rough from the ride. "Well," I said, tilting my head toward the sand, "guess this is where I let you off."

Jean nodded, not looking at me, just pulling my jacket closer like she could disappear into it. The sleeves swallowed her hands as she turned away, her shoes sinking slightly into the damp earth. She walked toward the water, leaving shallow footprints in the sand—footprints that were already softening at the edges, blurred by the wind and the tide.

Then—she hesitated.

Her shoulders went tight, like she'd walked straight into a memory she didn't want to see.

She stopped at the edge of the water, the waves stretching out before her, waiting. The lighthouse beam swept slow across the surface, making the ocean look like something alive, something shifting. Jean just stood there, still, like she was caught between two places—leaving, staying. Between the pull of what had been and the weight of what hadn't happened yet. The wind tugged at her. But she didn't move.

Not until she turned back.

Her gaze found mine, and there was something in her eyes. Something knowing. Not surprise, not even sadness. Just... recognition.

"You got to the end, didn't you?"

Her voice was quiet, nearly lost beneath the wind's insistent whine. But I heard it. And somehow, it was heavier than anything else she'd ever said.

I shifted my weight, feeling the cold settle into my bones. "Yeah," I said. "And you're right."

Jean tilted her head just slightly, like she wasn't sure if she wanted to ask what I meant.

I held her gaze. "You deserve more than this," I told her, my voice low, steady. "More than waiting. More than wondering. More than... than this town, this house, this fear that keeps you standing still."

She didn't move. Just let the words settle between us, heavy and untouchable, like something delicate she wasn't sure she wanted to hold.

I thought she'd laugh. Thought she'd throw up her hands, roll her eyes, maybe turn the whole thing into some abstract poem the way she always did when things got too real.

But she didn't. She just stood there, quiet, the ocean filling the space between us. Then, slow and certain, she walked back toward me.

She didn't look at me—not directly. Instead, she leaned against my bike, arms crossed over her chest, gaze locked on the waves. The lighthouse beam moved in slow, sweeping arcs, tracing the curve of her cheekbone, catching in the strands of her wind-tangled hair.

The waves rolled in heavy. Alive. Breathing.

Neither of us spoke for a long time.

"I have this dream," she said finally.

She didn't look at me when she said it. Just kept her arms crossed, watching the tide pull itself in and out, in and out. Like it had for all time before we stepped into its world. Like she was trying to match her breathing to it.

I waited.

She swallowed, jaw tightening just slightly. But she didn't stop.

"I'm drowning."

The words weren't dramatic. They weren't a confession. Just a fact. Just something she was stating, like she was talking about the weather.

I turned to look at her, but she didn't move.

"The water is so dark, I can't see the surface. And I don't try to swim."

Her voice was even, steady, but I caught it—just for a second. The way her breath hitched, just slightly, just at the end.

"I just let it take me."

Something cold twisted in my stomach.

The lighthouse beam cut across the horizon again, sending flashes of pale light skimming over the water, turning the waves into gleaming living things that shifted—sinister, swallowing, waiting. It passed over us, searching.

Then, as if it had seen enough, it moved on.

Jean stayed still. Her face unreadable, her hands tucked into the sleeves of my jacket like she was bracing against something colder than the night air.

I stayed still, too. Waiting.

She reached down, scooping up a handful of sand. Her fingers barely trembled, but I saw it. Just a little. She let it sift through her hands, grain by grain, carried off into the wind before it could ever touch the ground.

"Sometimes, I think that's the way I'm supposed to go."

Her voice was calm. Too calm. Like she wasn't even talking about herself. Like it was just a thought—some passing thing, barely worth mentioning. Like she'd considered it so many times, it had lost its weight.

My hands curled into fists against my knees.

"I come out here and just... stare at it," she went on, her voice barely audible over the wind. "It's not just water, Will. It's something else. Something waiting."

She exhaled sharply. Shook her head like she was trying to shake the thought loose.

"If I stepped in, I don't think it would fight me." Her voice dropped, something quiet, something almost... wistful creeping in. "I think it would just... take me."

The wind picked up, pulling at her hair, twisting it like seaweed caught in a slow current.

"I think it's been waiting for me my whole life."

Somewhere beyond the mist, a buoy let out a hollow, lonely chime, its voice swallowed up by the crash of the waves. The town was gone now, eaten by the fog, its neon glow buried under layers of gray. It was just us. Just the tide. Just the aching space between Jean's words.

I forced my voice to stay steady. "Jean."

She turned her head—just a little. Just enough. The lighthouse beam caught the edge of her profile, glinting off the distant shine in her eyes. But her expression stayed unreadable. Like the ocean itself —calm on the surface, but holding something deep and unknowable beneath.

"Sometimes," she said, "I think about putting on the heaviest boots I can find and just walking straight into it."

Jean's fingers curled against the fabric of my jacket, twisting it between her hands, knuckles tight, knuckles white.

The wind whipped a loose strand of hair across her face, but she didn't brush it away. She just stood there, arms wrapped tight around herself, staring out at the waves like they were the only thing left in the world.

Her eyes searched mine. "I wonder if it's supposed to be this way."

A cold weight settled in my chest.

Jean's fingers curled around her sleeves. "Maybe that's why I can't wake up." Her voice was quieter now, like she was saying it more to herself than to me. "Maybe that's why no one sees me. Why no one remembers I'm still here." She hesitated. Then, softer —"Maybe I was never real to begin with."

Then, in a voice so quiet I almost missed it—

"If you hadn't seen me that day, Will, I—"

The words caught. Stuck. Like they weren't meant to be spoken aloud. Like they weren't even hers—maybe they belonged to another version of herself. One she had nearly become.

She closed her mouth. Swallowed hard. Looked away.

Her breath hitched, shoulders trembling just slightly. Her fingers twitched against my jacket, gripping something unseen—something slipping through her grasp, something she wasn't sure she could keep.

Something inside me twisted, sharp and deep. Because I knew.

She inhaled—too sharp, too quick. Like she was trying to force something back down before it could escape.

But the moment cracked.

Her shoulders caved.

And then—like a fault line finally giving way—she lurched forward. Hard. Like something inside her had snapped. Like she'd been holding something in for too long, keeping it packed down, stuffed away, and now it was clawing its way out.

A sob tore from her throat. Raw. Desperate. It was the kind of sound that came from somewhere deep, from somewhere that had been locked up so tight, for so long, that breaking felt like the only thing left to do.

Her hands shook as she fisted them into my jacket, knuckles

tight, white, clinging like if she let go, she'd fall straight through the earth.

The crash of my bike hitting the pavement barely registered.

Because the only thing I knew was Jean.

I was already moving. Already reaching. My arms wrapped around her, pulling her in, holding her together, holding her like maybe if I held on tight enough, nothing could take her.

She sobbed into my chest, and the sound broke against me, hit me like a wave, like something I couldn't brace for. Her fingers curled tighter, twisting the fabric of my shirt, pulling herself closer, like she was trying to disappear into something solid, something real, something that wouldn't let her slip away.

I held her.

Held her through whatever this was—whatever was breaking inside her, whatever had already broken.

The wind howled around us, cutting through the cliffs, dragging at my jacket, Jean's hair, the edges of everything.

The ocean kept breathing. Steady. Unshaken. Rolling in and rolling out, like it had all the time in the world.

My throat burned, tight and aching. My ribs felt too small, my chest too full of something I couldn't name.

And then—quietly, like a promise—

"You're real," I whispered, my voice rough, thick with something unspoken. "You hear me? You're real, Jean."

She didn't say anything. Just pressed her face against me, shaking, her sobs wracking through her, through me.

We sank down to the damp earth, knees hitting sand and stone, the wind screaming past us, the world narrowing down to just this. Just us.

She clung tighter. I cradled the back of her head with one hand, the other tracing slow, steady circles against her back, grounding, anchoring.

"I'm here," I murmured, pressing my cheek against her temple. "I'm right here."

Her cries didn't stop. Not at first. But slowly—slowly—the tension in her shoulders started to unravel. The sobs turned into shaky breaths. The breaths turned into silence.

The ocean kept breathing, the tide pulling in and out, steady, unchanging.

I didn't let go. Not yet. Not until she did first.

CHAPTER SIXTEEN

Minutes passed before Jean finally shifted against me.

The wind had quieted some, but the night still hung heavy around us—thick with salt and mist, the scent of the ocean sinking deep into our clothes, our skin. It wasn't just a smell; it was a weight. Like the whole town had latched onto us, making sure we wouldn't forget where we were, even if we tried.

Somewhere down the coast, the waves kept up their slow, steady crawl toward shore. The same rhythm, over and over, carving patterns into the damp sand before pulling back—just to do it all again. There was something cruel about it, like the ocean knew how to let go, but only in a way that made sure it could still come back.

Jean pulled back just enough to look at me. Her eyes were swollen, red-rimmed, glistening in the dim light. She looked exhausted—not just the kind of tired that comes after crying, but the kind that settles deep. The kind that sticks. The kind you carry even when you're smiling. The kind that took years to build in you before you knew it was there. Then it was too late and you don't remember who you were—who you were supposed to be.

Her voice cracked when she spoke. "You don't have to—"

"I'm not leaving."

She blinked, like I'd just said something she didn't understand.

I swallowed hard and reached out, brushing a stray tear from her cheek. My thumb brushed over her skin, and for a second, I felt her lean into it—just barely, just enough for me to know she wasn't pushing me away.

"I don't plan on ever leaving Depoe Bay without you."

Jean's breath hitched again, but this time, she held it back. Her grip on my shirt loosened, but she didn't let go.

I exhaled, running a hand through my hair, trying to shake off the weight pressing against my chest. "You wanna know something?"

She sniffled, nodding.

"The day I met you—the only reason I was even on that beach? My friends convinced me to go for one last hoorah."

Jean's brow furrowed. "Last hoorah?"

I nodded, tilting my head toward the waves. "Yeah. I was finally gonna skip town. That was supposed to be it. One final day, one last look at the ocean before I took off for good."

Jean's fingers curled tighter into my shirt, like she thought if she let go, I'd slip away. The wind kicked up across the dunes, pushing strands of her hair into her face, but she didn't move to brush them away. She just stared at me, her eyes pulling in every word.

"But then you met me."

My lips parted slightly, my voice barely above the sound of the tide.

"Yeah," I said softly. "Then I met you."

Jean dropped her gaze, her hands settling in her lap, fingers twitching against the hem of her dress. The lighthouse beam swung overhead, its glow slipping across her face for just a second before fading again into the dark.

"But why me?" Her voice was small. "I'm a basket case."

I let out a quiet, breathy laugh, shaking my head. "Yeah? Well, welcome to the club."

She didn't smile. Just stared at her lap like the words had confirmed something she already knew.

I glanced out at the ocean, my voice steady, my hands resting lightly against my knees. "Because I've lived in that same old town my whole damn life, Jean. And never—not once—have I seen a fresh face apart from that day."

Her fingers twitched again, like she wanted to say something but wasn't sure how.

"Someone who didn't already know me. Someone who didn't already have their mind made up about me, always judging me."

The wind shifted again, stirring the tall grass along the cliffs, sending a spray of mist through the air. Somewhere up the road, the faint hum of a radio played from a parked truck, its driver half-asleep behind the wheel, letting the static-filled melody of an old love song carry him through the night.

"And you—you see the world and still want to love it anyway. And God dammit, Jean, I've never met anyone like that. You're the bravest person I know."

Jean sat there, still as stone, staring down at her hands like she was searching for something—something she didn't know how to name.

I stayed quiet. And I waited.

Jean finally glanced up, her gaze steady, searching.

"But—why don't people like you?"

The question settled between us, heavier than the wind, heavier than the night.

I hesitated.

The ocean kept breathing, the waves rolling in and out, slow and deliberate, like they knew the answer before I could say it. The lighthouse beam swung overhead again, cutting through the dark, tracing shadows across Jean's face.

She watched me carefully, waiting.

I let out a slow breath, my fingers curling around my knees, pressing against denim. The wind tugged at my shirt, and somewhere in the distance, the low murmur of a passing car rumbled against the cliffs before disappearing into the night.

"Because I tried to leave once before."

Jean's expression softened. "What happened?"

I swallowed hard, looking away. My chest felt tight—too tight—like my ribs weren't expanding right. Like my lungs had forgotten how to work.

I hadn't talked about this in months.

Not since him.

Not since the night everything went wrong.

I stared out at the ocean, watching as the tide swallowed the footprints we'd left behind, erasing any sign that we had ever been there at all. Just like that—gone. Like we never existed in the first place. Like the wind could pick up and carry us off too, and no one would even know to look.

I felt it creeping in, the weight of it. That night. That name.

"It was me and my best friend," I said finally, the words catching on something raw in my throat.

I stopped.

The name was there, right there, pressing against my ribs like something sharp, something jagged, something that would tear me apart if I let it out.

But I had to.

I forced it past my teeth.

"Tony."

Jean didn't move. Didn't speak. Just waited.

That was the thing about her. She never pushed. Never pried. Just let the words come when I was ready.

"We had it all planned out," I said, my voice low, almost lost beneath the wind. "We were gonna take off together. Just disappear."

Jean didn't interrupt. She didn't ask how. She didn't ask why. She just waited.

So I kept going.

"We didn't make it."

The words sat there, thick and heavy in the air, pressing against my chest like something I could physically feel. Too heavy. Like if I spoke them too loud, they'd pull me under, right into the dark water, right into the nothing.

My jaw clenched. My hands curled into fists against my thighs. The wind shifted—colder now, cutting through my jacket, threading through my hair—but it wasn't the wind I felt. It was asphalt scraping my skin, gravel biting into my palms. The burn of metal twisted in the wreckage. My breath shuddered.

"He—" I exhaled sharply. "He didn't make it."

And just like that, the past wasn't just creeping in. It was here.

I could still smell the gasoline. It clung to me, thick and acrid, like it had never really washed off. Like no matter how many times I scrubbed my hands raw, I'd still feel it between my fingers. The road was slick, shining in the headlights, and I remember thinking how strange that was—that something so broken could still reflect light.

The silence after the crash wasn't silence at all. It was the sound of something ending.

The headlights swallowed the night. I should have braked sooner.

The road lurched beneath us, tires screaming. I should have swerved left, not right.

Metal twisted. Glass shattered. The weight of Tony's body slammed into me before everything flipped—flipped—flipped—

I should have done something. I should have done anything.

My hands—God, my hands—were still on the wheel, knuckles white, breath torn from my lungs.

And Tony—

Tony's voice—

"Will—"

And then—

Nothing.

I tried.

Jesus, I tried.

I was still in the car when it stopped rolling. Blood in my mouth, ribs screaming, smoke curling into the night air like a dying breath. But I felt him.

Next to me.

Still there.

I reached for him, shaking, hands slick with blood, with sweat, with everything that felt too warm, too alive. I grabbed his wrist—tight, too tight—because I was afraid if I let go, I'd lose him.

And then...

He got colder.

Little by little, inch by inch, his body went from warm to something else.

And I just sat there.

Holding onto something already gone.

I gasped.

Jean's voice cut through the static. "Will."

I blinked.

The wreckage was gone. The ocean was in front of me. But the weight of it never really left.

I shook my head before she could say anything else.

"I don't talk about it."

Not because I didn't want to.

But because I couldn't.

Because the memories came too fast, too hard—the tires screeching, the road lurching beneath us, the headlights swallowing the night in a blinding rush of white.

Because I could still hear his voice.

Still remember the way he smiled.

I pressed a hand to my face, exhaling through my teeth. My pulse felt loud, too loud; I could hear it in my ears, matching the waves, crashing over me again and again.

"After that, people talked." My voice was bitter now. "They called me a screw-up. A bad influence."

They weren't wrong.

If it wasn't for me, Tony would still be here.

If it wasn't for me, he would have made it.

I didn't even go to the funeral.

Couldn't.

I couldn't face Polly. Couldn't stand in front of her parents and pretend I didn't put their son in the ground. I sat on the curb three blocks away while the whole damn town crammed into the church like it meant something.

And when the service ended, I kept walking.

"All of Depoe thinks I'm just gonna crash and burn like he did."

Jean stayed quiet.

The wind howled through the cliffs, rattling the sparse, crooked trees that clung stubbornly to the rock face. The kind that had been bent by the wind, by the salt, by years of standing in the same damn place, but still refused to fall.

Then, gently— "Is that why you got into that fight?"

My breath hitched.

She had pieced it together.

I swallowed the lump in my throat. "Yeah."

I could still hear the bastard's voice—the shit he said. The words had stuck to me, dug in like rusted nails, sharp and festering. They never really left. They just sat there, just under the skin, waiting to be ripped open again.

I could still feel the way my knuckles cracked when I swung. Could still feel the way the impact rattled up my arm, bone meeting bone, the force of it jolting through my entire body like a live wire.

Could still taste the blood in my mouth when I hit the pavement.

The weight of it all pressed against my ribs, thick and suffocating.

"He was the only person who ever really knew me. We were so close to finally escaping, but I ruined it." I exhaled sharply, shaking my head. "Polly hasn't looked at me the same since." My lip tensed. "We used to be thick as thieves, the two of us. But after the accident,

I was just another ghost in her life. Another silence that didn't get spoken about. And the funniest thing? I bet he would've loved you. But it doesn't matter now."

Even though it did.

Even if I didn't say it.

Even if I didn't want it to.

Even if I told myself it didn't.

It still mattered.

Jean moved before I even realized what she was doing.

Her fingers curled around my wrist, small and warm and steady, grounding me in a way I hadn't expected. Her touch was soft but firm, like she knew exactly how close I was to slipping under, and she wasn't about to let me.

The wind had picked up again, sending loose strands of her hair whipping across her face, but she didn't move to brush them away. She just held on.

"It matters."

I shook my head. "No, it doesn't."

Jean didn't let go.

"It does."

"I killed him."

The words scraped their way out of my throat, raw, jagged, barely above a whisper.

"I was the one driving. I should have—"

My throat closed before I could finish the sentence.

I finally looked at her.

Her eyes—God, her eyes.

Soft and deep and understanding, catching just enough of the moonlight to make them glow. Like she knew. Like she understood what it was like to carry something so heavy it bent you; crushed you beneath its weight.

The tide rolled in, reaching farther up the shore before pulling back again, leaving a thin film of water shimmering over the sand. The lighthouse beam swept across the horizon, carving brief slivers of light through the darkness. The world felt still—just for a moment.

My throat felt tight.

Jean squeezed my wrist, her voice barely above a breath.

"You didn't deserve that."

The way she said it—so sure, so unwavering—made something inside me crack.

A part of me wanted to argue. To tell her that maybe I did. That maybe they were right. That maybe I was exactly what they said I was—a screw-up, a lost cause, a kid too reckless for his own good.

But I didn't.

Because for the first time in a long, long time—I actually wanted to believe it.

I swallowed hard. My chest felt hollow, caved in, like something had cracked open inside me and I didn't know how to close it again.

"I can't lose you too."

The words came out on broken breath, but I didn't care. I meant them. I needed her to hear them.

A weak tear fell from my eye and she put a finger to it.

I let go of Tony.

I sat there and held onto his wrist until he was cold, until the sirens came, until someone pulled me away.

I never got to hold on tight enough.

Not this time.

I tightened my grip on Jean's wrist, pulling her in, my forehead pressing against hers, my breath shaking.

"You're the only reason I'm still here. If you go, I go."

My voice was shaking now, but I didn't care.

"Because God dammit, I love you, Jean."

Silence.

The kind that shouldn't have existed after words like that.

The wind pulled at her hair, her breath shallow against the cold. I felt her fingers tremble against me, holding on, holding on—

And then, before either of us could think better of it—

She kissed me.

It wasn't careful. It wasn't soft. It wasn't the kind of kiss you ease into.

It was desperate.

A crash, not a fall. A collision, not a choice.

Her hands tangled in my hair, my fingers gripping the back of her neck, like we were both afraid we'd slip right through each other's fingers if we let go. Like we weren't sure we knew how to hold on any other way.

The lighthouse beam swept over us, a flash of light and shadow, and for a moment, it felt like the only real thing in the world was this. Us. Here. Now.

When she finally pulled back, her breath was uneven, her forehead pressing against mine.

"I—I think I love you too," she whispered.

Maybe she wasn't sure yet. Maybe neither of us were.

Then she did it again.

THE NIGHT FELT DIFFERENT NOW.

Softer, maybe. Warmer, despite the wind. Like something heavy had finally lifted, leaving behind only the sound of the tide and the slow, steady rhythm of our breathing.

Jean was curled against me, her head resting on my bare shoulder, her fingers tracing slow, absent-minded shapes against my ribs. My jacket was beneath us, half-buried in the sand, and my shirt was somewhere off to the side—forgotten, unimportant. The cool night air exhaled over my skin, but I didn't feel cold.

Not with her here.

Not like this.

The lighthouse beam swung overhead, its glow sweeping across the dunes, over the water, catching on the scattered remains of our clothes. The wind carried the scent of salt and damp earth, wrapping around us like something alive, something listening.

Neither of us spoke.

We didn't need to.

Jean's fingers stilled against my side, her breath warm against my collarbone. I glanced down at her, brushing a loose strand of hair from her face. She looked peaceful. Tired in a way that wasn't exhaustion anymore, but something quieter.

Her eyes fluttered open, deep and searching, still filled with something I couldn't quite name.

I swallowed.

For her, this had been a first.

For me... maybe it should have felt different. Maybe it should have been just another moment, another night, another thing I didn't have to think too hard about.

But it wasn't.

Because it was *her*.

Because it was *us*.

The tide pressed higher against the shore, reaching, retreating, as if trying to pull the whole world under with it.

Jean's gaze drifted past me, out toward the ocean, watching as the waves rolled in and out, in and out, stealing back the footprints we'd left in the sand.

She was quiet for so long, I almost thought she wasn't going to say anything. But with her, silence wasn't a punishment. It was peace. It was comfort.

Then—

"Will?"

Her voice was so quiet, I barely heard it over the wind.

I turned toward her, but she wasn't looking at me.

She was still watching the tide. The way it kept returning. The way it kept leaving. The wind pushed a strand of hair across her face. Her fingers trembled slightly as she tucked it behind her ear.

Then, finally—

"If we run..." She inhaled, slow, shaky. "Do you think we'll make it?"

The answer lodged itself in my throat. I could hear the way she asked it. The way she said we. Like it was already decided. Like this wasn't just some late-night thought spoken into the wind—like it was something real, something she'd already let settle into her bones.

I held her gaze. The wind pulled at her hair. The tide rolled in and out, in and out, like it was waiting for my answer too. I swallowed.

"Yeah, Jean."

The words felt like a promise. I reached out, tucking a strand of hair behind her ear, my fingers brushing against her skin for just a second longer than they should have.

The lighthouse glow flickered across her face, catching in her eyes—deep and searching, full of something that made my chest ache. The silence stretched between us, hanging in the air like the last line of a poem you don't want to end. Then, finally, I said it.

"This time, we will."

Jean let out a slow breath, her shoulders easing, like something heavy had finally loosened its grip on her. Then, without another word, she leaned her head against my shoulder. We sat there, listening to the waves, letting the night stretch around us like an old song playing on a radio from somewhere far away.

Neither of us spoke. Neither of us needed to.

For tonight, being here was enough.

And maybe, for the first time, we weren't just waiting to leave.

Maybe, for the first time—

We were letting ourselves stay.

CHAPTER SEVENTEEN

The sharp cries of gulls cut through the morning, their voices slipping in and out of the mist, less like birds and more like echoes of something long gone—like a record skipping, playing back pieces of a song nobody remembers. It pulled me awake, not all at once, but in slow pieces. Like a tide dragging me back to shore.

The mist hung thick over the beach, rolling between the driftwood and wrapping around the dunes like it had a score to settle. Like it had come to take the whole place back. And maybe it would. Maybe a hundred years from now, there'd be nothing left of this town but bones under the sand.

The ocean stretched out before me—wide, endless, unfeeling. Used to be, I thought that was kinda nice. The one thing I'd miss about this place. The way the tide always came back, like it had a promise to keep.

But now? I wasn't so sure. Some things don't come back. Some things just drift further and further until they're nothing but a ripple on the horizon. And then nothing at all.

I let myself lie there a second longer, let the world settle around me like it was waiting for me to catch up. The salt-heavy air filled my lungs, thick and familiar, grounding me even as everything else felt like it was slipping through my fingers. My back ached from sleeping on the cold, uneven ground, muscles stiff like they'd forgotten what they were for. Somewhere in the distance, the tide murmured—a low, rhythmic breath, steady as a heartbeat.

It inched closer, wave by wave, creeping up the shore like it was listening. Like it had something to say.

Then I sat up.

Jean was gone.

I felt it before I even saw it, the absence settling in my chest like a rock in deep water.

I turned, scanning the beach.

"Jean?"

Nothing. Just the wind, the waves, the empty stretch of shoreline. And a silence that wasn't really silence at all, but something worse. A void waiting to be filled with the weight of nothingness.

My eyes found the footprints before my brain caught up, trailing off toward the dunes, fading into the shifting sand. My stomach twisted. I followed them with my eyes, willing her to step out from behind the driftwood, to call my name from down by the water, to laugh, to do anything at all—

But the beach just stared back. Empty.

And then I saw my bike.

It was propped back up, just where I'd left it.

The leather jacket I'd given her draped over the handlebar, its empty sleeves twisting slightly in the breeze—like it was still waiting for her to slip back inside.

I swallowed hard.

She left it behind.

I spent the whole day at the beach.

Waiting.

Watching the tide roll in and out, the water stretching toward me in slow, silver waves before pulling back again. Inhale. Exhale. Like the whole ocean was breathing. Alive. Like it was trying to say something.

It should've been calming. It wasn't.

I'd lost things before. But never like this. Never someone who felt like a second chance.

I kept telling myself she'd come back. Any second now, she'd slip out of the trees just like always—hair tousled by the wind, that quiet, knowing smile tugging at the corner of her lips. She'd walk up behind me, maybe toss a seashell at my back, laughing like none of this mattered. Like last night wasn't still sitting between us, heavy and unmoving.

But she didn't.

Not in the morning.

Not by noon.

Not when the sun dipped low, setting the sky on fire with streaks of gold and orange. The whole world burned while I sat there, hunger twisting in my stomach like a coiled-up thing, but I couldn't leave.

I couldn't miss her.

And the longer I waited, the more my thoughts turned inward, curling in on themselves like waves folding over one another, swallowing what came before.

Maybe it was too much. Maybe I pushed too far. Too soon. Maybe last night cracked something open in her that she didn't want to see.

That's the thing about telling the truth. Once it's out, it doesn't go away. It lingers. It stains. It shifts how you see things. And sometimes, you'd give anything to un-say it. But the words we speak out loud control us.

I thought about the way she had cried in my arms. The way I told her I wasn't leaving without her.

Maybe she regretted telling me everything.

Maybe she regretted giving me the book.

Maybe she didn't like what she saw in me.

Maybe she finally realized I wasn't someone worth knowing.

I let out a slow breath, dragging a hand down my face, my fingers pressing hard against my temples, like I could push the thoughts out of my skull if I just tried hard enough.

"Fuck!"

It came out low, barely more than an exhale, lost to the crash of the waves. *I should go. She isn't coming back.*

But then—

Just as I turned to leave—

I saw her.

A small figure in the distance, moving up the shore.

Slow. Careful. Like she wasn't sure she should be here at all.

The wind lifted the hem of the same dress she wore the night before, the fabric catching and twisting in the breeze as she walked through the sand. Her arms were curled around herself, her steps slow, deliberate, like she was carrying something too heavy to put down.

My breath caught in my throat.

She came back.

But as she drew closer, something shifted.

It was small—just a flicker of movement. Her hand reached up, fingers brushing through her hair, tucking loose strands behind her ear.

And that's when I saw it.

A shadow—no. Something more.

Something that didn't belong on her skin.

Like a stain that wouldn't wash away. Like something permanent.

Like ink bleeding through paper. Like a handprint pressed too hard into time itself.

A bruise.

No, not one. Many.

The kind of marks that don't just live on skin. The kind that live in memory.

The world around me dimmed.

The wind. The sea. The sky. It all blurred into nothing.

All I could see was the way the darkness bloomed beneath her collarbone.

Like someone had tried to erase her.

My stomach lurched. My vision tunneled. For a second, the whole beach felt unreal. Like I'd stepped out of time. Like nothing existed except the bruises and the weight of what they meant.

The moment passed in a breath, but it was enough.

I ran.

Sand kicked up behind me as I closed the space between us.

"Jean..."

I reached out before I even realized what I was doing, fingers barely grazing her shoulder before she tensed.

"Did she do this to you?"

The words came quieter than I meant. But they weren't calm.

They were sharp.

Dangerous.

Jean didn't flinch. Didn't step away. She just exhaled, her face unreadable, eyes clouded over like the tide pulling back before a storm.

"Don't, Will." Her voice was measured, steady. "Don't make this into something it isn't."

I let out a sharp breath, disbelieving. My hands clenched into fists before I even realized it.

"This isn't something?!" The words ripped out of me, too raw, too loud. "She's a monster."

Jean's head snapped up, her eyes flashing.

"You don't know anything about her."

I didn't back down.

"She put her hands on you, Jean."

Jean pressed her lips together, arms folding over herself. But it wasn't a defense. It was careful. Deliberate. Like she was smoothing herself out before I could see the edges fraying.

"I should've known better," she murmured, soft and even, like she was explaining gravity. Just a fact. "That's all. I made her upset."

I stared at her.

"No." My voice was firm, low, but the crack in it was impossible to hide. "No one makes someone do this. This isn't your fault."

Jean let out the smallest breath of a laugh—light and cool and brittle, like a glass cracking under pressure.

"Of course it is." Her gaze flickered toward the sea. "You think she wanted to? It's just... how things are."

I shook my head, hard.

"It's not, Jean. It doesn't have to be."

She tilted her chin up just slightly, keeping her expression careful, poised. But her fingers curled into her sleeves, gripping tight. Like she was holding herself together with the seams of her own clothes.

"This is what love is, Will," she said. "It's giving up pieces of yourself for someone else. It's knowing that if you get hurt, then you must have done something wrong. Because love is... sacrifice."

"Jean, don't—"

Her hands balled into fists. "No! You don't get it!" she snapped, and without thinking, she grabbed a piece of driftwood and hurled it into the surf. It landed with a flat splash and vanished beneath the foam. Jean's shoulders rose and fell with quick, shallow breaths, like she'd been holding that in for years. "You don't know what it's like to be told every day that love is pain. That it's your fault when it hurts." She looked away, jaw clenched. "You don't get to rewrite that with a promise and a motorcycle."

She swallowed, blinking toward the water. "Maybe I should have stayed home that day we met. Maybe I should have—"

She cut herself off, shaking her head, like she was slamming a door shut on the thought before it could take shape.

I took a breath, fists clenched at my sides.

"No, Jean, please—don't think like that! You're not a prisoner!"

The words came out too sharp. Too final.

And then—

Silence.

The way she looked at me.

The way my own voice echoed back in my head, unraveling itself.

Because that's exactly what she was.

Her gaze drifted past me, somewhere far away.

"She only does this because she loves me."

Jean's voice was steady. Too steady. Like she'd said these words before. Like she'd practiced them. Like she'd heard them a million times.

But her fingers twitched. Pressed against her sleeve. Tracing the fabric. Like she was holding onto something only she could feel.

"She cries harder than I do, after." A beat. Her voice dropped to something quieter, smaller, something almost not meant for me. "She prays for our forgiveness."

A breath.

Then, softer, almost to herself:

"Maybe she's the one who suffers the most."

My stomach twisted.

"Jean."

My voice barely made it past my throat. A whisper. A plea.

"She's going to kill you one day."

Jean didn't even flinch.

That was the worst part.

She wasn't scared of dying.

She wasn't scared of staying.

Of pain. Of regret. Of losing.

But leaving?

That was the thing that terrified her the most.

Because if she left, what was she without the cage?

If she left, who was she, if not the girl who endured?

If she left—what if there was nothing waiting for her on the other side?

It was like she had grown numb.

And for the first time, it hit me.

Not like a thought. Not like a suspicion.

Like a knife, slow and deep between my ribs.

Like the ground shifting beneath me. Like the tide pulling out too far, leaving everything exposed.

Jean didn't believe she deserved to be free.

She didn't believe there was a version of herself that could exist outside of this.

Like the cage wasn't just around her.

Like it was inside her.

Like she had swallowed it whole. Let it take root inside her bones.

But the truth is, she *was* the cage.

My chest caved in.

Because if I couldn't convince her, who could?

"Jean," I said again, softer now. "You don't have to live like this."

Something shifted in her face—like a door closing. Like the light in her eyes dimmed just enough to make me wonder if I imagined it.

She exhaled, turning her gaze toward the ocean. "You said it yourself."

I frowned. "What?"

She glanced at me, something distant in her expression. "If I disappeared, do you think anyone would notice?"

The words sat between us, heavier than the air, heavier than the tide.

I opened my mouth. Then shut it.

Jean gave a small, humorless laugh, shaking her head. "This town already thinks I'm gone. And the ones who don't? They look the other way."

I clenched my jaw. "Then we go to the police."

Jean flinched. "No."

"Jean—"

"No." The word came sharper this time, like a wound she didn't want reopened.

I stared at her. "They could help you."

She shook her head again, stepping back slightly, like she needed space, like the air between us had suddenly thinned.

"Nobody would believe me, anyway." Her voice was quieter now, but it wasn't weak. It was certain. Resigned. "They never did."

Something cold curled in my gut.

"What do you mean?" I asked carefully.

Jean inhaled slowly, like she was weighing something. Measuring it. Then she exhaled.

"When I was little... I tried."

I stared at her, my chest tightening.

"I tried to tell someone. The doctor, once. My aunt, over the phone before my mom yanked it from the wall." Her fingers curled slightly against her arms. "I don't even remember all the people I tried. But it didn't matter." She let out a quiet breath. "Because nothing happened."

I swallowed.

She gave me a small, sad smile, like she knew exactly what I was thinking.

"Maybe they knew. Maybe they didn't. But either way, they never interfered."

The wind stirred, pulling at her hair, her dress. The lighthouse beam swept across her face in slow, rhythmic arcs.

"Jean—"

"And if I left?" she interrupted, her voice measured, careful. "Where would I go? Wherever I would leave to, she would still find me..." She trailed off, stiffening.

Then, quieter—"You think you know her, but you don't."

I clenched my jaw. "I know enough. And I'll do all I can to protect you from her."

Jean inhaled again, slow, deliberate.

"You talk like she's some kind of monster." She exhaled, her voice quieter now. "But she's not, Will. She's just—"

She hesitated.

Let the words sit between us, hovering.

Then, softer:

"She's just afraid."

I let out a breath—sharp, disbelieving.

"Jean—"

"She grew up in a house worse than mine," she cut in, her voice suddenly edged, sharp enough to draw blood. "She watched her mother get taken away, Will. She didn't just lose her—she watched it happen. They dragged her off, locked her up, and threw away the key. Condemned to some nuthouse."

Her words came fast, hot, like they had been waiting just under the surface, ready to burst.

"You think my mother is cruel, but you don't know what it's like to grow up with that kind of fear pressing in on you."

Her gaze dropped to the sand, arms wrapping tight around herself, the sharpness in her voice fading into something quieter, something frayed at the edges.

"Her father was worse to her than she's ever been to me. And she never had anyone. Not until Patrick."

Patrick.

The name landed heavy between us. Jean didn't just say it—she let it settle, like it carried something more than just a man. Like it was a name that meant something sacred. Something ruined. I knew it.

Her father.

Jean turned, staring out at the waves, her voice distant, unreadable. "He was the only good thing that ever happened to her. The only person who ever made her feel safe."

A pause.

"And then she lost him."

"Jean—"

"She didn't even get to bury him, Will."

The words came out like glass—fragile, sharp. Like if she spoke them too loudly, they might shatter in her hands.

"Missing in action. Just—gone. No body. No grave. Just waiting. And waiting. And waiting."

Jean let out a soft, humorless breath.

"She still wears her wedding ring. Still talks to him like he might hear her. Maybe she really believes he can."

My throat tightened.

Jean's gaze stayed locked on the horizon, something strange and knowing in her expression. Like she wasn't just talking about the past—like it was still wrapped around her, refusing to let go.

I frowned.

"Jean, what are you saying?"

She nodded slightly, almost to herself, her voice drifting somewhere far away.

"On rainy nights, when she thinks I'm asleep, she stands on the back porch and talks to the ocean."

A chill curled through me.

"She asks him about me. What to do. What the right thing is."

Jean hesitated. The wind picked up, pushing strands of her hair across her face. She didn't brush them away.

"She prays he's still out there. And who knows? Maybe he is."

A dry, bitter pause.

"Maybe he just left us."

The air shifted, sharp and briny, cutting between us like a knife.

"But when Sandra drowned..." Jean trailed, her voice flattening.

Sandra.

Her sister.

The way she said it—empty, almost careless—sent a deep, cold unease through me.

Jean closed her eyes for a moment, long enough that I thought she might not open them again.

But then she did.

And when she looked at me, something in her had been shut away.

"I don't remember the day," she said, voice like glass, thin and breakable. "But I remember the thrashing. The waves pulling her down. I watched her die."

The words hit, heavy and unforgiving.

"You don't understand, Will. You never could."

Jean turned toward me then, her eyes burning with something too big, too raw to name.

"You think you know my life because you've read it in a book, but you don't. You can't. Because I have felt my mother's grief as if it were my own. And it is my own."

I swallowed hard.

The weight of her words pressed into me, thick and unmoving, like the air before a storm.

Somewhere, in the distance, waves crashed against the rocks, sending spray and foam up, confirming a life—a truth known.

Jean exhaled, arms tightening around herself again.

"She locks me away to protect me," she murmured. "To make sure I never experience the same pain she has. She believes if she lets me go, the world will take me, too."

Jean's lips parted, like she wanted to say something else, but she only shook her head slightly, her gaze dropping to the sand.

"Or worse," she whispered.

A pause.

Then, quieter, like the thought barely made it past her lips:

"She thinks I'll end up just like her."

"You said it yourself," I murmured, watching her carefully. "You think girls like you don't make it out at the end of their stories. But what if you're wrong?"

She shook her head, just barely. "You only think that because you don't know what it's like to want something and be afraid of it at the same time." Her voice cracked. "I want to believe you. But if I hope too hard... and this breaks..."

Her eyes flicked up to mine—hesitant, unsure.

"Listen to me. Maybe the girl does get out," I said. "Maybe someone helps her. Maybe I can."

I didn't say it like I was promising her something shiny and perfect. I said it like a man who'd already messed it up once.

Because the truth was, I didn't know if I was doing this for her... or for me. If trying to save her was just another way to rewrite what I couldn't fix with Tony.

But when I looked at her—really looked—I knew it didn't matter.

This wasn't about erasing the past. It was about *choosing her* now. Not because she was broken. Not because I needed to be forgiven.

Because I loved her.

And that had to be enough.

She finally looked at me again, her eyes dark and searching, like she was trying to make sense of something too tangled to unravel. Like she had spent her whole life pulling at knots that only tightened the more she tried to undo them.

"She's... she's not a monster, Will," she said, voice barely a breath against the wind. "She's just... broken."

I ran a hand through my hair, shaking my head. My chest ached, but I couldn't tell if it was anger or heartbreak.

Maybe both.

"Broken things can still hurt you, Jean," I said, voice low but firm. "That doesn't make this okay."

She held my gaze for a long moment, her expression unreadable.

Then, softly—too softly—

"I know. But she's my mother."

She gave a sad, fleeting smile, one that barely touched her lips before it disappeared. Like it had never really been there at all.

"We're all we have."

Her voice cracked on the last word, so quiet I almost didn't hear it.

Maybe she didn't either.

Maybe it slipped out before she could swallow it down. Before she could reshape it into something that hurt less.

Maybe it was a lie.

Something twisted deep inside me. A slow, sinking thing.

I reached for her again, but she took a step back, blinking hard, like she was trying to hold herself together, like one wrong move would shatter her completely.

"I can't just abandon her."

Her arms tightened around herself, her breath shaky. The wind tugged at the loose strands of her hair, but she didn't seem to notice.

Her eyes searched mine, desperate for something neither of us could name.

"I just... I don't know what to do."

The sky had darkened now, the last sliver of light fading. The wind howled against the cliffs, rattling through the silence between us.

Jean's voice was barely audible.

"She says the world already took my sister."

A beat.

"She won't let it take me, too."

Her voice was steady. Too steady. But something in her eyes flickered.

Something cracked.

Her fingers curled into her sleeve, pressing against the fabric like she was trying to hold herself in place. Like she was standing on a ledge, looking down. Like she could feel something shifting beneath her feet, and if she spoke it aloud—if she let it out—it would change everything.

For a second, I thought she might say it. For a second, I thought the world was about to shift beneath our feet.

But then—

She swallowed it down.

I nodded, slow, thoughtful.

"What do you think the world is?"

Jean didn't answer right away. She exhaled like she'd been holding her breath for longer than she realized, her chest rising and falling with a slow, careful rhythm. Her throat moved as she swallowed, and for a second, something flickered in her eyes—fear, maybe. Or doubt. Or something else tangled and deep that didn't have a name.

She looked out to the horizon. Not at me. Not even near me. Like if she met my eyes, the truth would spill out too fast, too loud, before she had a chance to stop it. Like the answer had been sitting inside her for years, and now that someone had finally asked, she wasn't sure if she wanted it out.

But I knew she had thought about it. You could feel it in the silence.

The tide crept closer, inch by inch, the water curling around the edge of the sand like it was trying to eavesdrop. Trying to listen in the way it always did. It moved slow, deliberate—like it wanted to be here for whatever came next. But I think it already knew.

We stood still. The two of us balanced in this strange place between things. Between the tide and the shore. Between the life she'd lived and the one she might still reach. Between everything she was running from and clinging to; everything I didn't understand yet and everything I knew to be true.

The wind cut through us—sharp, sudden—kicking up grains of sand around our feet. It sounded almost like a voice. A whisper tangled in the rush of air and salt. It didn't say anything, not really. Nothing we could understand anyway. But it felt like it wanted us to. Like it was waiting for something to happen. For something to be said so it could share its truth with us, tell us how things are going to be; how they were always going to be.

The air felt thick then. Like the kind of silence that wasn't just quiet—but charged. Like it was holding something heavy between its teeth. Even the tide seemed to slow, hesitating in its rhythm.

For a moment, everything felt suspended. Like the world couldn't move until Jean answered.

But she didn't.

She just stood there, still as stone. Staring at the horizon like it might hold something for her, something she'd been chasing without knowing it.

And for a second, I wasn't sure she ever would speak.

The silence stretched, long and wide, swallowing up the space between us. It didn't feel like quiet anymore—it felt like distance. Like we were a mile apart, standing on the same beach.

Then, the tide slid forward again, reaching for our footprints in the sand.

Wiping them away.

And just like that, we were gone.

CHAPTER EIGHTEEN

Time was up.

I could feel it in my chest, that tight, caged-animal kind of knowing. Like the walls were closing in, like the ground under my feet was shrinking by the second. I couldn't wait around anymore. Not while she kept making excuses. Not while she kept pretending this was normal.

Because it wasn't.

We tell ourselves things, sometimes. That we have time. That change happens slow, like the turning of the tide. That we'll see it coming, that we'll be ready.

But we don't. We aren't.

Change happens all at once. In a breath, in a heartbeat. In the space between one decision and the next, when you realize—there's no turning back.

The longer she stayed, the harder it would be to leave. I knew that better than anyone. This town had a way of getting its hooks in you, of wearing you down so slow you didn't even notice it happening. One day you're a kid with big ideas, big dreams, saying I can't wait to get out of here. Then, suddenly, you're thirty-five and stuck behind the counter at the gas station, telling some other kid the same thing, like the words themselves are a door you can step through if you just say them enough times.

I had waited long enough. Too long.

It was now or never, before this place did to Jean what it did to the rest of them.

Jean wasn't going to end up like him.

I couldn't let that happen.

Because people don't leave places like this. Not really. You stay long enough, and the town takes you. Binds you up in the past, in the version of yourself that never made it out. You start telling yourself maybe this is what you wanted all along. Maybe there was never anything else. That it was meant to be. For the best.

Jean was trapped. And if she wouldn't get herself out, then I was damn sure going to do it for her. She wasn't the only one haunted. I'd lived under a ghost too—Tony, my father, this whole damn town. Maybe that's why I still believed escape was possible. Because I had to.

So, I told her. Straight to her face. No way to dodge it, no way to smooth it over.

"Run away with me."

Jean froze. I saw it first in her hands—fingers twitching like a phantom had walked right through her, rattled something loose inside her bones. Then in the way her breath hitched—small, almost nothing, but I caught it.

"I can't keep watching you disappear. I need you to want this too." I continued, my voice a fragile plea. "I don't care where we go. North Carolina, up to Washington for your aunt—I just need you with me."

The ocean dragged against the shore in slow, heaving sighs, the kind that pull you under if you let them. The sky above us was bruised with the last light of day, the moon too bright, too early. Its reflection stretched thin across the darkening waves, unraveling like thread. The sand under my boots was cold and damp, flecked with broken seashells, tangled strands of seaweed. A distant buoy rocked in the harbor, its dull bell ringing out in the distance—a sound that should've been peaceful.

But it wasn't.

It sounded like something ending.

Jean let out a breath, shaking her head. "Will, don't say things like that." Her voice was soft, but the words were weighted, careful. Like stepping over broken glass. "You know it's not that easy."

I frowned. "Why isn't it?"

She lifted her chin just a little, a challenge, but not the kind she wanted to win. "Because I don't get to just—go. People like me don't leave, not really. Even if we run, we carry it with us. It's stitched under the skin."

The wind picked up, carrying the briny scent of the tide as I clenched my jaw. "She doesn't own you."

Jean's mouth pulled into something almost like a smile, except it wasn't. "That's where you're wrong." Her gaze drifted past me, past the shore, past anything I could touch. Like she could already see the spirit of her mother reaching for her. "She's in my head. In my bones. I could wake up a thousand miles away and still hear her voice telling me what I am. What I owe. She'll always haunt me. I can't abandon her."

I nodded. Not because she was doomed to this place, but because I felt the same thing. The same way this town gets into you. Quiet. Permanent. You don't even feel the chains until they've rusted into your skin.

Her fingers twitched like she wanted to reach for something— me, maybe—but didn't.

I wasn't going to let this be the end of it. If she couldn't run, maybe I could shift the ground under her. Give her another option. Get her mom to see her differently. Or see me. Or make a mistake.

"Introduce me to her."

Jean blinked, startled.

I kept going. "Let me meet your mom. I'll do this properly. I'll ask for your hand like a gentleman, and then I'll get you the hell out of there."

"That sounds like a fairytale," she said. "But in those stories, I'm not the girl people love. I'm the one they warn you about. The one with the curse. You don't really see me, Will. Not all the way."

Her laugh was soft, but there was no joy in it. She tilted her head, studying me like I was something small and breakable. "You don't know what you're asking."

I wasn't brave, not really. But for her? I'd knock on the Devil's door if it meant seeing her smile again. If it meant she didn't have to be afraid anymore.

I shrugged. "It worked for her and Patrick. Why are we any different?"

Jean turned her gaze to the horizon, chewing her lip. The ocean rolled in and out, a restless pulse beneath the night sky. The salt air clung to us, cold and heavy, wrapping around her bare shoulders, felt but unseen.

I could see it—the war inside her.

The part of her that wanted to believe in this, in me. The part of her that knew better. If she couldn't walk out yet, I'd walk in. I'd take the hit. Prove to both of them that it could be different.

Her voice was quiet when she spoke. "You wouldn't like me if you knew what my home was like."

That hit me like a fist to the gut. Not the kind you see coming— the kind that lands when you're already down, when you're already trying to breathe through one you haven't recovered from yet.

I leaned in. Close enough that she had to look at me, really look at me. Close enough that she couldn't pretend I wasn't there, that I wasn't all in on this, on her.

"Try me."

Jean swallowed hard.

A long silence stretched between us, heavy with things she wasn't saying. It sat between us like a third person, like something alive. The waves licked at the shore, retreating like whispered secrets, the night so still it felt like the world was holding its breath.

Jean's fingers curled against her palm, like she was bracing for something. For me. For herself.

Finally, she dropped her gaze, exhaling slowly.

"Meet me here," she whispered. Then hesitated. Just for a second. Just long enough for my stomach to twist up tight. "Later tonight."

She turned before I could respond, bare feet sinking into the damp sand like the earth itself was trying to hold her down.

Like it *wanted* to keep her here.

Like it *always* did.

For a second, she lingered, wavering on the edge of something, just enough to make my heart ache.

Then she continued, walking away, the wind pulling at her hair, her shadow stretching long behind her as she disappeared into the dark.

I watched her go, my pulse hammering in my ears.

She slipped into the shadows behind the cliffs—there one second, gone the next, like a phantom swallowed by the night.

The lighthouse in the distance flickered once.

And then it was gone.

Taken by the dark.

Just like everyone else this town didn't know how to love.

CHAPTER NINETEEN

The ride home was a blur of cold wind and engine noise, the night stretching wide and empty around me like it was trying to swallow me whole. The Harley beneath me growled low and steady, the only real thing in a world that felt like it was flickering in and out of focus. I tightened my grip on the handlebars, my bare fingers stiff from the cold, the bite of the air sharp against my knuckles. The leather of my jacket flapped against my sides, the smell of oil and gasoline clinging to me like a second skin.

Streetlights flashed overhead, casting long shadows that twisted and coiled across the pavement, like they were trying to grab at my tires, like they wanted to drag me back.

Didn't matter. I had a job to do. No hesitation. No second thoughts. Just movement. Just momentum.

The road stretched on, dark and endless. My heartbeat matched the steady thrum of the engine—fast, rhythmic, controlled. I kept my gaze locked forward, past the dim glow of the old gas station, past the diner on the corner with its neon sign buzzing weakly against the cold air. A part of me wanted to pull over, maybe sit at the counter, let Norma pour me a cup of coffee from a glass pot whose chipped plastic spout told a thousand tales. But stopping meant thinking, and thinking was a luxury I couldn't afford right now.

By the time I pulled into the driveway, my fingers were aching, stiff with cold, the tips raw where they curled around the handlebars. My chest was tight, full of something nameless, something thick and pressing, like a fist wedged between my ribs, but the only thing on my mind was Jean. How I'd always thought I was the kind of guy who didn't get a happy ending—but she made me want one. Not just want it—but believe it might be possible.

The house loomed ahead, dark except for the dim glow of the kitchen window, the porch light above the front steps buzzing like it was barely holding itself together. The old Buick sat in the driveway, its chrome bumper catching the light just enough to remind me it was there, silent and heavy, waiting for someone who never came back.

I killed the engine and swung my leg over the bike, boots scraping against the pavement. The silence that followed was deafening. It pressed against my ears, filled up the space where the roar of the engine had been, left me feeling weightless and off-balance.

Inside. Keep moving.

I shoved the door open harder than I meant to, the frame rattling like it wanted to fight me on this. Alright. My room next. It was exactly as I'd left it—messy, half-lived-in, like I was already halfway out the door before I even knew I was leaving. Clothes draped over the back of my chair. An old turntable on the desk, half-buried under notebooks and loose papers, the latest Everly Brothers record still resting on it. A single lamp casting weak light over the chaos.

I yanked my duffel bag from the closet, the canvas rough under my fingers as I unzipped it and started stuffing it with whatever I could grab—clothes, my lucky shorts, a wad of cash from the dresser drawer, a couple of keepsakes that meant something even if I'd never admit it. Too much, not enough—everything and nothing, all at once. My hands shook as I worked.

I zipped it up, threw the strap over my shoulder. I was ready. I wasn't.

I turned for the door, but before I could take a step, I heard it.

"Will?"

I froze.

Eddie stood in the hallway, blinking like he'd just woken up but had never actually gone to sleep. His hair was a brown, mussed-up mess—flat on one side and sticking up at the crown, like he'd been running his hands through it all night. He wore an old white under-shirt, the kind with a stretched-out collar, and a pair of plaid pajama pants that hit too short at the ankles. He was barefoot, toes curling slightly against the hardwood floor, like he was trying to brace himself for whatever came next.

There was nothing flashy about him. No posturing. No perfor-mance. Just Eddie. Tall for his age, still filling out, freckles softened by the low hallway light. A little gangly. A little too kind for his own good. And still, somehow, the most grown-up person in the house.

"Are we doing it? Is it go-time?" he asked, not a whisper, not a demand. Just a question.

I exhaled, forced a lopsided smile. "Yeah, something like that."

His gaze flicked to the duffel bag, my posture, the way my fingers had gone white around the strap. He wasn't dumb. Never had been. He saw things. Me included. Probably better than I ever did. His face didn't shift into shock or confusion—just this slow, steady realiza-tion settling behind his eyes, like he'd already worked out what this was and was just waiting for me to confirm it.

"Far out." he said, nodding slightly. No judgment. No drama. Just understanding. And that—God, that was worse.

"You want me to pack a bag? We breakin' Jean outta Alcatraz or what?"

I let out a quiet laugh, shaking my head. "I think this one's going to have to be a solo mission, Watson."

Eddie grinned. "Fair enough! I'll get the couch made up for her—can't wait to meet the Ghost Girl for real."

My stomach twisted. "That's the thing, Eddie. I don't think I'll be—"

"Will?"

Another voice.

I turned.

Mom stood at the end of the hallway, her silhouette framed by the warm light spilling from the kitchen. She was still wearing her house dress, her cardigan draped over her shoulders, her hands loose at her sides. Her posture was easy, steady. Not tense. Not angry.

There was no surprise in her face. Just something soft. Something that made my throat tighten.

"Come sit," she said.

Not a question. Not a demand. Just an invitation.

THE KITCHEN SMELLED LIKE COFFEE, like home. Like a hundred slow mornings and a thousand late nights, all of them blurring together into something warm and familiar. The light above the table buzzed faintly, flickering every few seconds like it was thinking about going out but wanted to keep up, to fulfill its duty.

The clock on the wall ticked out slow, steady beats, filling the spaces between words we hadn't spoken yet.

I sat with my duffel bag at my feet, one hand drumming against the tabletop, the other curled into a loose fist in my lap. Eddie sat beside me, his legs stretched out now, planted there, solid. His feet pushed at the linoleum like he was grounding himself, like he could provide reinforcements just by staying still enough.

Mom was across from us, hands folded neatly on the table, her eyes scanning my face like she was trying to commit every inch of it to memory.

Like maybe if she looked long enough, I wouldn't disappear.

She exhaled through her nose, quiet but deliberate. "Is this it? Are you finally leaving for your trip?" She paused. "You're not coming back, are you?"

It wasn't really a question.

I swallowed hard. "No, Mom," I said, voice scratchy. "I'm not."

She nodded like she'd already known. Maybe she had. Maybe she'd known longer than I had. Maybe this was always in the walls. Since the day I first rode my bike past the county line and didn't look back.

For a long time, none of us spoke. It should've felt suffocating. Instead, it felt... right. Like some invisible weight had finally shifted, settled in the right place.

"You come back to visit, alright?" Mom reached into the pocket of her cardigan, pulling out an envelope. She set it on the table and pushed it toward me. "Even ghosts come home sometimes." Her fingers lingered there for a beat longer than they needed to. Just enough to say everything she couldn't. "It's not much... but it's all I have."

I stared at it. The paper was thin, worn soft at the edges like she'd been carrying it around for a while. Like she'd been waiting for the moment she'd have to hand it over.

"Mom—"

"Take it." Her voice was firm, but not unkind. Just steady. Just final. "You'll need it more than I will."

My throat felt tight as I picked it up, turned it over in my hands. It felt heavier than it should have, like it carried more than just cash inside. Like it carried every quiet thing she didn't know how to say out loud.

I tucked it into my jacket pocket. It felt safe there, pressed against my chest.

Eddie shifted beside me, his fingers tracing invisible lines on the tabletop. He wasn't looking at me when he spoke. "I always figured you'd blow this popsicle stand someday." He smirked. "Gotta say, the circumstances are a bit more... colorful than I expected, but hey— makes for a heck of a story."

Something in me uncoiled at that. Like I could finally let out a breath I'd been holding for years.

"I love you guys," I said, voice quieter than I meant it to be. "I mean it."

Mom smiled, something soft and infinite in her eyes. Something sad and proud and full of understanding. "We know, sweetheart."

Eddie looked at me, and for a second, I thought maybe he'd say something deep, something that'd stick with me when I was miles away from here. Instead, he just smirked, nudging me with his elbow.

"Just don't go forgettin' the little people when you strike it rich or sail off with your mystery girl, alright?"

I huffed a laugh, ruffling his already messy hair. "Like I could."

Eddie paused, then looked at me deeper, the smirk never falling from his face. "Be careful out there, Will. And don't worry— I won't let anyone forget you're real."

"That's all I could ask for," I smiled back.

And just like that, the weight in the room shifted again. Not gone, not lifted, just... settled. The silence wasn't heavy anymore. It was just there. Just us.

For once, that was enough.

THE NIGHT STRETCHED WIDE and quiet around me as I walked down the driveway, pavement protesting beneath my boots. The weight of the envelope was still solid in my pocket, heavier than it had any right to be.

The air was sharp, crisp with the scent of cut grass and something salty rolling in from the shore. The kind of night that made everything feel still, like the world had pressed pause just for a second, just long enough for me to realize how much I was leaving behind.

I stopped beside my Harley, running a hand through my hair, fingers gripping tight for a second before I let out a slow breath. My chest felt tight, like I'd been holding something in all night, something that had nowhere to go.

Keep moving. Just keep moving.

I reached into my bag, digging past clothes and crumpled bills until my fingers found the pen tucked between everything. Clicked it open with my thumb. Stared at the envelope for a long second, the paper dim in the porchlight glow. Then, carefully, I scrawled across the front:

To: Eddie.

Get yourself a set of wheels. Or better yet, a whole auto shop. Happy Birthday, Kid.

I ran my fingers over the ink, smudging it just a little.

It wasn't enough. But it was something.

I stepped up to the mailbox, lifting the lid and slipping the envelope inside. Paused for half a second. Pressed the lid shut.

That was it. Done. Sealed. No taking it back.

I turned on my heel, swung my leg over the bike. My fingers found the handlebars like they belonged there, like they were the only thing keeping me tethered.

The key turned easy. The engine came alive under me, low and steady, a sound I knew better than my own heartbeat.

I could've looked back.

Could've taken one last glance at the house, at the light still glowing soft in the kitchen window, at the place that had been mine for so long it almost felt like a part of me.

But I didn't.

Not once. Because looking back meant I wasn't ready. And I was.

So, I twisted the throttle, felt the pull of the road under me, and let the night swallow me whole.

CHAPTER TWENTY

I rode my Harley back to the shoreline. Parked it right where I had the night before. Right where it was when she fell. When I pulled her into my arms. When everything cracked open like a bad dream you can't wake up from.

The bike had a scar now. A long, jagged thing running alongside the spot where it hit the ground. Funny, how things could remember better than people ever could.

I cut the engine. Pulled the strap of my duffle over my head and tossed it aside before taking off toward the beach. The sand was damp, sticking to the soles of my boots, slowing me down.

"Jean?" I called, the wind carrying my voice off into the dark.

Nothing. Just the waves rolling in, quiet, steady. Like they weren't even listening.

I cupped my hands around my mouth. "Jean?!" My voice cracked somewhere in the middle, but I wasn't about to let that mean anything.

The shore stretched out before me, empty. Hollow. An endless, starless night pressed in from all sides.

Maybe she wasn't here yet.

That was fine. Nothing weird about that. I told myself she was late. Maybe she got caught up. Maybe she had to wait for her mother to fall asleep. Maybe she was up there on the cliffs right now, watching me from the shadows of the wind-beaten pines the way she liked to, counting the minutes until she could come down.

So I waited.

First for minutes.

Then an hour.

Then another.

And with every second that passed, the cold crept in a little deeper.

I stared out at the water. The waves whispered against the shore, dragging away everything like they'd never even been there. The bike, the scar, the ground where she had fallen—those things remembered. But the tide? The tide didn't care. It just kept coming. Kept taking.

Was this... was this my answer? For me to just leave without her? No. She wouldn't do that. Not to me.

The night stretched out in front of me, endless and indifferent, swallowing my excuses one by one as time kept marching on.

I never thought I'd need someone like this. Not again. Never thought needing someone could feel so much like drowning and breathing at the same time. But maybe this was it—the lesson I kept refusing to learn. That it's just me against the world. That I can't save anybody. That waiting is nothing more than a quiet kind of death, and hope is just another way of watching the tide pull everything away, piece by piece, until all that's left is the hollow space where something used to be.

That maybe—just maybe—this was my fault.

I had pushed everything too soon, too fast. But she was trapped, dammit. Couldn't she see that?

The ocean breathed, steady and slow, rolling in like a thing that knew better than me. The tide crept up the shore, inch by inch, swallowing the footprints I'd left behind, like it had been waiting all along to erase me. The waves moved with a rhythm I couldn't follow, their dark surface rippling beneath the silver glow of the moon. Slow. Deliberate. As if mocking my stillness. My waiting.

I didn't move.

Instead, I knelt in the damp sand, pressing my finger into its cool, shifting surface. The grains clung to my skin, sticky with salt and memory, as I traced each letter into the earth.

J E A N.

A name pressed into something that could never keep it.

I traced the letters again and again, pressing hard enough that the sand fought back, the grains lodging into my skin like tiny splinters, like maybe pain could hold something in place. Like maybe, if I pushed hard enough, the earth would keep her for me.

The first drop of rain landed on the back of my hand. Cold. Indifferent. Then another. Then more.

And before I could stop it—before I could even think to stop it— she was gone.

Not with a crash, not with a scream.

Just... gone.

No protest.

No flash of light.

The rain took her.

Washed her name away like it was never here to begin with.

Like she had never been here at all.

A hollow ache spread through my chest. Like something sharp slipping beneath my ribs. Like she was slipping through my fingers, disappearing faster than I could hold onto her.

What if the town was right? What if I was losing my mind—chasing after someone long gone? What if she was never real in the first place? What if I was the only one who saw her—because I needed her to exist?

My chest tightened.

No.

I thought of the movie, Jean, sitting beside me in the dim glow of the screen.

Her fingers pressed into the armrests, bracing herself like she was holding onto something unseen, something vast. The flickering colors spilled across her face, wide-eyed and unguarded.

She leaned in, barely moving, barely breathing.

And then, in a voice so soft, so certain—like she had just figured out something the rest of us hadn't—

"It's like stepping into another life."

My throat tightened. Because she had been right.

For a little while, in that dark theater, she had stepped into another life. She hadn't been trapped. She hadn't been forgotten. She had just been a girl.

She was real. I knew she was. And people saw her.

The memory tilted. Shifted. Slipped.

Charlie. Polly.

Outside the theater.

The sharp click of Polly's heels against the pavement. The slow, lazy drag of her cigarette. She had looked at Jean like she was trying to place her. Like there was something nagging at the edge of her memory.

And then—

That pause.

The hesitation.

Polly had smirked all night, had thrown out sharp-edged comments like she wanted to cut deep. But that was just who Polly was.

Until—

Jean had spoken her name.

And for the first time, Polly had—changed. She had gone still. Blinked. Something in her face had shifted.

"Jean?"

Barely a whisper. Barely there at all. Like the air had changed. Like the ground wasn't quite as solid beneath her feet. Like she had seen something impossible. Like she was staring at the dead.

The realization struck something in me, hit like the snap of a rubber band pulled too tight.

Polly knew something.

My pulse roared in my ears, matching the rain, the waves, the storm. I turned toward the road. I moved before I could think.

Polly had looked at her like she'd seen something impossible. Like a memory she couldn't place.

Why?

The thought crashed through me, shaking something loose, something raw and unsettled.

Polly knows her. Knows Jean. I have to find out why.

Soaking wet, I climbed onto my bike.

The engine roared to life beneath me, the only solid thing in a world that felt like it was slipping through my fingers. The beam from the lighthouse flickered once behind me as I revved the throttle. And then it was gone, swallowed by the cold, as I shot forward into the dark.

CHAPTER TWENTY-ONE

The main road into town felt different now.

Same cracked pavement. Same flickering neon signs. Same rusted-out cars that hadn't moved since before I was born. But something about it felt meaner in the dark. In the rain. Like the streets were watching, waiting for me to make a wrong move.

Like the people in the diner windows and on the motel balconies —the ones huddled under awnings, cigarettes glowing between their fingers—were watching too.

They didn't turn away when I passed.

Didn't even pretend.

Behind the fogged glass of the diner, I caught them—Earl behind the counter, arms folded like always, except this time he wasn't looking at his coffee. Marge sat statue-still, her plate cooling in front of her. Gil hadn't even touched his fries. All three of them staring out like they'd been expecting me.

The throbbing pulse of the engine was the only sound protesting the splatter of raindrops on the road, but their faces didn't change as I rode past. I felt it. That tension. Like the town had taken a breath and decided not to let it go.

They weren't watching *me* anymore. They were watching a story play out.

I didn't have to hear them to know what they were saying.

That boy Will... he's been seen talkin' to her, hasn't he?

Reckon he'll be next.

A car door slammed.

I flinched.

"Hey, Will!" a voice called out.

I turned just enough to see Danny standing by his truck, one foot still on the running board.

He was already back here—dragged back to Depoe Bay. It didn't make sense. He just left for school— I thought, then Jean's voice echoed in my head. *Some places don't let you leave so easily.*

Danny squinted against the rain, a half-grin on his face. "What're you still doing here?" he yelled as I whipped past. I didn't answer. Didn't wave. Didn't slow down. I twisted the throttle and let the roar of the engine do the talking.

Didn't matter what Danny thought. Didn't matter what any of them thought. I only had one thing on my mind—and nothing was going to hold me back.

POLLY'S HOUSE sat at the edge of town, past the old church with its leaning steeple and the abandoned general store where kids swore you could still hear voices if you pressed your ear to the boards.

I never tried. Didn't need to.

The town was already full of legends.

I pulled up to her house, tires sloshing against wet pavement. Big, clean, cold. The kind of house that belonged to someone who had money, but not much else. Light glowed from the windows, but the place still looked empty.

I killed the engine, swung off the bike, and hit the ground hard, boots splashing into puddles. Rain rolled off the roof, off the gutters, sliding over my jacket, my hair, soaking straight through. Didn't stop me from taking the steps two at a time. Didn't stop me from knocking.

Once. Twice.

Hard enough to sting.

Silence.

Then—

The door swung open.

Dr. Parker.

Same pressed shirt he always wore, same tired eyes that've looked at me for years, but this time, there was something sharper beneath them. No indifference. Just anger.

He looked me over, slow and deliberate, like he was deciding whether or not I was worth his time.

"You got some nerve."

I wiped the rain from my face, forced a smirk. "That's what they tell me."

His expression darkened. "William Charleson, if you don't get off my porch, I'm calling the police!"

The smirk faltered. Just slightly.

"I'm warning you, I'll have the sheriff here in two seconds flat!"

I held up my hands, took a slow step back into the rain. "Whoa there, Daddy-o. I just need to talk to Polly."

"I don't give a damn what you're here for—"

"Dad. Cool it. It's fine."

Polly's voice cut through the tension, sharp and steady. Dr. Parker's jaw clenched, but she was already stepping past him onto the porch. He hesitated like he might say something—might drag her back inside, slam the door, end this before it could begin.

But he didn't.

He let out a sharp breath through his nose, turned, and walked away. The door clicked shut behind him.

Polly lit a cigarette, slow and practiced, cupping her hand against the wind. The flame flared before catching, and she took a drag, exhaling smoke into the cold air.

She wasn't dressed like usual. The red lipstick was gone. No cat-eyes, no glossy ponytail. Just a half-tucked tee and a cardigan slipping down one shoulder. Her hair hung loose and uneven, curling at the ends like it forgot what it was supposed to do. She looked like someone who hadn't planned to be seen. Someone who didn't care if she was.

But she still stood like a queen guarding her porch.

"What do you want, Will? Say it quick—I'm not in the mood to play detective."

She sounded like him, sometimes. When she was tired. Or done pretending. I shook out my sleeves, flicking water off my fingers, but it didn't help. My clothes were already soaked through, rain running down my face, sliding into my collar, sticking everything to my skin like a second layer I couldn't shake off.

Polly stood just inside the overhang, dry, arms folded, cigarette balanced between two fingers. She took a slow drag, watching me through the smoke like she was already bored of this conversation.

"Answers."

She let out a short, humorless laugh. "Well, ain't that somethin'. You came to the wrong porch, gumshoe."

"Pol."

She didn't look at me. Instead, she turned toward the street, like there was something more interesting out there in the rain, something worth looking at.

Like she was already done.

But I wasn't.

"She was your friend." My voice came low, steady. "Jean. You knew her. I know it. She told me. She said she was friends with the doctor's kids. Was that you? Huh?"

Polly's jaw tensed.

I kept going.

"What do you know, Pol. Tell me why no one knows about her. Tell me why you looked at her like you'd seen a ghost."

She flinched. Barely. Covered it well.

But I caught it.

Her arms tightened around herself, and she took another drag, exhaled slow, like she was buying herself time.

"I don't know what you want me to say, Will."

"Tell me the truth."

She pinched the bridge of her nose. Or maybe she was just holding something in. "You wouldn't believe it if I did."

I stepped closer, boots sinking into the flooded gravel.

"Try me."

She licked her lips, shifted her weight, but didn't speak.

I pushed harder.

"Your dad—he has to know something. He was their doctor, wasn't he?"

Something flickered across her face. A hesitation. A crack.

I swallowed, pressing on.

"He must've seen Sandra and Jean's bodies." The words felt heavy in my mouth. I barely knew what I was saying. "Did he—" I stammered, shaking my head, running a hand through my hair. My fingers trembled. "Does he—"

She shook her head, cutting me off.

"Don't."

Her voice was sharper this time. Almost desperate.

The air between us thickened.

I clenched my jaw, rain pressing down on me, dragging me under. The weight of all of it—the town, the whispers, Jean—settled deep in my ribs.

Polly exhaled, but it didn't sound like relief. More like she was getting ready to say something that hurt.

"Jean's dead, Will. They both are."

Something twisted in my chest. A slow, sick curl of dread unfurled along my spine.

"No. No, you saw her." My voice came out rough, uneven. I took a step forward, almost pleading. "You saw her and you knew!"

Polly didn't answer.

Rain slid down my face, cold creeping into my collar, my sleeves, my bones. I shook my head, hair clinging to my forehead. "Don't tell me you didn't!"

Still nothing. No argument. No denial.

And somehow, that silence felt worse.

Something inside me cracked open.

The rain kept falling, steady and relentless, filling the silence between us. Every drop seemed to stretch the space wider, until it felt unbearable.

Finally, Polly said, "You always do this, don't you? Show up, full of fire, thinkin' you can fix the whole world with a pack of smokes and a leather jacket. You wanna save someone, Will? Start with yourself."

It hit me sideways.

"What are you saying?"

Her voice was quiet, flat. Then she added, "I'm saying you talk a big game. But do you ever actually think about leaving this place— for good? Or do you just like the drama?"

I swallowed. "I think about it all the time."

She nodded once. Slow. Like that didn't surprise her.

She kept her eyes on the street, watching puddles collect in the cracks, watching streetlight reflections ripple and break apart.

"Yeah. He did too."

She didn't have to say his name. I already knew.

Tony.

"Dreamed about getting out, same as you. Maybe more." She took another drag from her cigarette, then exhaled long and low. "I don't blame you, y'know."

I let out a sharp breath. "Don't lie."

A hint of a laugh slipped out of her, almost too soft to catch.

"Fine. Maybe I did. For a spell."

Then she looked at me.

Really looked at me.

"But truth is, I was more burned you left me out."

I felt something shift. My chest tightened.

She shook her head slowly. "He said I was comin' too—that I'd be riding off into the sunset with you both. Guess he forgot to loop you in." Her voice cracked just a little. "I don't know if he meant it."

She hesitated.

Then, softer—

"Who knows what would've happened if I'd been in that car." She looked down at the sidewalk, anywhere but my eyes. "Maybe nothin'." She didn't look up. "Or maybe I'd be six feet under right next to him." Her words hit harder than she probably meant them to.

I couldn't breathe.

She let the silence hang for a second. Then, with a sharp exhale, "Bet you never thought about that, huh?"

My mouth opened. Nothing came out. He never told me. Not once. I didn't even know she thought she had a seat in that car. I tried again.

"Polly, I—I didn't know. That wasn't the plan. I swear, it—"

She cut me off with a bitter little laugh. Not cruel. Just exhausted.

"You were my brother's whole damn world, Will. Not me. Not our folks. Just you."

The words sank deep. Like a punch to the ribs.

"That's not true," I said. Barely.

She shrugged. "Isn't it?"

No edge in her voice. Just... tired.

"I don't hate you, Will."

I looked at her. Swallowed hard. "Then what? What is all this?"

"I just... I don't think you ever learned how to stop runnin'. You keep thinkin' there's somewhere better, someone cleaner. But all you do is leave messes behind." She sighed, running a hand through her hair before flicking the burnt-out cigarette into the water pooling near my feet.

"We all make our choices, Will."

I stared up at her. "And what's yours?"

Polly took a step back toward the door.

"To stay."

I stared at her. "Why?"

Polly exhaled, long and slow, like she was trying to let something go.

"Because somebody's gotta. And it sure as hell ain't gonna be you."

Her voice was steady. Resigned.

Then—

"Whatever it is you're huntin' for—I've got nothin' left to give you."

She finally looked at me. Really looked. Her gaze caught the porch light, something sharp beneath the dark, something I couldn't reach.

"You want answers?" Her voice didn't waver. Didn't hesitate. "Go knock on Betty's door."

She took a step back. Not big, not rushed. Just enough to put space between us.

"You already took enough from this house."

The words landed in my chest like a slow punch.

I swallowed.

She gripped the doorknob, fingers tightening around the brass.

"This one ain't mine to give."

And then—

The door clicked shut. And somehow, that felt worse than a goodbye.

The rain kept falling. I stood there, staring at the house, taking it in one last time. It looked different now. Like I had never been here before. Like I hadn't spent half my childhood sneaking through that window upstairs, or whispering plans to Tony in the dark, or watching Polly roll her eyes as she stood guard on the porch.

Like none of it had ever happened.

Like none of it ever mattered.

Because the truth was—

Tony was gone.

And Polly had nothing left to say.

Still, Dr. Parker had to know something. That much was clear. But Polly was right. There was only one person left who could tell me the truth.

I turned. Walked down the steps, rainwater splashing against my boots, rolling off my sleeves. Didn't run. Didn't rush. Just walked.

The town was quiet now. The storm swallowing whatever whispers had been left behind. Obscuring the twitches of lace curtains that hid evening watchers. I reached my Harley, brushed the water off the seat—not that it mattered—and swung one leg over. The engine rumbled beneath me, low and restless, like it already knew where we were going.

I twisted the throttle. Didn't hesitate. Didn't look back.

And headed straight for Betty's house.

CHAPTER TWENTY-TWO

The house stood at the edge of the cliffs, where the land dropped into the sea.

19 Crescent Ave.

It had been there longer than I'd been alive, longer than anyone could remember. One of those places that shouldn't still be standing but just was.

A house that didn't belong to a person, but to time. To salt. To the wind that tore at its bones but never quite managed to break them.

We told stories about it as kids. About the woman inside who never left. About the things she did to keep herself alive. About the cellar out back, half-swallowed by the earth, waiting for the next body to be buried inside.

Nobody ever got close enough to see if the stories were true.

Until now.

I pulled up slow. The Harley grumbled beneath me, wheels sinking into the road, thick with mud. The rain had turned the dirt into something slick and sucking, like the earth itself wanted to pull me under. I cut the engine. The silence didn't feel like silence at all—

just a different kind of noise. The wind roared across the cliffs. The ocean pounded against the rocks below. And the house...

The house just watched.

It looked abandoned, but not in the way that meant empty. More like something had settled inside it. Something old. Something patient. The roof sagged, buckled under the weight of too many years. The windows were wrong—some boarded, some gaping and black, like empty eye sockets staring out into the dark. The porch leaned forward, not in welcome, but in expectation.

The rain came down in sheets. Thick. Unrelenting. It sliced through the night like knives, soaking through my clothes, chilling me straight to the bone. My hair stuck to my forehead. My breath hitched in my chest. My pulse pounded like a drum in my ears.

I hesitated.

I pulled off the road, cutting the engine.

I swung my leg off the bike and kicked the stand down into the rain-soaked ground. The bike tilted, awkward, like it didn't belong here.

Honestly, neither did I.

For a moment, I just stood there. Hands still on the handlebars. Breathing hard without meaning to.

The house loomed in front of me, dark and hunched against the storm. Its edges blurred into the sky, more shadow than structure. No lights in the windows. No movement behind the curtains. Just blackness—and not the kind you walk into. The kind that swallows you.

Jean's voice was soft, and warm, and alive. This house didn't feel alive. It felt like it had erased anything that had ever been part of it.

I adjusted the duffle bag slung across my shoulder, fingers tightening around the strap, but I didn't move. Didn't speak. Didn't even blink. The wind tore through the trees around me, branches grinding against each other, whispering things in a language I didn't want to understand.

I pushed myself to go near it, my thoughts hesitant, chaotic, mangled between what I knew to be true and what everyone else had told me about this place, this family, their history. I put my forehead against the glass and glanced deeper into one of the windows.

Nothing. No flicker. No silhouette. Just a whole lot of nothing staring right back.

The duffle slid off my shoulder with a reluctant scrape. I let it fall, and it hit the mud with a wet, exhausted thud. Heavy, but not loud. The sound barely registered.

I stepped forward, toward the front door.

The porch groaned beneath my boots—not sudden, not sharp, just slow. Like it was exhaling after holding its breath too long. Like the house had been waiting for someone, anyone, to come join it, test it, challenge it. It had been waiting for me.

The worn wooden railing was slick with rain. The posts were warped, swollen from decades of weather and whatever else had happened inside. I grabbed one to test it. It held. Barely.

Didn't like the feel of it. Didn't like any of this.

It didn't feel like walking into someone's home.

It felt like stepping into a memory being played out in some horror movie; one that had never belonged to me.

I reached for the door. Lifted a fist. Hesitated.

Then knocked. Once. Twice.

Nothing.

The rain slipped from my sleeves and dripped off my knuckles, pattering against the wood. I shifted my weight and knocked again —harder this time. The kind of knock that should echo through every empty hallway, stir the shadows, startle something awake.

But it didn't.

The sound just vanished. Like the house took it in and didn't feel the need to answer.

No footsteps.

No voice.

Just the storm creeping in around me, and the ocean, louder now, angry and alive beneath the cliffs. Protesting what was, what might have been.

I turned slightly, glancing down the side of the house.

The cellar doors were sunken into the ground, almost hidden beneath layers of mud and moss. Their wood was split and water-warped, the iron handle eaten through with rust. The kind of rust that looked darker than it should have. The kind you didn't name out loud.

They looked sealed. Untouched.

But there—just barely visible through the runoff and muck—were footprints. Fresh ones.

Leading toward the cellar.

Not away.

I pounded on the front door again, this time with the full weight of my fist. The frame shuddered under the force. Thunder rumbled low in the near distance.

Then, finally—a sound.

A creak.

Soft. Slow.

A faint light came on from somewhere deep inside.

The door cracked open just an inch, and the faintest strip of yellow light spilled onto the porch. Barely enough to see by. Just enough to remind me that the house was still alive. Still watching.

And then—

She was there.

Betty.

Jean's mother. I had only seen her in photographs, but I knew her the second our eyes met.

She didn't move. Didn't speak. Just stood there, eerily still, perfectly composed. Not tired. Not angry. Not even confused. Just there.

The orange light from inside caught the harsh angles of her face, casting shadows that stretched and sharpened, making her look carved from stone. Her hair was swept back into a neat twist—not a strand out of place. Her nightgown was starched stiff, the kind of fabric that didn't move right—too heavy, too clean. It didn't wrinkle, even as the wind from the open door sent the hem fluttering like it didn't belong to her body. The color was pale—bone white or faded blue, hard to tell in the dark—and it clung to her in places, loose in others, like it had been worn too many nights in a row. Like it had learned to shape itself around her silence.

She tilted her head—slow, deliberate. Her eyes scanned me. Not curious. Not suspicious. Just... certain. Like she already knew what I was. Like she'd known before I even showed up on her porch.

There was no weariness in her face. No anger. Just stillness and waiting.

Then, in a calm, practiced voice—like she was greeting a child who had wandered too far from the picnic—she said,

"You shouldn't be here."

Not rude. Not shaken.

Just... matter-of-fact.

A chill crept down my spine.

She started to close the door.

I didn't move. Didn't blink. Just braced my hand against the wood before it could shut me out.

The rain dripped from my jaw, rolling off my skin, soaking into my collar. A slow, steady rhythm. It pooled on the warped wooden slats beneath my boots, turning the porch into something slick, uneven, precarious. The wind screamed at my back, trying to shove me away, push me out, but I stood my ground.

I squared my shoulders.

Lifted my chin.

Met her gaze head-on.

"Ma'am." My voice came even, steady, despite the storm howling around me. "I know you don't know me. And maybe you don't want to. But... I'm here to ask you some questions about your daughter. Jean."

For the first time, something flickered in her expression.

Not shock. Not anger.

Something else.

Something I didn't have a name for yet.

The silence stretched between us, thick as the saturated storm clouds pressing down on the town. The wind rattled the trees. The ocean groaned against the cliffs. The house just stood there—watching.

Betty stared at me for a long, slow moment. Her eyes were unreadable.

Then, without a word, she stepped aside.

The door eased open a little wider—and the house breathed.

The wind slipped through the cracks in the walls, dragging the storm inside with quiet little whispers. The air shifted, thick and heavy, pressing in from all sides. The doorway gaped open—warm, dimly lit—but wrong.

I didn't know why. I just knew.

Inside, the floorboards didn't creak, didn't groan under the weight of time. They just waited.

The air wasn't just stale. It had weight, like it had been held inside for so long it didn't know anything else. Like Jean.

Every part of me screamed to turn around. To leave. To walk back into the storm and never come back. But I had already come this far. And before I could stop myself—

I stepped inside.

CHAPTER TWENTY-THREE

Everything inside me screamed that I was making a mistake.
What was I doing here? What if everything the town said was true? What if I was just losing my mind?
The house swallowed me whole. Like a mouth snapping shut behind me, the air inside stagnant, old, the scent of must and decay mixed with—what was that? Not just the scent of mildew, not just the damp clinging to my skin like a second layer. No, this was something deeper. Something patient.

Something that had been waiting like some beast in a cave waiting for the right fool to enter.

It pressed against me, threading through my ribs like fingers, curling into the hollow spaces between bones. Holding its rancid breath like it had been doing it for a long, long time.

The damp crept in first, heavy at the back of my throat, thick enough to choke on. It tasted like dust and rot, something almost alive, something that had been left too long to fester. Beneath it, the mildew clung sour and sharp, twisted up with something worse—something deeper, something rotting from the inside out.

A smell that didn't belong to the house.

The walls sagged under the weight of time. Wallpaper peeled in jagged, curling strips, flaking like dead skin, exposing the yellowed plaster beneath—bone under an old wound that never quite healed. Water stains bled down from the ceiling in dark, clawed streaks. The kind of damage that came from slow, quiet suffering.

Or maybe not suffering. Maybe just waiting.

Faint rectangles still marked the walls, shadows where pictures used to be. Remains of a family that had once existed here. The frames were gone, but the outlines remained, bruises left behind in places no one bothered to touch.

No coats by the door. No shoes left kicked off in a hurry. No clutter, no warmth, no signs of life.

Just space. Too much space.

The floor groaned beneath my boots—a slow, aching sound. Like a whisper, like a warning. I glanced around. No signs of Jean. No movement, no sound.

But the silence wasn't empty. It moved.

It stretched too long, pressed too hard. It curled thick and slow against my skin, like breath against the back of my neck. A thing with weight. A thing with patience. A thing that had been waiting for me to step inside.

Did Jean really live here? Was she here now? She had to be, I could feel it. I could feel it the way you feel a storm before it breaks, thick in the air, pressing at the edges of your lungs. But the house wasn't ready to let me know that yet.

"Pardon the mess," Betty said, her voice syrup-thick. The kind of sweet that sticks in your teeth. "It's not often I have company anymore."

Her words slithered in under my skin. She moved ahead, leading me past a living room that didn't look lived in. There was furniture— a couch with threadbare cushions, an old recliner sunken at the seams, a side table, and lamp, laying broken on the floor. No pillows. No books. No knickknacks or clutter. Just the suggestion of a life, staged and silent. Like someone had moved out years ago and left the ghosts behind to keep it warm.

She never looked back, but I could feel her eyes on me all the same. Even when her gaze stayed forward, spine too straight, shoulders too still. Like she was listening to something I couldn't hear.

We reached the end of the hall, and she paused—just for a second—before drifting sideways through a doorway. Her hand brushed the frame as she passed, fingers grazing the wood like she was warning it. Like she was asking permission. The walls stretched long, shadows stretching longer. The light grew brighter. It felt like something pressing inward, closing in. My gut twisted, coiled tight.

Inside, the kitchen was too small. Too close.

The walls pressed inward, the ceiling too low. A single bulb buzzed overhead, its flickering glow jittering against the stained walls. Water marks ran down in spidery streaks, creeping like roots, like fingers, like something alive, vines ready to engulf, entangle the innocent. The countertops were lined with old jars, their glass fogged, the contents thick and murky. Something about them felt wrong, like looking into an aquarium that hadn't been cleaned in years.

Betty gestured to the small wooden table. "Go on now, sit. It's rude to linger in the doorway."

I did.

The chair wobbled under me, one uneven leg tapping softly against the cracked linoleum floor. Betty moved slow, deliberate, fingers skimming the countertops, the back of my chair—too slow. Too deliberate.

Her hand drifted over to the knife block.

A casual touch.

Not an accident. Not absentminded.

A choice.

She tapped the handle once. Twice. The sound barely reached me over the blood rushing in my ears.

"William Charleson... My, my. You've grown into quite the picture. I suppose I shouldn't be surprised."

Her voice was too even. Too polite. The kind of polite you use when you're holding something sharp behind your back.

I nodded once.

Betty settled across from me, folding her hands neatly over the table. Her nails were short, clean. But her knuckles were rough. Lined with tiny white scars. A thick amber-colored ring sat on her finger— too large for her hand, too bright for the room. It caught the light when she moved, glowing orange like a lit coal.

The rain tapped lightly against the window. Betty's gaze flicked to it. Just for a second. Quick. Like she didn't mean to. Like she didn't want to. Then—back to me.

The way she said it sent something cold down my spine.

I met her gaze, steady. "How do you know who I am?"

She smiled. That same eerie calm, that same unsettling stillness.

"Oh, sweetheart. A mother notices things. Your story was in the paper. That poor face of yours, all torn up like that... You looked so lost. Such a tragic thing. All that blood, all that screaming... but you survived. That's what matters, isn't it? Why, you even have the scars to show for it."

I hesitated. A half-second pause. Then slowly, I pulled my arms back from the table, resting my hands in my lap.

"If it's alright, I wanted to ask you some questions about Jean."

"We'll talk about Jean. But tell me—how is George? Your father was always such a proud man. Loud. The kind that filled a room before he opened his mouth. I haven't seen him in ages."

I didn't like the way she said his name. Like it wasn't really a question. Like she already knew the answer and just wanted to hear how I'd say it.

"No, I suppose you haven't," I said carefully. "He's—"

The rain picked up. A steady rhythm, tapping against the window. She cut me off, her jaw tightening. Just like that. Sharp.

Deliberate. Like she was cutting through the conversation with a blade.

"And your mother... Judith. She must be exhausted, poor thing. Two boys all on her own. Though, if I remember right, Judith was always good at... *multitasking*."

My blood went cold.

"And Edward—he must be what, sixteen now? A dangerous age for a boy. That's when they start thinking they know everything."

Eddie.

She said his name like she knew him. Like she had seen him.

The words slithered under my skin, cold and slow, twisting in deep. My jaw tightened.

This wasn't small-town gossip. This wasn't the usual whispers passed between neighbors over laundry lines and grocery store aisles. This was something else. Something older. Like she had been studying me. Studying my family. Sitting in this house, in this silence, waiting for this exact moment.

Like she had been waiting for me long before I ever knocked on her door.

I didn't let it show. Didn't let the cold spread past my ribs.

Didn't hesitate.

"Like I said before, ma'am," I said, voice even. "I'm here about Jean."

The smile didn't falter. Not shock. Not anger. Just that look.

Something slow and creeping, sinking its teeth into my skin, dragging itself deeper. Something that told me I shouldn't have come.

Tap. Tap. Tap.

Betty's fingers flexed. She exhaled through her nose, shaking her head slightly—like I was a child who didn't know any better. A foolish boy. She stepped away from the table, my eyes tracking every movement.

"That's right. Always comes back to Jean in the end. Poor thing. Can't even rest without someone digging her up." she paused. "You boys never stop and think, do you? What it's like for a mother—answering the same questions, reliving the same loss, over and over like it's nothing."

I stared at her. "I—I know how this might come across, especially given the time of night. But please. Can you tell me about her? What happened?"

Another pause. "Of course I can. I remember everything. Jean and my Sandra... my precious girls. The ocean takes what it pleases, and no amount of screaming ever brings it back."

I hesitated, a fraction of a second. But my mouth ran before I could catch it. "But ma'am, I've seen her. Jean. I know she's alive."

It looked like something inside Betty broke.

"You think you've seen her. That's what they all say. You boys with your stories and your shining eyes. You think love is enough to call someone back from the dead?"

"It's true! I've seen her by the shoreline, she—"

"Someone always comes knockin'," she murmured. "Every few years, like clockwork. Different name. Same foolish heart. They come looking, thinking they'll find something the rest of the world missed. But this house doesn't like visitors. And neither do we."

She didn't seem to notice what she'd said.

But I did.

The word hung there—*we*—like a thread pulled too far. Like a door left cracked just wide enough to see the light behind it.

"What do you mean, 'we'?"

Her fingers drifted—casual, careful—to the knife resting beside a small plate of pears.

Not like she had just decided to do it. Like she had been waiting for the right moment.

Her fingers curled around the handle, nails tapping once against the grain—like knocking on wood, like a superstition she didn't know she had.

The blade caught the dim kitchen light as she began slicing.
Press. Slide. Press. Slide.

Rhythmic. Practiced. Like a prayer. The wind rattled the windows. Betty inhaled, slow and measured.

"That Jean," she spoke into the blade. Almost fond. Almost sad. "She always finds someone, doesn't she? Thinkin' they're the one. You ever wonder why you never met them?" Betty smiled—too sweet. Too knowing.

"What are you saying? That the legend's true? That they all—"

"I'm saying boys like you always think you're different." Betty cut me off, "You think you can save her. You think she picked *you*." Betty tilted her head. "Tell me, William... have you ever wondered why it's always the ones like you?"

I blinked.

"The ones like me?"

"The ones about to run," Betty let out a low chuckle, shaking her head. "Always just about to leave. Pack up, vanish. And there she is, right when you're looking for something to hold on to."

A beat.

Betty's smile didn't falter.

"You think you're the first boy she's lured in?"

Press. Slide. Press. Slide.

"You're all the same," Betty said, and now her smile was gone. "All these pretty boys with broken parts. So full of longing. So easy to convince themselves it's love." she gazed back at me. "And I'm sure you think you love my daughter, don't you, William?"

I didn't flinch.

"That's a very strong word. *Love*."

"I know what I feel," I said, steady. "And with your permission, ma'am..."

I met her gaze. Didn't look away.

"I'd like to marry her."

CHAPTER TWENTY-FOUR

The knife never stopped. *Press. Slide.* The slices fell into neat, even crescents.

She didn't look up. Didn't acknowledge the words, not really.

Her lips curled—not quite a smile. Something else.

"She's very impressionable, you know. She listens too closely to people who shouldn't be speaking to her." *Press. Slide.* The slices stacked, even and perfect. "She gets... confused sometimes. Not that it's her fault. Her mind was always too soft for the world."

My jaw clenched.

The soft thud of the blade tapping against the cutting board filled the silence. A steady beat against the storm outside.

Betty sighed, shaking her head, like she was disappointed. Like I had already failed some unspoken test.

"She may not tell me things. Not everything. But I always find out, William. Always." she continued, tapping the flat of the blade against the wood. Once. Twice.

"Things about you. About the things you say to her. I don't

imagine you think much before you speak. But words linger. They grow in her head."

The air shifted. Heavy. Thick. The rain hit harder. The wind howled through the trees.

She flinched—so small I almost didn't catch it.

I did.

A weight settled in the room, pressing against my ribs.

"But I have eyes everywhere in this town. Depoe Bay's a small place. People notice things. And they tell me. They always do. And *you*, William, don't care about marriage. Don't care about love. All you want is to take her away from me. And what will happen then? If I let her go, she'll vanish like the others. You're just like the boys who've come before you. You come here full of dreams, thinking you know best. But you don't love her. You don't even see her for what she really is."

A muscle twitched in my jaw. "What do you—"

"I've watched you at the beach. During the moments she thought she was free." Her voice was soft. Too soft. "She plays pretend, poor thing. Pretends she's alone. Pretends I'm not watching."

She set the knife down.

"Freedom." She almost laughed. "People throw that word around like it's a gift. Like it's meant for everyone."

My fingers curled into fists in my lap.

"She says she's trapped. Says I've kept her locked away. But she forgets..."

Betty tilted her head slowly.

"She forgets what she did. What she cost this family. She forgets that it was *me* who kept her safe after all that."

Her words sat between us like a loaded gun.

Betty leaned in slightly, watching me, waiting. Her voice cracked —just barely.

"And she knows what would happen if people ever heard the truth."

She didn't blink.

"That's why she stays. Not because she has to. But because she *owes it* to me."

My breath caught in my throat, but I didn't let it show. Kept my face blank.

She was waiting for me to react.

If I gave her something, anything, she'd take it. She'd twist it, wrap it around my throat like a noose.

The thunder outside barely registered over the pounding in my ears.

Betty reached for the radio, her fingers whisping over the dial.

"Do you mind if I turn on the radio?" she asked sweetly. "The rain gets inside my head."

Click.

Static crackled to life, humming low, shifting, searching for a station.

"I can't stand storms anymore," she said, barely louder than the music.

"The night they told me Patrick wasn't coming home... it was raining. The sky never stopped crying." Betty smiled—just a little. The kind of smile that didn't need an answer. That didn't expect one. Then softer—almost a lullaby:

"That's when it all changed. That's when I started hearing the house breathe."

The storm outside howled, rattling the windowpanes. The radio hummed, warbling between frequencies, caught somewhere between the past and the present. And the knife sat between us on the cutting board, glinting under the flickering light.

She didn't wait.

The dial turned. Static pulsed and wavered, an aimless, drifting hum, like voices lost between stations. Searching. Trying to find something solid.

Then—music.

Midnight, the Stars and You.

Al Bowlly's voice slipped through the old speaker, mellow and golden, but wrong. Warbled. Slowed in some places, stretching too long before snapping back into time. Like it was trying to keep up and losing.

The melody drifted between us, soft and strange, the kind of song that belonged somewhere warm, somewhere safe. But here, in this dim, rotting kitchen, it felt like something else entirely. Like something playing in a dream you couldn't wake from.

Betty slid the plate of pears toward me. She claimed her seat once again at the table, her eyes never leaving mine.

"Jean never told you, did she?" Her voice was softer now. Heavier. "About Sandra. What she did."

I looked at the plate, then back at her. My fingers flexed in my lap, but I kept my mouth shut.

"Oh, don't go quiet now." Her smile barely moved. "Eat."

I hesitated.

She didn't blink.

"That's a mother's fruit, William. Picked from our tree. Grown with care. It won't bite unless you do."

I reached for a slice. It was warm against my fingertips, slick, almost slimy. A second too long in my grasp and I could swear it pulsed, like something still alive.

She watched me the whole time.

"My Sandra was eight years old," she said. "Only eight. Do you know what it's like to carry someone that small in your arms? To feel every heartbeat, every breath? You love her before she has a name. And then one day..."

She stopped, eyes flicking to the window. The rain hit harder.

"One day you come home and everything you've built has been torn down by your own child."

She looked at the plate. Her voice didn't rise, didn't break. It cracked in places, but never slipped.

"Jean says she was just a little girl. But little girls don't drown their sisters, do they?"

I gripped the edge of the table. Betty leaned in just slightly, her voice dipping low.

"I did everything right. I warned them about the tide. I kept the rules. I gave them everything."

Her hand drifted, slow, toward the edge of the table.

"Jean insisted Sandra didn't scream when it happened. Not once. I like to think she didn't suffer."

Betty's voice was almost tender now. Almost proud.

"She had such pretty hair. Jean stayed beside her all night, brushing it, like nothing had happened. Just humming that song I used to sing."

She smiled again—wistful, distant.

"And when I asked her... Jean looked me right in the eye and said, 'She's just sleeping.'"

Silence.

Betty's hand pressed flat to the wood.

"I pulled back the blanket, and the water had soaked through everything. Through the sheets, the mattress, the floor..."

She inhaled deeply. Slow. Controlled.

"...through my whole life."

A slow chill crawled down my spine.

The storm raged outside. The radio hummed, warbled, slowed.

Betty's eyes glassed over with something unreadable—grief, blame, something deeper. But her smile never wavered.

"But still, I would do anything for my children," she said. The words came soft, almost reverent. "A good mother does what's necessary. Even the hard things."

She didn't blink. Didn't flinch. Just kept watching me. "Especially if it means keeping them safe. Safe from people who don't understand what it means to protect someone."

The pear sat in my hand, untouched. A weight. A thing.

"Tell me," she murmured, tilting her head like she was admiring a photograph. "Can you really do that for Jean? Keep her safe?"

The rain tapped against the window. Betty's fingers twitched.

I saw it then.

She was holding herself together. She was trying not to look at it. Trying not to listen.

I swallowed hard, forcing my voice even. "I can only hope to do my best for her. I love her with all my heart."

Betty scoffed. "Your best?"

She leaned forward, just slightly, just enough for the light to catch the gleam in her eyes. Her smile looked practiced—something worn too often to mean anything.

"Tell me, William. Was that enough for Tony?"

A slow beat.

My blood turned to fire in my veins.

"You don't know—"

"Oh, but I do." Her voice was still soft. Still sweet. But colder now. "I know what boys like you leave behind. I know what happens when you promise and promise... and let go anyway."

She let that hang in the air.

"I tried my best too, you know. I did everything right. And when I came home that night..." Her eyes drifted toward the plate. Her voice didn't crack. But it wanted to. "...Sandra was already gone."

Tap. Tap. Tap.

A muscle twitched in her jaw.

She froze.

The tapping. The rain. The static.

Betty jerked her head toward the window, her fingers digging into the table, her breath caught somewhere between a sigh and a snarl.

Then—she roared.

"DON'T INTERRUPT ME WHEN I'M SPEAKING TO HIM!"

Her voice ripped through the air. Her hand slammed against the table. The thunder cracked, rattling the room.

My fingers felt numb as I placed the pear back onto the plate. My throat was dry, my pulse hammering in my ears. I suddenly felt like a child. Like I had done something wrong. Like I was the one being scolded. Then, she turned back to me.

"Jean is a dangerous girl, William." Betty's voice didn't waver. It was calm. Patient. Like a mother explaining why the family dog had to be put down. "She lies. She hurts people. She can't help herself."

She smiled faintly, not with joy—but with certainty.

"She's always known how to get what she wants. Even as a little girl. That kind of cunning doesn't go away."

The rain battered the windows harder. The radio warbled, a voice caught between songs. The room felt like it was listening.

"You think your love will save her? That you'll fix whatever's broken?" Betty tilted her head slightly. "Your best won't be enough. It never is. Not with girls like Jean."

The rain battered against the window. The radio whined in the background.

"God takes what He must. He doesn't care how hard you try. The truth always catches up." She tilted her head slightly, watching, waiting. Letting the weight of her words settle in. "So, tell me, William," she said, voice light, sweet, disturbingly casual. "Is that why you're here?"

A pause. Then, gently—

"To free her?"

The knife on the cutting board gleamed under the flickering light.

"To be her hero?"

Her fingers brushed the plate, tapping against the porcelain.

"Or has she already done it—made you believe you're the only one who's ever understood her? She's clever like that. Poor boys never stand a chance."

My throat was tight, but I forced the words out anyway.

"She's not a monster."

Betty didn't move. Didn't blink.

"You don't know her," I said, the words sharp-edged, carved from something deeper than anger. "You don't know what she dreams of.

Who she is to me. Who she's going to be one day. I just want to show her that there's more than this house. More than you."

A slow, measured inhale.

Betty's eyes softened. Just a fraction.

Almost pitying. Almost affectionate.

Outside, the storm cracked open the sky, lightning flashing white-hot through the window like a warning not to tell or a prompt to continue. The house trembled under the weight of it.

"You're still just a boy," she murmured. "Still trying to prove something." she said it like she was mourning something. Like she had already grieved me, long before I even stepped inside.

Another roll of thunder. Closer this time.

"You trust too easily," she said, shaking her head like she was looking at a child who hadn't yet learned the hard lesson. "You think love is just...wanting something bad enough."

The words dripped from her mouth like something spoiled. Something that had been sitting out too long, curdling in the open air.

She sighed, slow and deliberate, and suddenly the room felt too small, too close, the air thick and pressing down.

"Boys like you," she whispered. "You get swept up. You think you're choosing her. But it's the other way around."

A sharp pinch against my knee. My fingers dug into the fabric of my jeans before I even realized. A grounding instinct. A quiet, desperate need to stay upright.

And Betty—

She didn't blink.

She leaned forward slightly, voice quickening, curling tighter around the space between us.

"And she knows, William. She knows what happens to girls like her." A pause. Just long enough to sting. "The world either eats them whole... or lets them live long enough to wish it had."

There it was.

The way she said it.

The way her voice curled around the words, like something poisonous.

Like I had already lost.

Like this wasn't a conversation—just the slow, deliberate way a spider wraps silk around its prey.

"You're... wrong." The words barely made it past my lips. But I held her gaze.

Betty didn't move. Didn't breathe. For a second, the only sound was the static-soft hiss of the radio, Bowlly's voice stretched thin beneath it. The rain lashed against the window, beating hollow against the glass.

Then, slowly, Betty turned—her gaze sliding past me, past the table, past everything—settling on the window above the sink.

Beyond it, lightning shattered the sky.

Thunder slammed against the house, shaking the floor beneath me.

And then, she moved.

Fast.

"Fine! Don't listen. But don't say I didn't try to save you."

She grabbed the plate, her fingers white-knuckled around the porcelain. The sound of it shattering against the sink tore through the room, splintering through my skull.

She flipped the switch.

A grinding hum swallowed everything whole.

The garbage disposal screamed. Metal teeth clashed, snarled, tore. The air reeked—spoiled fruit, rust, something burnt that shouldn't be burning. The sound was too much, drilling into my skull, into my ribs, rattling the floor beneath my feet.

Then she reached for the knife.

No hesitation. No buildup. Just one clean motion—then another, and another. She brought the blade down hard, stabbing into the sink where the rotten pears sat piled like festering wounds. The first strike hit with a wet thunk. The second drove deeper. By the third, the fruit was gone—shredded pulp spinning into the drain, pulled into the grinding maw of the garbage disposal.

Betty watched it happen. Not frantic. Not angry. Just... watching. Like the mess had offended her, and now she was correcting it.

Her fingers tightened on the handle as the machine howled, loud and vicious beneath her hands. The noise swallowed everything— the thunder, the rain, even the old radio still warbling in the corner. The outside world didn't exist anymore. There was only the kitchen. Only her. Only that brutal, mechanical sound of destruction.

It got into me. The vibration of it traveled up through the floor-boards, crept into my legs, crawled up my spine. A raw, grinding shriek that didn't just sound hungry—it sounded like it knew how to chew through flesh.

My knee bounced under the table, my pulse hammering out of rhythm. I didn't even realize I was holding my breath until—

She flipped the switch.

Silence.

Betty didn't move. Just leaned forward against the counter, arms braced on either side of the sink. The overhead light buzzed faintly above her, painting her in pale, flickering color.

She stood there. Completely still. Like she was listening for something.

Or like something was listening for her.

I couldn't take my eyes off her hands. One gripped the edge of the sink. The other still clutched the knife, juice running down her fingers, dripping onto the floor.

Then she breathed in—slow, sharp, like it hurt. Her hand slid up across her face, wiping away the sweat or the juice or maybe nothing at all. I couldn't tell. The radio hissed, caught in static.

She let the breath out and smoothed the front of her dress, quiet, methodical. Like she was getting ready for company.

When she turned to me, her smile was calm. Too calm. The kind of smile you wear at a dinner party, when you're about to serve dessert.

"If you'll excuse me," she said sweetly, "the rain brought Patrick home again. I don't like to keep him waiting."

The knife was still in her hand.

She moved toward the back door without another word. The wind outside slammed against the walls, howling through the cracks like it was begging to be let in. The radio warbled, catching for a moment on a distorted line of music before slipping again into chaos.

The door creaked open.

And the storm took her.

The wind rushed inside like a scream, swallowing the room whole.

I didn't move. Couldn't. My heart was thudding against my ribs, my fingers twitching against my knee. The rain hit the roof harder now, urgent and deafening, as if the house itself knew something was about to snap.

Then finally—I breathed.

And I knew.

This was my chance.

CHAPTER TWENTY-FIVE

The wind rattled the house, low and guttural, a bone-deep groan slipping through the walls. It was the kind of sound that got under your skin, crawled right up your spine like a bad feeling you couldn't shake. The radio still hummed in the background, its warbled melody stretching thin over the silence, barely clinging to life. But Betty was gone.

For now.

I didn't move right away.

I listened.

The house breathed—settling, shifting, stretching itself into place like an old man cracking his joints. But the back door didn't creak. The wind didn't carry her voice. The rain did, though—hammering against the roof, seeping into the walls, filling up the spaces she left behind.

Now or never.

I pushed back from the table. Slowly. Quietly. The chair wobbled beneath me, one uneven leg tapping soft against the linoleum. Too loud. Way too loud. My pulse was in my throat now, knocking hard like it was trying to break out of my skin. I clenched my jaw, swallowed it down, forced myself to move.

"Jean?"

I whispered her name, barely more than breath. Just a test. A sound sent out into the dark.

The house didn't whisper back.

I moved forward, keeping to the edges of the room, my steps careful, avoiding the warped parts of the floor that might groan beneath my weight. The air was stale, thick with mildew and something else—something older, something deeper. The kind of scent that made you think of locked doors and things left too long in the dark.

The hall stretched ahead of me, long and narrow, the kind of dark that felt full. Like it wasn't just empty space, but something solid.

I didn't turn on the lights.

Couldn't.

Instead, I crept forward, the storm outside throwing jagged shadows across the peeling wallpaper. Deep clawed streaks marred the paneling. Some were small—fingernails dragging, slow and deliberate. Others were deeper, rougher, frantic. The kind of marks someone makes when they're not thinking about it. When they're just trying to get out.

My throat tightened.

"Jean? Where are you?"

Another whisper. Another silence.

The first door on my left was cracked open just enough. Not wide enough to see inside, not closed enough to keep me out. I pressed my fingers against the wood, gave it a slow push. It creaked, long and low, a sound that settled right in my chest.

A bedroom. Small. Cramped.

The mattress sagged in the center, the sheets thrown back in a mess, like someone had been yanked from them in a hurry. The air was thick, dust swirling in the dim light, caught in the edges of the storm's glow through the nailed-up windows. Not boarded—nailed.

Violently, desperately. Someone had needed them to stay closed. The rusted heads stuck out at odd angles, biting deep into the wood. No way in. No way out.

A sewing machine sat against the far wall, old and black, the kind that looked like it weighed a hundred pounds and could crush your foot if you looked at it wrong. The chair beside it had been pushed back slightly, like someone had left in the middle of something, like they meant to come back. A scrap of fabric lay folded next to it, half-stitched, the thread still caught in the needle.

This must've been it. Jean's room I exhaled slowly, the sound getting lost in the thick air.

The closet door was open just enough to show the row of dresses inside—identical, muted colors, perfectly pressed. Jean's whole wardrobe, lined up like museum pieces. The fabrics were soft creams, pale blues, faded yellows. Styles that didn't belong in 1962. They weren't new, but they weren't worn. Not the way clothes should be. Not the way Jean should've been allowed to wear them.

My fingers brushed over a sleeve, the fabric smooth, untouched.

A needle was still threaded through the hem, the stitching incomplete.

She hadn't finished it.

Or she hadn't been allowed to.

I took a step back.

Everything in here felt like her. And God help me, I wanted to hold on to every last piece—even the painful ones.

A few books were scattered near the bed, some stacked against the wall, others lying open, their pages curling at the edges like they'd been left too close to something damp. The spines were cracked, the covers frayed, worn soft from too much handling.

I crouched, reached for the closest one. My fingers brushed over the cover, the fabric stretched thin at the edges, the kind of soft that only comes from being held too many times.

Inside the front cover, a name.

Jean.

Small, careful, deliberate—the kind of handwriting you have when you're still figuring out how letters are supposed to sit next to each other.

Then, beneath the book, something else.

Something half-hidden under the pile.

A photo.

I picked it up. It was old, but not ancient. The kind of thing you'd expect to find tucked between the pages of a forgotten book, not left out in the open. Not just lying here, waiting to be seen.

Jean, maybe four years old, stood in the center, small and uncertain, her hands curled into tiny fists at her sides. Beside her, another girl, a little older—Sandra.

And then—two more kids.

A boy and a girl, standing just slightly apart, like they hadn't quite been part of the picture but had ended up in it anyway. Or maybe like someone had let them be there, but only just.

I flipped it over, my thumb catching on the worn edge. On the back, in faded ink:

Jeanie (4) - Sandra (8) - Anthony (4) - Pauline (3)

I stared at the names.

Tony. Polly. Christ. It's the missing photo.

The air inside the room pressed a little heavier, thick and unmoving.

I flipped the photo back over, running my eyes over the faces again, slower this time. Jean, looking straight into the camera, wide-eyed, mouth slightly open—caught mid-breath, mid-thought, mid-something. Sandra, standing taller, one arm wrapped tight around her sister's shoulders. Like a shield. Like a promise. The shell necklace still dangling around her neck. The other two, Polly—Tony—grinning, loose and easy, like he was having fun. *He never changed a day.* My eyes began to well. *Her name wasn't Jenny, but damn, you were close.* I took a breath, continuing like it was a prayer. *I'm just... glad you really got to meet her, buddy. Thank you for being our friend.*

A tear rolled down my cheek as I turned to Polly's expression, caught between a smile and something else. Something less certain. *And I'm sorry, Pol. I should've been there for you. I just didn't know how.*

The wind rattled the house, shaking the nailed-down window behind me. The photo suddenly felt too thin in my hand, too fragile, like it could crumple just from me holding it. Like it didn't want to be looked at too closely.

I slid it into my jacket pocket gently, then moved on.

The wind groaned against the walls.

The storm pressed in, slipping through the cracks in the foundation, thick and waiting, like something holding its breath.

"Jean?"

A whisper.

Still no answer.

My pulse picked up as I turned, slipping back into the hall.

Across from Jean's room was another door. Even before I touched the handle, I knew.

Sandra's room.

The air was different here. Still. Like stepping inside meant stepping into something else, something sacred. A monument. Or a tomb.

I pushed the door open, slow and careful, and the scent of dust and rotting fabric pressed thick against my tongue. The room was untouched—preserved, frozen in time, like someone had built a shrine and then walked away.

An old radiator was rusted beside the door. Dolls lined the shelves. Their glassy eyes caught the dim light, their lips frozen in tiny, unmoving smiles. The kind of smiles that didn't reach their eyes. Some were missing hands, others their eyes. One lay discarded on the dresser, its body curled unnaturally, its head tilted toward the ceiling, mouth slightly open.

I exhaled through my teeth.

The bed was too small. Too small for someone who should've outgrown it.

The blankets were still neatly tucked, the pillow untouched. But the mattress sagged toward the center, dark water stains spreading from underneath, bleeding outward. Some of them looked fresh.

I took a step back. The window beside me rattled, and my breath caught—

Betty.

She was outside, standing on the porch, barely illuminated by the storm.

She wasn't looking at me. She wasn't looking at anything.

Her lips moved—whispering. Talking. But no one was there. No one I could see.

The wind howled through the trees, tugging at her dress, sending the hem fluttering against her legs like something trying to pull her back inside. Like something trying to keep her from leaving.

She didn't move. Didn't flinch. Just kept talking, her lips forming words I couldn't hear, her fingers twitching at her sides like they were itching to hold something.

I blinked.

She was gone.

My breath left me in a slow, unsteady drag.

Move.

I tore myself from the window and slipped back into the hallway, my steps faster now. I didn't stop at the other doors. Couldn't.

But Jean had to be there.

I hurried back to the kitchen.

The lights flickered overhead, buzzing, casting deep shadows against the stained walls. The radio still played—faint, distant, its song unraveling like it was struggling to keep up.

And Betty—

Betty was standing in the center of the room.

The knife in her hand.

The air between us tightened, thickened, wrapped itself around my throat.

She smiled.

"Now, William... what exactly do you think you're doing?"

CHAPTER TWENTY-SIX

The house felt wrong, obsessed. The storm rattled the windows, the back door slamming open and shut behind Betty, rain sweeping in across the floor. The wind carried in the smell of wet earth, salt, something sharp and rotting beneath it.

And she stood there. Soaked to the skin. Hair plastered to her face, eyes sharp and glassy in the flickering kitchen light. Her dress clung to her legs like seaweed, twisted and heavy with water. And in her hand—

The knife.

It caught the light just right. Steel flashed like lightning.

But she didn't flinch. Didn't shiver. She just stood there. Watching me.

"Oh... you were looking for her, weren't you?"

Her voice barely rose above the wind, but it cut straight through me.

I swallowed. Forced my hands to stay still.

"Betty," I said, steady. "Where is she?"

She didn't blink. Didn't breathe. Just took a step forward. Slow.

Careful. Like the house was hers now and I was the stranger trespassing in something sacred.

"Still trying to save her?" the words slithered out, soft and knowing. Like they already knew they were going to win.

My chest tightened.

"She's here somewhere, I know it. You locked her somewhere."

Betty exhaled, low and patient, like a mother talking to a child
who just wouldn't understand. "I'm keeping her safe, William."

I took a step back. The kitchen creaked beneath us, the air thick
as wet wool, hard to swallow.

"You're depriving her of everything," I said. "A life. Friends.
Memories. Sunlight." My voice caught. "How is that saving her?"

Betty's fingers flexed on the handle of the knife.

"She's alive, isn't she? Because of me. I was her whole world. Her
mother. Her protector. And still—she ran. That's what girls like her
do. You give them everything, and they spit it right back."

Her other hand twitched—some little muscle pulling at the air
like it wanted to strike too.

My stomach twisted. "What about the doctor?"

That got her.

A flicker. A pulse behind her eyes.

The rain roared through the open door, flooding the kitchen with
the smell of sea salt.

"Dr. Parker," I said again, louder now. "His kids. Jean used to play
with them. You remember that?"

I pulled the photo from my pocket, holding it up between us like
a shield.

Betty tilted her head. Her mouth curled. Not a smile. Not really.

"Oh, that picture. She was such a darling little thing, wasn't she?
Always smiling for strangers."

The knife gleamed again.

I could feel the pulse in my neck. Too fast. Too loud.

She looked at the picture, not like it meant something—but like
it used to. Her gaze drifted, unfocused for a second.

"You used to let her out. Be free. What happened? You said you like small talk. How is Dr. Parker tied up in this?"

Betty laughed. Low. Dry. Not like something was funny. Like I was.

"If you really want to know," she murmured, "this was his idea."

The house groaned like it heard her. Or like it didn't like what she said.

"What do you mean?" I asked.

But her smile only widened.

Lightning split across the sky outside.

It lit her up from behind—made her silhouette show through her nightgown.

"He helped me." She said it like she was proud. Like it was a favor. "I called him. That night. After I found my Sandra." Her eyes clouded, but her voice didn't waver. "There was nothing left to do. She was cold. Still. He looked her over, said it was trauma. That maybe it was a rock, maybe something else—but it didn't matter."

My throat closed up, like the storm had crept inside me. "And Jean?" I forced out.

Betty's eyes narrowed. She exhaled through her nose, sharp, tired, like I was some slow student who couldn't follow the lesson.

"Oh, she told him everything. Like she was proud of it. Like she didn't even understand what she'd done."

I felt it in my gut. Like I'd been punched.

The storm shoved harder against the house—wind rattling the windowpanes, the screen door banging like something trying to get in.

"So, you begged him," I muttered.

Betty smiled. "I did. I begged." she admitted.

And then—

Her expression cracked. Just barely. Just enough to let something darker crawl through.

"You think I wanted this? You think I had a choice?" she said. The words curled at the edges, sharper now. Bitter. Her grip on the knife shifted, knuckles paling around the handle. "I lost Patrick overseas. Then Sandra. I couldn't lose her too. Not Jean. She was all I had left."

The sentence hit the air like a snapped bone.

She smoothed her hands down the front of her dress, slow, deliberate. Rain dripped from her sleeves, spattering against the tile.

"Dr. Parker knew what it would do to me," she murmured.

The screen door banged again. The wind clawed at the frame.

"So, he helped."

My stomach dropped. My pulse climbed up my throat. "How?"

She didn't blink. Just smiled. That same flat, saccharine smile that never quite reached her eyes.

"He signed the papers. Said he'd take care of it. No one asked questions, except that pesky funeral director." she said. "But I took care of it all. His widow was more than understanding."

The words dug under my skin.

"You ever wonder why there wasn't a funeral?" she asked, like it had only just occurred to her. Like she was letting me in on a joke I was too slow to catch.

"There was a funeral," I said, too fast. "I was there—"

But even as the words left my mouth, I wasn't sure anymore.

Betty shook her head. Her voice dropped lower, warmer. The kind of warmth that burns.

"No, sweetheart." she said. "There was a sermon. A headstone. A few old pictures in a box." She tilted her head. Her wet hair clung to her cheek, limp and stringy. "But no body."

I couldn't breathe.

"No Sandra. No Jean." she said. "Just a story to keep the town quiet."

The house swayed with the wind. The walls seemed to breathe in quiet gasps. The air felt wet in my lungs.

My voice scraped out, raw. "So, what, Dr. Parker forged the death certificate, and that's why everyone thinks she's really gone?"

Betty's smile widened like she'd been waiting for me to catch up. "Exactly. No one asked any questions until poor Mr. Boyle got in the way. That's why she can never leave, William," she whispered. "Everyone who pries into our lives just keeps... disappearing."

I could feel it—something coiling beneath the floor, in the walls, in the air itself.

"Believe me, Jean's dangerous." She hissed. "A bad omen."

Betty shifted her weight. The knife caught the light.

And her voice—

soft, steady, sweet as poison—

"She belongs here."

The storm screamed behind her.

"With me."

Her eyes locked onto mine.

"And now..."

She took a step.

"...so do you."

She moved before I even saw her.

One second she was standing there—knife in hand, storm behind her—

and the next—

She burst forward.

Not stumbling. Not screaming. Just full-speed fury. Sprinting like she'd already made peace with the end of it.

The knife caught the light, bright and sudden. A flash of silver in the dark, a slash of rain-lit steel cutting through the air like it had been waiting its whole life for this exact moment.

She was coming for me.

I didn't think. Didn't plan. There wasn't time.

My hands went up—reflex, not reason. A move to survive, not fight.

The chair between us wasn't strategy. It was instinct. Panic with legs.

I shoved it forward. It scraped loud against the linoleum, crying out like it didn't want to be part of this either.

She hit it square, arms out, dress soaked and clinging, hair plastered across her face.

It didn't stop her. Didn't even slow her down.

But it bought me a breath.

One.

And that's all I needed.

I grabbed her wrist mid-swing—

just as the knife came in low.

The blade caught in the light, trembling between us. Inches. Maybe less. Close enough that I could feel the cold of it. Smell the metal.

Betty didn't flinch. Didn't jerk back. She just held her ground, arm locked like iron. Her breath hit my neck. Hot. Sharp. "She's my baby, William. And I won't let anyone take her from me. Not again." She wasn't yelling. She wasn't pleading. She was promising.

Her whole body shook. Not from fear. Not even from anger. From effort. From grit. From holding back a wave that had been building in her bones for years.

I pushed back. Hands tight around her wrist. Fingers aching.

The knife wobbled. Tilted. Jerked.

An inch forward, and it would split my throat wide. An inch back, and it'd carve hers.

And she knew it.

She wanted me to know it too.

The rain crashed through the broken door behind her, turning the floor into something slick and glassy. Wind screamed through the kitchen, raking its fingers along the walls.

And we stood in the middle of it—me and her, locked together. Still. Like statues. Like this was what the house had been building toward all along.

Her breath came sharp and wet and alive, her chest heaving, but her eyes never moved, locked on mine.

This wasn't about fury. Or grief. Or revenge.

This was certainty.

This was a mother doing what she thought had to be done.

A final move in a game I hadn't even known I was playing.

And somehow—

Somehow, I knew—

I was exactly where I was always meant to be.

Right here. Right now.

Trapped in the ribs of this dying house, with a woman who was ready to bleed for a lie.

The knife shook in her hand. In my hand. Between us.

The whole world narrowed to that blade.

And the sick, sinking truth that I might not be able to stop it.

CHAPTER TWENTY-SEVEN

I didn't think.

There wasn't time to.

It wasn't courage, wasn't strategy. It was instinct—the kind that lives in your gut and breaks things before you even realize you're moving. One second she was bearing down on me with that knife like she meant to carve the truth out of my ribs, and the next—

I shoved her.

Hard.

My shoulder hit her midsection with a sick kind of force, enough to lift her slightly off the ground. Enough to break something that had been building between us from the moment I walked into this house.

The knife caught my jacket on the way out—split through the leather like paper, kissed my ribs just long enough to remind me it could've been worse.

Betty reeled back, arms flailing, bare feet sliding on the linoleum. Fingers reaching for purchase, for something solid.

There was nothing.

She hit the counter with a thud that echoed wrong. Her body folded, a shape no human should make.

And then—

Crack.

Her head hit the corner of the overhead cabinet. Sharp. Sudden.

A wet sound. The kind that doesn't echo. The kind that sticks.

Something in my chest pulled tight.

She dropped.

Like a puppet with every string cut at once. Arms and legs bent wrong. Her dress soaked from the rain. Her hair matted to her cheek.

And then—

Stillness.

The storm roared through the open door behind me, howling like it had a name, slamming wind and rain into the kitchen, demanding to be seen. But inside—

Nothing moved.

I couldn't breathe. Couldn't think.

I watched her chest, waiting for it to rise, waiting for something, anything—

But all I saw was the ghost of a breath. Then even that disappeared.

The wind hit the back door again. Slammed it open. Slammed it shut. Over and over. A warning. A threat. A heartbeat.

Open. Shut. Open. Shut.

The sound filled the house. Swallowed it. Swallowed me.

The walls groaned. The floor beneath her was slick with water, rain pooling around her body, climbing the tiles like it meant to drag her down with it. Like the house was trying to bury her. Or keep her.

Everything twisted.

My knees buckled. I grabbed the counter to stay upright. My vision tunneled, the corners of the room curving in like I was inside the mouth of something much bigger than this place. My hands wouldn't stop shaking.

I took a step back. Then another.

Her limbs didn't move. Her eyes didn't flutter.

I should've checked. Should've done something.

Instead, I stood there. Useless. Breathing too hard. Listening to the sound of the storm rip the world apart.

And then—

A new sound.

Faint. Wrong. Pounding.

Not thunder. Not the storm.

Inside.

I turned, heart climbing up my throat, scraping past my voice box, demanding to be let out.

BANG.

Again.

BANG. BANG.

Somewhere deep in the house.

I stumbled forward, legs numb. Past the counter. Through the narrow kitchen door.

The house didn't feel like a house anymore. It was alive. It was breathing.

I could feel it shifting around me—old wood groaning, wallpaper peeling at the corners like it wanted to whisper something, like it had been waiting to exhale.

The pounding again.

Closer now.

Steady. Desperate.

Like someone had been knocking this whole time, and I'd only just started to listen.

I didn't call out. Didn't ask who it was. I already knew. And I ran.

MY BOOTS HIT the floor hard, too loud in a space that wanted quiet. The storm was trying to get in through every crack. The house was trying to keep something in.

The pounding didn't stop. It only got louder. A tempo. A signal.

Like the house was telling me where to go. Like it wanted me to find her. Or maybe... it just wanted me to see.

I moved fast—

Past doors that didn't feel like doors. Past wallpaper that curled like old skin.

The hallway breathed with me. No, against me. Walls bending inward, pressing down, like the whole house was leaning in to listen.

The pounding kept going—sloppy, uneven, desperate.

The door at the end looked wrong. Too swollen, like it had been drinking from the walls for years. Black veins ran up the sides, the wood so warped it barely fit the frame anymore. The brass knob had rusted down to a dark, angry red.

Not a door.

A barrier.

I reached for it anyway.

Tried the knob.

Nothing. Didn't even wiggle. Of course not. Then—

BANG.

The door jumped in the frame. The sound hit me like static—loud, sudden, familiar. Not just noise. Something buried under it.

"Will—"

Her voice.

Jean.

My body locked. That voice cracked me open from the inside.

"Jean!"

I braced my feet, threw my shoulder into the door. It thudded, heavy and solid, but didn't move.

"Move back!" I shouted.

I didn't even know if she could hear me. Didn't care. Again. Harder this time.

The hinges cried out. The lock groaned.

And the third time—

SNAP.

The door cracked open like a wound. It bled darkness. The air behind it wasn't just stale. It was thick. Muggy. The kind of air you find in the belly of something that's been digesting you for years.

I stepped inside.

The rot clung to the walls. Black mold bloomed up from the base-boards. Everything glistened like it was sweating. Breathing.

The cellar was flooding. Stormwater pooled from the hatch outside, crawling in slow waves over the stone foundation like the house was drinking itself to death.

The steps bowed under my weight. I heard them creak—not like wood. Like bones.

And then—

She was there.

Jean. Standing in water up to her thighs, soaked to the bone. Her dress floated around her like seaweed in the brine, her hair sticking to the sweat on her face. She once told me she'd never felt seen. But I saw her. And God, she made me want to be seen too.

The moment her eyes locked on me, she bolted. Like she thought the moment would vanish if she didn't get to me fast enough.

I jumped the last three steps and landed in the water with a splash that echoed like a scream. Cold hit me fast. Sharp. I wrapped my arms around her, holding her tight.

"Jean." It cracked out of me. Not a name. A prayer. Like I could speak her into being real.

She clung to my jacket, but something in her hesitated. Like she wasn't sure if I was real either. Like I might disappear the second she looked away.

"Will," she breathed. "How—how did you know where to find me? That she locked me down here?"

I wanted to tell her everything. About Polly. The doctor. The lies. But she was already standing in too much. So I lied. Sort of. I smirked —crooked, useless. Forced it into my face like it belonged there.

"We swapped addresses, remember?" I made it sound like a joke. Like something normal.

Jean let out a breath that wasn't relief. But close. Then her voice dropped. Tight. Careful.

"Where's my mother?"

She already knew. I could hear it in the way she asked. Not scared. Not sad. Just... ready.

Her fingers clutched at me, but looser now.

I hesitated. Should've told her it didn't matter. Should've told her we didn't have time. But I knew. And she did too. So I said the only thing I could.

"Jean... we need to go."

Her eyes flicked past me, back toward the hallway, like she could still feel her there. Betty. Soaked into the walls. Breathed into the wallpaper. The house wasn't empty—it just wasn't speaking yet.

"She tried to stop me," I said.

Jean's breath caught mid-throat.

"She—she came at me with a knife, Jean."

Her fingers locked around my arm. Tight. Desperate. Like if she held on long enough, she could stop the world from moving.

Her voice broke apart trying to hold itself together. "Is she—?"

I shook my head, jaw clenched so hard it hurt.

"I don't know. I didn't—I didn't stay to check."

Her face twisted—something between relief and horror—like she didn't know which one she was supposed to feel first.

She squeezed harder. "You weren't supposed to be here," she whispered. "I—I didn't want you to see this. I tried to meet you at the beach, but she—"

"It's alright, Jean. I'm here." It came out sharp. Fractured. Shaky. "After you didn't show, I—I wasn't gonna let you disappear."

I didn't even know I was trembling until she gripped my hand like she could feel it too.

Then she looked at me. Really looked at me. Like she hadn't let herself until now. And something behind her eyes flickered.

This was it. I could feel it.

Maybe she'd let me carry her out. Maybe we could crawl out of this thing still whole—just cracked around the edges.

I turned. Pulled her with me. One step. Two.

And then—

The air changed. Heavy. Cold. Like something old had woken up behind the walls.

Jean went still. Her breath caught and stayed there. Frozen.

"Jean?"

She didn't answer. Just gasped—

And slipped.

Gone.

The water took her like it had been waiting. No splash. Just silence and then chaos.

Her hand vanished from mine. Her scream barely made it out before the water ripped her under.

"Jean!" I dropped. No thinking, just instinct—shoved into the black. The cold punched up my spine. My breath went tight.

Then—

Her hand. A flicker. Fingers breaking the surface like a flare. Then yanked back down.

I caught her wrist. Just barely.

She was thrashing, panicked, the water rolling over her.

"Hold on!" I barked. My grip slick, my arms burning.

She didn't say anything. Couldn't. Her eyes were wide, unfocused. Something had her.

Her dress was twisted tight, yanked hard in the dark.

Snagged on something.

I forced myself to look, to plunge my head under the murky water.

But what I saw—

Had been waiting for her longer than either of us could've known.

CHAPTER TWENTY-EIGHT

My pulse blew open behind my eyes.

I grabbed the back of Jean's collar, fingers locking in soaked fabric, twisting hard, yanking like my life depended on it. The fabric tore with a sound I don't ever wanna hear again. Like paper. Like skin.

She broke the surface with a gasp that cut the air clean in half, hair slicked down to her cheeks, her eyes wild, mouth open like she couldn't believe she was breathing again.

And then something followed her up.

Dragging behind.

Rising.

Wrong.

A hand.

Brittle and pale, warped from the water, bones exposed through what little flesh was left. The fingers clawed mindlessly at the hem of her dress, tangled in old threads and the limp clump of what might've once been hair.

It didn't know what it was doing. That was the worst part.

It wasn't a monster with teeth or claws or hunger. It wasn't even alive. It was just... reaching. Not out of anger. Not out of need.

Just memory.

Jean spun, saw it, and the scream that ripped from her throat hit like shrapnel. Her leg shot out, kicking hard—once—twice—until her heel connected with the wrist.

The bone snapped like driftwood.

The hand vanished with a splash that sounded too loud, like the house didn't want us to break the silence.

Gone.

Not defeated. Not gone for good.

Just... gone.

The cellar shifted, like the house had sucked in air through its teeth. The water slapped against the beams in lazy pulses. The smell twisted up from beneath the surface—wet dirt, old mildew, something sour that lived where light didn't.

Jean stood still. Frozen. Her eyes on the water.

So were mine.

It shifted again. Just enough.

And then we saw it.

Small. Fragile.

A body floated up in slow motion, like it wasn't ready to be seen. Like it had forgotten it was supposed to stay hidden.

The ribs were curled inward, collapsed like a hand clenched too tight. The skull—half-gone—angled toward us, hollow where the eyes used to be.

And there, still clinging to bone, was a necklace.

A cheap little seashell charm.

Jean's hand slipped out of mine. She backed up—slow at first, then fast. Her heel skidded. Her fingers went to her mouth like she was trying to keep something in, but her breath broke through anyway.

I pulled her toward me. Held her.

She didn't react. Didn't move. Didn't even see me. She was somewhere else now.

"No..." she whispered. Not a scream. Not a question. Just... realization.

I didn't ask. Didn't need to.

Sandra.

She was still here. Still in this house. Still beneath her mother's feet.

The storm outside rattled the beams, but in here, it was quiet. The kind of quiet that hums in your ears. That creeps between your ribs. That waits.

The house felt like it was listening.

Watching.

Holding its breath.

I remembered something dumb—something from English class. Some line about how houses could rot from the inside. How grief could crawl through the wood like termites, hollowing everything out until there's nothing left but walls pretending they still hold anything up.

Back then I thought it was just a metaphor. But this place? This place wasn't haunted. It was sick. Starving. And Jean had been sleeping above its open mouth.

I looked at her—really looked at her—and tried to understand how she'd done it. How she'd lived here. How she breathed with bones just below her feet.

Unless—

She didn't know.

Or worse—

She did.

I reached for her hand.

It was cold. Trembling. Like she wasn't fully in her body anymore. Like her skin was holding her in place while everything else tried to disappear.

"We need to go," I said. Voice low. Even. Trying not to shake.

She nodded, but not really. Just muscle memory. Just a flicker of movement like her brain hadn't caught up to her legs yet.

Then—

I heard it.

Not loud. Not clear.

Just... there.

A whisper, thin as breath, underneath the floor.

Jean froze.

Her grip crushed into mine. Bone on bone.

The air thickened, turned heavy, damp—like it was exhaling through wet teeth. Every wall felt like it was sweating. The cellar started to feel too small. Too deep. Too alive.

We stood frozen in water that lapped at our sides. The dark held its breath. The storm had teeth again.

And then I heard it clearer.

Dripping.

Soft. Incessant. Not from inside—From everywhere.

Jean turned her head, eyes locked on the far wall.

The cellar door was sealed shut. Braced. Barred. But the hinges had started to bleed. Water leaked through, slow and steady. Like it had all the time in the world.

Drip.

Drip.

Drip.

But then—

Crack.

The house groaned. A low, animal sound. Like something deep beneath the floor rolled over in its sleep.

Then the flood came faster.

The storm clawed in through the stonework. Rain shoved through the seams. The foundation started to sweat rivers. Water bleeding from the mortar like the house had opened a vein.

Jean gasped. Stepped back too fast. She slipped into me, her fingers digging into my arm.

"Will—" she said, but her voice collapsed under the weight of it.

Because something else had surfaced.

No splash. No warning.

A second body.

Then another. And another.

The water kept rising. Thick and black and filled with too much memory. It crawled up the walls. Seeped down the stairs. The house let out another long moan—bones flexing, breath hitching like it was about to be sick.

"Up," I snapped, grabbing Jean and turning her toward the steps. "Now!"

She scrambled ahead, fingers clawing at the rail, feet slipping on wet wood.

I followed, water pushing my stomach, swallowing the steps in front of me.

But something bumped against my back.

I spun—

Another body. Male. Gray. Green. Bloated. Hair like seaweed drifting in the tide. Lips peeled back. Cheeks caved in. Teeth bared, like it was smiling. Or screaming. Dog tags were still around his neck, swinging like he was still breathing.

His mouth opened—

And a tooth floated out.

Drip. Drip.

I choked, scrambled higher, pushing past him. I caught up with Jean at the top of the stairs, standing beside where she'd stopped at the landing.

She stared down at the water, frozen.

Then I saw it too.

All of them.

The boy with the boat—skin bloated, fingers curled, a floating keychain still wrapped around his wrist. The boardwalk worker—his belly ballooned, jaw split, sunglasses somehow still hanging from a torn ear.

The water was full of them.

Floating. Watching. Eyes gone, but gazing up at us.

Jean backed up against the doorway, her arms tight at her sides, her knees locked. "I—I told him to help me," she whispered, her voice barely hers. Her eyes bounced from body to body, panic filling her like a scream she couldn't let out.

"Jean—don't tell me—"

"It's all of them," she cut me off. "All the boys who came before you." Her voice cracked. "They're all here."

Another hand surfaced, palm up. A wedding ring was still on its finger—tarnished black, clinging to a bone-white finger like a curse.

I felt my throat close. "You're telling me the story was real?! That it's all true?!" My voice cracked like ice. "You told me I was the first! Jean—how many were there?!"

Her whole body shook. Like the truth wouldn't stop coming out. "I don't know!" she cried. "I didn't know— I thought they didn't believe me. I thought they left—"

The water hit the second to last step. It didn't rise slowly anymore. It climbing, charging forward.

This house wasn't just filling. It was vomiting.

Coughing up everything it had swallowed.

Everything it tried to bury.

I grabbed her hand again—tight. Too tight.

"We have to go."

"Will—Do... do people know?" Her voice cracked. "About this? About them? Why didn't anyone—why didn't anybody stop her?"

I looked her in the eye. Didn't flinch. Didn't blink.

"People knew," I said. "The town. The doctor. Everyone." The words tasted like rust. Like something I should've choked on. "They buried it in folklore and called it a ghost story."

Jean's breath caught in her throat. She didn't speak. Didn't even nod. Just stood there, trembling, her breath coming in shallow bursts like her lungs were trying to bolt without the rest of her.

"This is..." she started, voice cracking. "This is all my fault."

I opened my mouth, but the house answered first. A deep, shuddering groan echoed through the walls, like the trembling of an earthquake. But it was something deeper. Like the place itself was protesting. This place was alive and it didn't want to let go.

Somewhere behind the foundation, a rock shifted. Then—*pop*. A wet, unnatural sound, like something inside the walls had given way. Then, a fresh stream of water burst through the far side of the cellar, cutting a line across the wall like the house had split an artery. The water poured in, fast, messy, bleeding into the cellar with a hiss.

Behind us, the dim light filtering form the kitchen flickered. Once. Twice. Then went black, plunging us in total darkness.

A moment later, lightning flared through the windows—blinding, white-hot. For a second, the whole world froze under it. I saw the swollen stairs, the water climbing, the bloated corpses bobbing like rotten apples, their empty sockets catching the flash.

Then thunder. So loud it rattled the walls.

And beneath that—beneath the storm and the rain and the hum in my ears—I heard something else. Something that didn't belong.

It wasn't just sound. It was weight. A presence. The kind of noise you don't hear with your ears, not really. You feel it in your ribs, your teeth, your spine. And Jean felt it too.

Her body went rigid in my hands, her pulse hammering like a warning. Her head turned slowly, eyes searching the dark.

There was a shuffle.

Not the storm. Not the house settling. Something deliberate. Something heavy. Dragging.

Jean gasped—just a breath, sharp and afraid.

I squeezed her arm as something shifted behind us in the dark. Not quickly. Not slowly. Just steady. Like it didn't need to rush.

And I swear to God, it felt like the house was holding its breath.

Whatever had been waiting in the quiet all these years?

It wasn't quiet anymore.

It took a step. Then one more. Wet. Muffled.
Then—
It ran.

CHAPTER TWENTY-NINE

The glint of a blade swung for my throat in the darkness.

I ducked on instinct, but not fast enough. The flat of the knife caught the side of my head, fast and sharp—like lightning slicing skin. Betty's body hit mine like a wave, and we crashed into the wall. Something cracked. Could've been bone, could've been the house. Either way, it hurt.

"Get your filthy hands off my daughter!" she screamed, and it sounded like the storm had crawled down her throat. Wet, jagged. Static crackling in her lungs.

My boots slipped across the flooded floor as we struggled. We slammed into the plaster again, and I swear I felt the house flinch. Her breath hit my cheek—hot, heavy, and feral.

Then her knee came up, hard and fast. It caught my ribs just right, knocking the wind clean out of me. For a second, I couldn't breathe. Couldn't even swear.

Her nails raked across my cheek, tearing skin. My vision swam.

I swung—reflex. A wild punch that caught her forearm, knocking the knife from her grip and onto the floor with a sharp clatter as it skidded out of reach.

My chest heaved.

"Jean!" I rasped. "Get out of here! Run!"

But the dark didn't answer. No voice, no footsteps. Just that thick, creeping black that swallowed everything in the room. It wasn't night anymore—it was something else. Something heavier. Something hungry.

Betty crashed into me again, knocking me backward. I hit the floor hard. The boards groaned, something beneath them cracking. Maybe the house. Maybe me.

Her weight dropped onto my chest, pressing the air out of my lungs like she was trying to bury me with her body.

I twisted, fought to get free, but her hands clamped around my wrists like iron.

"Jean, darling," she cooed, low and syrup-sweet. "It's alright now. Mama's here. Everything's going to be just fine."

"No—" I gasped, twisting under her. "Jean, go. You have to go!" I screamed it with my last ounce of breath.

But I didn't know if she could hear me. I didn't know if she was even still there.

Betty leaned closer. Her voice curled around me like wire.

"Oh, sweetheart," she whispered. "All I've ever wanted to do was protect her. Can't you understand that? That's what mothers do. That's what good mothers do."

My breath came in broken gasps. My wrists burned under her grip. I could feel my pulse in my teeth.

Then she shifted, pressing closer. Her nails dug in deeper, curling into bone.

And then her voice dropped—low, knowing, the kind of quiet that cuts deep.

"You think you can protect her? Look at you," she whispered.

I froze.

"I see it in your eyes. You're still clinging to a dead boy's hand. You never let go of him, did you?"

She pressed her forehead to mine. Her skin was damp, clammy. Her breath stank of something spoiled.

"Poor thing. You were there, weren't you? Holding on."

Something inside me twisted.

Because suddenly, it wasn't her breath anymore. It wasn't even her voice. It was inside me—rattling around behind my ribs, echoing off my bones like it had been there all along.

"And then—"

The hallway vanished. The floor, the walls—gone. I was somewhere else. Somewhere cold. Somewhere wet. My knees on pavement. Rain on my face. Blood on my hands.

She leaned in, her mouth brushing my ear.

"You let him die."

The words didn't hit me.

They burrowed.

Slid under my skin. Took root. Spread.

I lost it.

Shoved upward like I could physically throw her off me, like I could shake her voice out of my body. But she held. Held tight. Held like she knew this moment—had been waiting for it.

I couldn't see. Couldn't breathe.

But I snapped.

And spat.

Right into her face.

Betty blinked.

Then she laughed.

It was high, thin, glass-sharp. It wasn't rage. It wasn't surprise. It was joy.

Then her head snapped back—

And came down like a hammer.

CRACK.

Pain tore through my skull, white-hot and blinding. Something split behind my eyes—clean and fast.

My nose.

The world tilted. My ears rang. Blood poured over my lips, into my mouth, thick and metallic, hot as it soaked my shirt and collar.

I gagged on it, coughed, tried to push her off.

"Get—off me—"

She didn't move. Didn't flinch. Didn't blink.

She just leaned back again.

And slammed her forehead into mine a second time.

THUD.

My head slammed against the floor. A white-hot bolt of pain cut through everything, blooming behind my eyes. The edges of the room disappeared. My ears rang—sharp and shrill, like a busted radio dial stuck between channels. That high whine of static filled my skull, like something trying to claw its way out.

Then came the next hit.

Her forehead cracked into my cheekbone—lower this time. Off-kilter. Bone on bone. No cushion. No warning.

I felt something give. A pop. A shift. A crunch.

I didn't know if it was her or me. My hands jerked uselessly beneath her grip, wrists slick and numb. My pulse fluttered, then staggered, then dropped. The room slid sideways, like gravity didn't know where to land.

And through all of it—she smiled.

"Oh, but you know it's true. You've always known." she whispered, breath sticky against my temple. Her voice dipped into something softer, something wrong. The kind of gentle that curdles in your stomach.

"It was your fault, William. It was always your fault."

Lightning flared through the windows. Thunder rolled hard and mean. The storm outside screamed. But inside—she was calm. Too calm.

She grinned through the blood streaked across my face, like she was drinking it in.

"That's why I kept Jean safe—from boys like you. From a world that chews you up and forgets your name." she murmured. Her lips brushed my ear. I could feel every word. "She doesn't belong in that place. She never did. Not with someone who lets go when it matters most."

She stayed there, straddling me, breathing heavy in my ear. But suddenly it wasn't her breath anymore.

It was his.

Tony's.

His last breath.

I blinked, but the house was gone. The floor beneath me morphed into pavement. The rain falling too fast. My knees cut up from the gravel. Blood on my palms. His blood. My hands wrapped around his wrist, trying to feel something—anything.

I promised I'd hold on. Swore I wouldn't let go.

But his fingers twitched once. Then stilled.

Nothing after that.

He was gone.

And I was alone.

Again.

A memory. A curse. A trap.

Lightning split the sky again and lit up the room. Just for a second. Just long enough to see her.

Betty.

Her head twitched hard to one side—too far, too fast, like a puppet on frayed strings. Her jaw dropped open—not wide enough to scream, but wide enough to be wrong.

She didn't blink. She just smiled. And for one terrifying second, I knew it wasn't her anymore. Something else was pulling the strings.

"If you'd just held on..." she whispered.

But her lips didn't match the words. They came from somewhere deeper. Through her.

"Just a little longer..."

Her hands clenched tighter. My blood smeared down my arms, hot and slick. Her weight crushed me, pressing into me like she wanted to live inside my skin.

I couldn't breathe.

"Stop it—" I choked out, twisting under her, trying to break free.

But she didn't stop. She didn't even blink. Just smiled wider. Hungrier.

Another flash lit up the room like a warning flare. In it, I saw her —Jean. Standing frozen. Her hands behind her back, her eyes locked on us. She wasn't moving.

Betty didn't notice. Didn't care.

"You should've walked away when I gave you the chance," she said. Her tone dropped into something soft. Reassuring. Final. "I gave you a story—something simple, something clean. The kind everyone else was content to believe. But you just had to dig. You had to pry."

She let out a breath—almost a laugh.

"And now, well... now you see." she whispered, almost fond. "I'm the only one who can keep her safe. I always have been. Because in the end, William..."

She leaned in again, her lips grazing my ear.

"You killed Tony."

Something cracked inside me.

"I didn't," I rasped. Then louder. "I DIDN'T! I TRIED! I TRIED—!"

The words tore from my throat like they were being dragged out with hooks. My voice cracked. My whole body trembled.

"Then why is he dead?" she hissed.

I broke.

"IT WASN'T MY FAULT!"

I screamed it in her face, spit and blood spraying between us.

She didn't flinch.

Tsk. Tsk.

Betty clicked her tongue and shook her head, slowly, like she pitied me. Like I'd disappointed her somehow.

"Still lying. Even now." she said, her eyes locked on mine. "See, Jean? He never truly loved you. They never do. Not like I do. I've always been here, haven't I? When everyone else left. When the world forgot you."

Her voice softened again. Too much. Too smooth. She wasn't trying to win—she was trying to end it.

"Not him. Not anyone else. Just me. It's always been just us, baby. We don't need anyone else. And you know I can't finish this alone."

And then—

Another flash.

Jean stepped forward. Close now. The blade in her hand caught the light.

Betty didn't turn.

Jean's voice floated across the dark, light and calm.

"I know, Mama."

My blood froze. My body locked up.

Betty leaned in close, almost lovingly.

"Well then..." she whispered. "Consider this a gift, William. You and that poor boy of yours—finally free of this place. Depoe Bay won't miss you."

Then came the inhale—a sharp, high gasp of breath. A shift in air. A blur of motion. The knife raised.

I didn't breathe. Didn't blink.

Then—

Jean slammed the knife in—hard, deep, past flesh and bone. The sound it made was wet, awful. Lightning tore across the room as a gasp ripped from Betty's throat, strangled and raw.

Her whole body seized, fingers twitching, spine locking, eyes rolling back. Her arms flailed behind her, reaching, but she didn't fall. Like she refused to die.

Jean pressed harder. Her breath came shaky, uneven. But her voice? Steady. Unwavering. "I'm sorry..."

Betty gulped at nothing. Her body arching back, but she was still alive.

"But it's time for me to go." Jean twisted.

This was my chance.

With all my effort, I bucked.

Betty tilted, then slammed face down onto the cellar landing with a sickening thud.

I forced myself to my feet, standing beside Jean.

"You—You don't know what you're doing—!" Betty huffed, her body twitching against the wet wooden floor.

I wiped the blood from my face on my sleeve, and walked over to her, kneeling above Betty's broken body.

"We all have choices, Betty," I said, my voice hoarse, shredded. "And Jean just made hers."

I drove my heel into her shoulder. Hard. The force rolled her into the dark. She tumbled down, arms flailing as she crashed into the water below.

The cellar swallowed her.

That black water didn't churn. It didn't rise. It just... waited. Still and thick. Not just stagnant. Not just old. It was dead. A grave without dirt. Depth without bottom. The kind of dark that pulls you in and forgets you were ever there.

Then, her head broke the surface. Her shriek tore through the shadows like a blade. "Jean!"

Her voice hit a pitch that didn't sound human anymore—thin and feral and desperate.

I gasped and stumbled back, dragging air into my lungs like it was a lifeline. My hands shot out, fumbling for the open cellar door. I slammed it shut behind us just as Betty's fists collided with the other side.

BAM. BAM. BAM.

The whole frame shook with the impact.

"Jean! Don't leave me!"

I threw my body weight into the door and clutched the handle with both hands, white-knuckled. My voice cracked as I shouted, "Jean—get me something! Anything! We have to lock it—tie it—just —now!"

She hesitated, just a second too long.

BAM. BAM. BAM.

The door shuddered behind me again. Her fists kept coming, relentless.

"Jean!" I snapped.

She turned and bolted. Her footsteps slipped and echoed across the hall, disappearing into the house. I held my ground, bracing with everything I had left. The door groaned against the force behind it.

Then, Jean came back. Breathless. Soaked. Holding an old frayed laundry line.

She tossed it to me. I caught it midair, looped it quick, tied it to the rusted radiator bolted in Sandra's bedroom. The rope went taut, groaning under the tension. The frame creaked. The wood wailed like it wanted to give, but it didn't.

Then, silence.

For one second, the world just... paused.

And then, slowly, the door pulled open—just an inch. Then another. The rope strained, fighting back, but the wood bowed under the pressure. Cold, rotted air spilled through the crack. A hand reached through—Betty's hand. Soaked. Pale. Bone-white. Her fingers twitched once, then curled around the edge of the door.

SLAM.

The rope yanked her back, hard. The door clapped shut. Behind it came a scream, low and wounded, and something skittered across the floorboards—her ring. That ugly orange stone catching the light for just a second before spinning to a stop near the wall.

Then the door pulled again.

SLAM. BAM. SLAM. BAM.

A rhythm now. Like a heartbeat that refused to die.

Then it slowed.

"Please..." Betty's voice cracked. "Baby, don't leave me. I love you."

The pounding faded to a series of soft, broken sobs. Then a thud, like her body sliding down the back of the door, defeated.

Jean didn't say a word. Didn't move. Just stood there, staring at the door like she could still see through it. Like it had teeth, and it was smiling.

The rope groaned again.

But it held.

And then—nothing. No sound but the storm beyond the walls, the occasional drip from the ceiling tapping the floor. Plunk. Plunk. Like the house was counting down to something we couldn't see.

It wasn't over.

I looked at Jean. Her shoulders trembled, but she wasn't crying. Her eyes were glassed over, stuck in some distant place I couldn't follow. Somewhere deeper than the cellar. Somewhere older.

"She's still alive," Jean whispered. "How is she still alive?"

I reached out and took her hand. It was cold and damp, trembling. She didn't pull away. But she didn't hold on, either. Her gaze stayed fixed on that door, like it might open again at any second.

"What if the knot doesn't hold?" Jean's voice barely made it out. Paper-thin. Faded at the edges. "What if she gets out?"

I held her hand tighter. "Then we run," I said. "As far as we can go."

The words hung there between us, simple and empty, and still somehow the most honest thing I'd said all night. I swallowed, my throat raw. My voice wanted to fall apart, but I pushed it forward. "This is our chance, Jean."

She didn't answer. Didn't look at me. Her eyes stayed locked on the cellar door.

"Please," I added, quieter this time.

Her fingers shifted slightly in mine. Just a twitch.

And then, behind the door, the voice came back.

Not a scream. Not a threat.

Soft. Low. Like a lullaby hummed in the dark.

"Jean..."

Betty's voice drifted through the wood, cooing and tender. "Baby, it's okay now. Mama's not mad."

Jean blinked slowly, like it took effort. Like her body was still here, but the rest of her... wasn't.

"You can come back," Betty continued. Her voice was sugar-slick, sweet enough to rot. "I won't be mad. You know I love you, don't you? I've *always* loved you..."

She breathed the last part like a prayer. Like a promise she had said too many times.

"You were mine before you were anyone else's."

Jean's shoulders stiffened. Her weight shifted forward just a little, a lean so subtle it might've been imagined. But I felt it. I felt the way her center of gravity moved, like her name was being pulled through the door and she wasn't sure if she should follow it.

She didn't speak. Didn't cry. But I could feel her slipping.

I gripped her hand harder. Not just her hand—her. Every part of her that was still listening. Every broken piece that still wanted to believe the voice might be telling the truth.

"Jean," I said, voice low. "It's over."

She didn't move. Not at first. Because it wasn't over. Not for her. Not yet.

Some part of her was still in that basement. Still staring into that water. Still waiting to hear something different in the voice that haunted her. Still hoping for a mother who never existed.

The wind screamed outside, loud enough to rattle the windows. Somewhere in the house, glass trembled in its frame.

Jean didn't flinch. Then—finally—she nodded. Small. Barely there. But enough.

We didn't say anything else. We didn't have to.

And together—

We ran.

CHAPTER THIRTY

We didn't stop. Not to breathe. Not to think.

The front door blew open like it had been waiting—like the house wanted us gone. Maybe it did. Maybe it knew. That this was the end. Or at least the part where the screaming stopped.

We tore through the yard, soaked and half-feral, the storm bearing down like it had teeth. Trees whipped in the wind, branches snapping like bones. The whole world smelled like rain and rot, like the house was finally decomposing now that it didn't have Jean to hold hostage.

Lightning split the sky. The flashes were quick and mean, carving the woods into pieces, showing everything that didn't want to be seen.

Jean didn't let go of my hand. Not once. Her grip was all bone and adrenaline, like she was afraid I'd vanish if she loosened up even a little. Like I was the only thing keeping her tethered to the now.

Behind us, the house sagged in the dark, bloated with secrets and stormwater. I didn't have to look to know it was still there—its silhouette burned into the back of my eyes like a bruise. A carcass. Its windows empty. Watching.

Some part of me expected the cellar door to snap open. For her to come back.

Betty.

Dragging herself out of the flood, snarling, soaked, rotten from the inside out. Clawing up the steps with one good hand and a mouth full of lies. Coming for Jean. Coming for me.

But she didn't.

All we heard was the storm. And the soft, slow caving of the roof. Like the house was collapsing in on itself. Like it didn't have the strength to stand without her. Like it knew it was time to bury the dead.

Jean kept running. Bare feet slapping through mud, dress soaked and clinging to her legs like it didn't want to let go. Her whole body trembled, but she didn't stumble. She moved like someone who had dreamed about this night so many times it had started to feel like a myth.

Maybe she thought it still was.

I didn't know if she was crying. Didn't ask. Her face was unreadable, too much lightning and rain to tell what was real and what was memory. But I could feel her pulse in her grip. Fast. Alive.

We didn't speak.

We didn't look back.

Not once.

By the time we reached my bike, I could barely keep my hands steady. My boots skidded across the gravel and I nearly lost it, catching myself against the handlebars. I plucked my soaked duffle from the mud and threw it over my shoulder. Frantically, I dug in my pocket, fingers numb, the keys slick with rain. Every second stretched thin.

Behind us, the wind howled through the trees, screaming through the cliffside like it wanted to pull us back.

Jean climbed on behind me, arms locking tight around my ribs.

Her hands curled into the leather of my jacket. She held on like she was afraid she'd disappear if she let go. Like she was still half-inside that cellar.

The key slid in. Turned.

Nothing.

The engine sputtered. Died.

I swore under my breath and tried again.

Still nothing.

My stomach twisted. The wind hit us hard enough to rock the frame.

One more time.

The bike roared awake, the sound sharp and sudden and loud enough to push back the dark. A clean break. A door slamming shut.

Jean's grip didn't loosen.

I looked back.

Just once.

The house was barely there anymore. A shadow with a spine. A coffin the size of a life.

And then we were gone.

Not free. Not yet.

But gone.

THE WHEELS TORE across the pavement like they were trying to erase it. Water hissed under the tires, spraying up behind us in fractured sheets that scattered like broken glass in the leftover storm light. The wind screamed past my ears, clawing at our clothes, pulling at my sleeves like it still hadn't given up on dragging us back.

But we were already gone.

We flew through the outskirts, engine howling under me, riding the edge between control and collapse. Past the motel—light still off in the front office. Past the diner, where Norma stood behind the window, leaning on the counter with a cigarette between her fingers and that same unreadable look in her eyes.

She saw us. Didn't wave. Didn't blink.

Just watched us go like she always knew we would.

Like maybe she'd known everything.

Jean's arms were tight around my waist, her fists clenched into my jacket. Her breath hit the back of my neck in bursts—warm, uneven. Not scared. Not anymore. Just trying to believe this was real. That we were actually out. Actually free. Her whole body trembled against me, and I couldn't tell where the storm ended and she began.

Did the town ever really believe she was dead? Or was that just easier? Simpler than admitting they'd let her disappear. That they'd looked the other way and called it a ghost story. Because legends are easier to tell than truth.

We passed Mile Marker 126. And just like that— The storm faded behind us. No warning. No build-up. The wind stilled. The sky cracked open, and just a little—the clouds peeled back like skin after a sunburn, ragged and soft around the edges. Light bled through the cracks in long, gold ribbons. The kind that don't feel real at first. The road shimmered ahead—wet, but gleaming. The kind of shine that comes after something bad. Not exactly clean. But clearer.

Jean's fingers loosened, just a little. Her grip easing as the cold began to lift. Her head still pressed to my back, but her breathing started to steady. Less like panic. More like... breath.

I didn't say anything. Didn't need to.

The road stretched out in front of us, open and wet and wide. But behind us? Behind us was a town that buried things. And not just Jean.

I found myself wondering what else they'd covered up with stories. What other specters walked those streets while no one looked up. Maybe Jean wasn't the first. Maybe she wouldn't be the last. Legends make it easier to forget what you've done. But truth? That gets messy. That clings.

The sun came up slow behind the cliffs, dragging the world out of black and white and back into color. The kind of color that aches. Too gold. Too alive. The ocean flashed beside us as we rode—endless and glittering like it had never seen the storm. Like it had waited for us.

Jean let out a sound. Barely more than breath. Somewhere between a sigh and a laugh. I saw her face in the side mirror. Just the edge of it. A smile breaking through the wreckage. Not a big one. But it was real.

We kept riding. Wind in our ears. Salt in our lungs. Town shrinking behind us, second by second. I didn't know it at the time, but I had stayed because of her. Because I was already in love with her before I even had the words. We never looked back as Depoe Bay faded away. Not because we were strong—but because we knew if we did, we might start to wonder about everything we left behind. And right now—we didn't need doubt. We needed speed.

Still, we knew freedom wasn't about running. It wasn't the road, or the engine. Wasn't the coast or the sunrise. To me, it was about her. It was *us*. It was about making it out alive. And for the first time —I wasn't the only one who got to live.

And as we passed the highway sign, one thing became clear.

We were heading to Washington.

AFTERWORD

Afterword

Thank you for joining Will and Jean on their journey through silence, fear, and first love. *Written Just For You* was born from the idea that even in the darkest corners—behind closed doors, under years of grief—there is still hope. Still fight. Still the possibility of something beautiful trying to grow.

This story is, at its core, about reclaiming your voice. About breaking cycles, naming wounds, and daring to reach for someone when the world tells you not to. Writing it challenged me emotionally in ways I didn't expect, and if it challenged you too, I hope it also offered something in return—whether that's understanding, catharsis, or simply the comfort of being seen.

To every reader who made it to this page: thank you. Your time, your trust, your heart—it all means more than I can say. To my editor, beta readers, and the friends who read pieces of this book late at night and told me to keep going: this wouldn't exist without you. Truly.

A Note on Themes

Written Just For You touches on difficult and emotional topics, including psychological abuse, trauma, grief, isolation, and the complicated bond between love and survival. These themes are central to Will and Jean's story, but I understand they may resonate deeply—or painfully—with some readers. If certain scenes left you feeling raw or unsettled, please know that you are not alone. There is no shame in needing to step back, reflect, or seek support.

Helpful Resources

If you or someone you know is struggling, the following resources are available:

- **National Suicide Prevention Lifeline (U.S.):** 988 or 1-800-273-TALK (8255)
- **Crisis Text Line:** Text HOME to 741741
- **SAMHSA Helpline (Mental Health/Substance Use):** 1-800-662-HELP (4357)
- **For international support:** www.befrienders.org

Disclaimer

This novel is a work of fiction. Any similarities to real people, places, or events are purely coincidental. The characters and their stories are creations of the author's imagination, written to explore emotional truths through fictional means.

A Reminder

Sometimes, the scariest thing isn't the house or the secret—it's believing that no one will ever find you. But someone will. Or maybe you'll find yourself first. Either way, you are not beyond saving.

If this story stirred something in you, I hope you carry that feeling into your life—whether it's a quiet kind of courage, or the start of your own escape. You deserve joy. You deserve peace. And you deserve to be written into something better.

Thank you, truly, for reading.

Respectfully Yours,

Lincoln James

ACKNOWLEDGMENTS

A special thanks to these fantastic people who helped make this book possible:

Adri

Ana

Bree

Cossy

Elena

Gogi

Jack

Jessie

Joanna

Kamran

Keaton

Lee

Mason

Maureen

Mike

Mila

Nadia

Rob

Ross

ABOUT THE AUTHOR

Lincoln James, your favorite author's favorite author, is known for his haunting love stories, vintage thrillers, and slow-burn suspense. His characters feel, ache, and bleed, often trapped between the past and the people who won't let them forget it. When he's not writing, James is a Communication professor in New York City and cherishes moments with friends and family, proving that the most thrilling tales lie in the love and laughter shared with those closest to us.

www.ingramcontent.com/pod-product-compliance
Lightning Source LLC
Chambersburg PA
CBHW050149120726
47903CB00002B/559